THE LATTE
SEGMENT

A novel

Zoe Landon

For Sydney.

CHAPTER ONE

A rabbit sat in a coffee shop. It was Sunday, about 3 o'clock, so this was expected. Her absence would be more surprising, more worthy of report. It had become so predictable an event that her order was almost ready before she even finished paying – a latte, medium, improved with a hint of mint no matter the season. When the barista wasn't too busy, he would draw a sprig of mint in the foam. It was how she had her first coffee years and years ago when she was in college. There was no reason to change it.

She wore the local uniform, jeans with a durable button-down shirt. She was tucked away in the corner, a simple wood chair supporting her, a laptop glowing blue-grey light onto her face. There, the noise of a half-empty cafe was whittled away to a fine din. Her brown ears, half-perked, kept the light from falling onto a painting behind her. It was an impressionist take on the look just a few blocks up the street; she was fond of it. The corner was slightly dark, tucked away from the September sun. Still, there was enough light in the back. If anyone there wanted to see the painting, they would be able to.

Sarah fidgeted and the corner creaked. She was worrying about money.

Her finances were safe, by most reasonable standards, yet there was a nagging sense that she should be doing better. Perhaps she could save a little more. She could go to fewer movies with Sean and their whole circle of friends. She couldn't get rid of her television like Sean did; she relied on it too much for work. But she could stop coming to the Deadline Cafe every Sunday. It did feel like the lattes got more expensive the last year or so.

Everything in Portland felt like it was getting more expensive lately. Most of it was inevitable. She moved here when things weren't very good anywhere, and now things were especially good here. New businesses were popping up in her neighborhood left and right. Businesses that, for one reason or another, she rarely went to.

Some of the growth was probably her fault. At least, it was the fault of the swarm that started moving into town in the last few years. She knew she was part of it.

So making plans made sense. Sarah wanted to be a sensible rabbit. She wanted to keep enjoying the city, to keep on going without having to cut back too much.

The Deadline was a home away from home. It almost felt like more of a home than her cozy apartment up the road. The walls here were caked with artwork. Scenes of local attractions and raw emotion, the output of the city's remaining artistic heritage. Tall windows kept the front well-lit in the summer, with only subtle ambient light filling the area Sarah preferred.

Maybe I should keep the lights low at home, she thought. *It would cut down the electric bill, at least. Probably wouldn't mind it.*

What she did mind was the pair of foxes sitting halfway across the room. She was always instinctively on edge around foxes, but these were more distracting simply because they were so loud. The cafe was never silent, but the pair had apparently decided to try to compete for the loudest source of noise. They were putting in a gold-star effort.

Sarah tried not to eavesdrop, but her focus was repeatedly ripped from her laptop by their laughing interjections. Howls of "you're serious?" and "oh hun, I know!" were favorites. Their loudest cries grabbed the attention of the entire back room, including a coyote on the other side of the room. He stumbled onto eye contact with Sarah, his face broadcasting the same silent exasperation.

She tried to avoid focusing on the two and let her mind float in the air. A breeze from the vent pushed her thoughts to a wire sculpture. It hung from a thin string, high against the bare rafters. It was a silver skeleton of pyramids, interlocking and staggered. Its construction probably held no particular significance, but it was familiar to Sarah.

Her neighbor, Carl, had something similar on his apartment door. It was simpler and flatter, but it showed the same geometric approach. It had been there since she moved in years ago, never coming down, not even for holidays. It was one of those things that she knew him by; he was The Hyena with the Sculpture above anything else.

She shook her head quickly to regain focus, her ears flopping loosely. All this effort and worry around budget was starting to feel like a pointless exercise. After all, things were going fine. She wasn't rich – not by her own standards – but she didn't need to make sacrifices. She wasn't struggling to make rent. She could even afford that trip to Washington to help Alex with his gallery showing.

Hell, she thought, *I have savings. Nobody has savings.*

The uncertainty still hung on her face. Even if things were good now, she was convinced they wouldn't last. Her routines would have to change someday. A surprise would be hard to manage.

She sipped her coffee as if part of a ritual, closed her eyes, and took deep meditative breaths. Her focus returned. She started thinking of scenarios that could affect her finances.

What if I find a new job? Would make things easier, sure, but I doubt it'd be that much... And that's best case anyway. What if I lost it? I mean, Roger likes me too much so I'm not gonna get fired, but even then, I should be fine for a little while. Like, four months? Maybe five if I cut down a little. I can find a new job by then. Moving would... no, I can't do that, rent's too crazy. Well, I guess I could split a place with Sean if he'd want to, but... I don't think he'd really want to...

The tangents were useful, she'd tell herself, even if they were unlikely. She found success at work by letting her mind wander. Her marketing job was rarely creative, but when it was, her wandering mind led to impressive results. And besides, the whole point of her coming by on a pleasant Sunday afternoon was to prepare. What good is it to only be ready for things that were likely to happen?

But she knew she wasn't getting anywhere. And as her latte cooled and neared its end, the mint aroma all but vanished, she conceded the point. Her head was only filled with half-thoughts, each trailing into the next, none of them offering any meaningful action or idea. There might be some small nugget of gold buried in there, but she wasn't going to find it today. Her mind was stuck in mud without the strength to pull itself out.

She sighed and closed her laptop, fitting it into her bag. As she stood, she glanced again at the hanging wire sculpture. It, like everything else that decorated the cafe, had a price attached to it. $65.

It wasn't going in the budget.

CHAPTER TWO

September had only just started, and the weather had not gotten the memo. The sun still hung in cloudless skies, as warm and bright as Sarah ever wanted summers to be. She was starting to miss the spring rain and looked forward to the autumn muck. It wouldn't be comfortable or even pleasant weather, but it was coming. After living there four years, she knew what to expect.

Compared to so many of her neighbors, though, she was an outright veteran. Her building was old, but its residents had mostly moved in after her. Only two or three others in the building were there longer. The new neighbors were split into two camps: either they came to town as part of the soggy gold rush that was the local tech scene, or they were trying to downsize out of a neighborhood that the gold rush made too expensive. The Alphabet District was far from the most expensive area (that was the Pearl District, by all estimates), but it did have its price. Yet, it also had its appeal. Sarah couldn't blame anyone for wanting to move here.

She always left her apartment door open when she got home. Hers was a corner apartment, as far from the stairs and elevator as it gets, so nobody ever passed by her door. Carl lived across the hall, but that was it. So leaving the door open became something she just did.

This confused Sean. He was the kind to lock his door, and double-check the lock, and even then be a little wary that he forgot. He worked in software, and, as a result, became tensely aware of his own privacy and security.

At the same time, he was a raccoon. By his telling, he was a loner growing up as well. The combination made others just a tiny bit unsettled, if only subconsciously. But Sean noticed. He had developed a fear of his own reputation. He kept the fact quiet, but around Sarah, he was willing to share.

As far as she was concerned, his reputation was clean. Perhaps even admirable. He was something of a leader for their group of friends, a cobbled-together set of imports who needed others in their new town to be friends with. She admired anyone who could keep them organized.

The group started doing whatever was around. Small street festivals, holiday events, trivia nights, anything that sounded interesting. Sean wasn't in charge when things started, but nobody minded it when he took charge. He was happy to do anything that didn't exist back in his corner of California. That was the whole reason he moved – he needed to do something new.

Sarah let him into the building and led him back up to her still-open apartment, watching as he rolled his bike along. He was slightly taller than Sarah (unless they had their ears perked) and, despite riding several miles to Sarah's place, still wore the programmer's typical hoodie and dark jeans. He paused when they reached the apartment door.

"Okay, seriously," Sean said, "why is your door still open?"

"It's hot." For September, it was. "Besides, it's not like it's a big deal. I mean yeah, people steal shit, but the building's locked. It's fine."

Sean nodded. "I guess I always worry someone's just gonna, like, swoop in and steal my laptop and boom, it's gone."

"Well, that's 'cause your computer is, like, your whole life."

Sean feigned indignation. "Not all of it! I have the bike too."

The two bonded over movies. The group made a ritual of going to a small theater every other weekend. Sean and Sarah made a habit of going to each others' place on the other weekends. Other members of the group used to join in, but lately, it was just the two of them.

This week was the same. Invitations came back with a batch of "no"s, along with some "maybe"s that everyone knew to treat as a polite rejection. Sean said he might call it off entirely at this point. Kate was starting to talk as if Sarah and Sean were dating, and with how much time they spent together, they were both running out of arguments to the contrary. But Sarah liked the routine. She liked the movies they picked. And, though she wouldn't admit it, she liked Sean.

"So," Sean said, "I need you to explain something to me. How in the hell have you not seen *Young Frankenstein?*"

Sarah shrugged. "I haven't gotten into Mel Brooks yet. He's not my style."

"But he's-"

Sean cut himself off. He loved debating movies with friends. Most of them were even good for a snappy quip in return, the sort of friendly banter that endeared Sarah to the whole crowd. Sean played well off Kate in particular because she was so loud. Sarah, a more mild-mannered rabbit, wasn't a good foil.

Mel Brooks was Sean's kind of thing. Sarah wasn't as much of a fan; she liked Hitchcock and Kubrick, any sort of slow and brooding drama. But she was never very interested in defending her tastes, so if Sean wanted to argue, well then, he could argue.

"Right. We need to get you to see *History of the World* at some point."

"I saw that," Sarah said. "You got me to watch that last time we had this argument."

"Well, then, there you go. You've seen the best Mel Brooks movie."

"So, good, we're done."

"I didn't say that!" He grabbed the remote. "It's *Young Frankenstein*, or it's *Spaceballs*, whichever one is around..."

Sean trailed off. Sarah's face was back to the same expression she wore in the coffee shop, her cheeks drooping as she stared at the idle TV.

"Look, I'm sorry about arguing."

Sarah chuckled. "No, dude, that's half the fun."

He tilted his head and examined her face. "Well, is something wrong? You look kinda..."

"I know. I'm just... I dunno. Been thinking about work, and the apartment..."

"Things not going well?"

Sean was one of the few people Sarah knew she could open up to. "Two guys on my team both quit lately. One went off to another startup, no surprise, but the other left town for somewhere cheaper. And I keep hearing about stuff like that, things getting too expensive, and I'm just like... I don't know if I'm ready in case I have to worry about that."

"Well, your job's going fine, isn't it?"

"Yeah. Not gonna lose that anytime soon."

"Then don't worry. You know what you're doing."

Sean dropped himself on the couch, swiping his tail to the side. Sarah joined him, leaning back and tucking her tail between the cushions.

"You know better than to tell me not to worry."

"This is true," Sean said with a slight smile.

"Besides, you're the one with the good job." Sean nodded meekly. "So you've definitely got nothing to worry about."

"Well, you've got a good job too."

She didn't enjoy working in marketing, but she had to admit, it did pay well. "I guess. I just... I feel sorry for people."

Sean nodded, more confidently this time. "This about Alex?"

Sarah dithered. "Maybe, a little?"

"How's she doing?"

"He," Sarah said.

"We're going with 'he' now?"

"Last we talked."

Alex was known to move around with what pronouns he preferred. Sarah was always willing to oblige, but it was the sort of information that needed to be passed around.

He was one of the first people Sarah got to know in Portland. He was offering art lessons at the time, and Sarah took him up on the offer. He fit Sarah's idea of the eccentric, androgynous artist to a T: a small, curiously fashionable otter, soft-spoken with an excitable and scattered brain. Just the kind of character Sarah wanted to get to know.

"But yeah. He's surviving, still working at that bar. Sold a couple of pieces."
"Well, that's good. He still looking at that guild thing?"
Sarah sighed. "Didn't sound like it."

The guild was one of Sarah's many attempts to help Alex out. He was a starving artist, at times literally, and Sarah felt a motherly need to help him. She caught wind of a graphic designer guild in town – more of an industry support group than anything serious – and suggested it to Alex. Most of the members were artists, so she assumed he would fit in fine. Perhaps he would even get a more meaningful job than waiting tables at yet another bar. At this point, he seemed as well known in food service circles as in art circles.

Sean and Sarah didn't run in either of those. Their circle was, tonight, focused on a cheap couch and a modest TV in a cheap and modest apartment. It was nowhere near perfect. Sarah would definitely prefer it if the apartment were bigger or if the couch were more inviting. But it was okay, and she was satisfied.

CHAPTER THREE

For the big-business enterprise-scale world that Sarah spent her weekdays in, the end of the quarter was something of a sacred period. One worshiped by all and approached with the fear of angering an unseen and unpredictable god. By the time the mood worked its way down to her level, the doctrine and ritual had disintegrated into sheer chaos. Even with weeks left in September, the quarter would end too soon. So everything must happen now, if not yesterday. Otherwise, the stock market may become angry and start throwing lightning bolts.

Sarah could only deal with these months. She didn't enjoy the chaos. After four years at this job, however, she learned to manage it. She was in charge of managing marketing campaigns for two different clients, and she kept tabs on them gradually. Her approach was measured; chaos would only bring more chaos. An email here, a meeting there, a phone call on occasion, delivered slowly and when necessary. They weren't the projects with the best performance or most spend or anything that her bosses cared about, but she kept organized and planned ahead. For that, she was well-liked.

That was a modest consolation. Things took a dip a year after she started, and other well-liked marketing managers got the ax in the process. (Her survival was rabbits' luck, as far as she was concerned.) Being well-liked didn't make her job any easier or more exciting. It was just something she did, and she did it well enough, and it paid well enough. That was all.

"So, Sarah, how'd your weekend out in the woods go?"

Michelle did enjoy her job. She was a perky middle-aged wolf dressed in a vibrant green that nearly matched the walls. Perfectly on brand, whether intended or not. Her desk, neighboring Sarah's, was full of papers and notes, wherever she hadn't situated photos of her kids. Sarah's desk was barren in comparison.

The office space was open rows of desks all the way around. There were no cubicle walls to block windows, but that also meant they couldn't block noise. The result was a steady din of keyboards and chatter. It was like working in a coffee shop, with the smell of coffee replaced by a faint sting of lemon cleaner.

Sarah paused to process that yes, Michelle had started a conversation, and yes, it was with her. "Oh. Fine, I guess."

"First time up Multnomah Falls?"

"Yep," Sarah said, now thoroughly distracted. "You kinda have to, sooner or later."

"Definitely! I'm just waiting until I know the boys can handle it. It can be a tough hike."

"I know. Guess I'm not quite in the kind of shape I want to be."

"Oh, pshaw," Michelle said. "You're fine. You just have to pace yourself. That's all there is to it."

Sarah watched her drink yet another soda. It was mid-afternoon, and she was on her third or fourth of the day. *Maybe you should pace yourself too*, she found herself thinking before a rush of guilt came over her.

No. Stop being judgmental. Stop it.

Even if Sarah was well-liked and had a good standing in the office, the moment she stepped into it she started being hard on herself. When things got especially tense with a client, she started to panic. Roger, the marketing director, would have to reassure her that things were going to be fine. He'd remind her that she consistently rated herself low on her self-evaluations while everyone else rated themselves highly.

It bled into thoughts about the rest of her life. She felt fine at home, but here, suddenly she became critical of everything. Her impulse was to criticize Michelle for her diet, to get a little stab at a wolf. But she worried more about her own. She was healthy, as far as she knew, but there had to be room to improve. Maybe she should go to that Thai restaurant less often. The portions were huge, and besides, they don't get tofu right and sometimes still leave the eggs in...

She would even beat herself up for letting her mind wander. The job always had plenty of tasks to offer. There was always a little more customer research to do, a little more communication with the clients. Even in the meetings that required hardly any focus, she felt an obligation to be productive. Otherwise, she feared she would lose her job, and she didn't like the budget she made for that.

The office did have private rooms, designed for someone to use as their exclusive space, which were instead the venue for conference calls and the like. They were all too claustrophobic to use for meetings, but they were soundproof. A relief on some days.

Sarah had a call coming, so she claimed one by laying her laptop on the desk. These calls never required much focus. Everyone was somewhere else, and her only function on them was to keep things organized. This group of creatives and production managers was particularly self-organizing. She didn't even feel necessary.

Maybe she should practice drawing. Ever since the lessons with Alex ended, she had let the whole art thing slide. She had her notepad, its yellow pages still virgin and crisp. She had a pen that still worked. Nobody could see if her mind was elsewhere, and she could imagine Ben and Kim doing the same while the more business-oriented attendees went on about logistics. There was no reason to feel guilty about it.

After everyone picked up their phones – late, of course – and Sarah kicked off the meeting, she immediately started staring at the blank page. Her pen tapped gently. Something had to come out. She tried random, nondescript swirls. Then, she traced over them and layered echoes and ripples around them. She was doodling, technically, but she felt uninspired. After a few minutes, she tore the sheet off the top of the pad in disappointment. The attempt at distracting herself instead left her more focused, listening keenly to the conversation just in case she had to chime in with something.

But she didn't. She never did. She knew she never did. These meetings ran themselves, more or less. They made people feel good, as if they achieved something meaningful in the process. And they chewed up time. For a time when everyone claimed to be busy, there was plenty of time being wasted.

All of her meetings that day followed the same refrain. She was present in body, but barely in mind. Virtually unnecessary, yet always required. It was productive on paper, but she couldn't ignore the feeling that her time would be better used doing something else.

When evening came, Sarah walked back across the street to the parking garage. Her head hung slightly, her ears drooped. On the corner was a trash can, stuffed with plastic lunch trays from the food carts nearby. As she passed it, she threw a crumpled piece of yellow paper with a soft grunt, not even turning to make sure it fell in.

CHAPTER FOUR

Sarah had a routine for most things, and returning home after a work day was no exception. She would swing around the side of her apartment building, parking in the furthest corner of the lot. There was a parking spot near the front that was always available and would be more convenient, but she never took it. Instead, she went to the back entrance. It was a beat-up old door beneath the fire escape, surrounded by moss. The mailboxes sat there. There was rarely anything important, mostly circulars and credit card offers, but it was a ritual. It was such a habit that she found herself checking the mail when she returned from running Sunday errands.

The building was far from the nicest in town, or even the nicest in the neighborhood. When an apartment opened up, its ad contained words like "vintage" and "cozy". Nothing more than euphemisms. They tried to give appeal to a building nearly 100 years old and far more modest than the flashy new complexes that were popping up.

The building showed its age. The heat didn't come on as quickly or consistently as it should; the windows had a strange way of opening and years of rust that made it a physical feat; the floorboards creaked so softly yet frequently that their absence would surprise Sarah. None of these were problems in the newer buildings like the one where Sean lived. She had reasons to complain about the place if she wanted to.

But she didn't. Not often, at least. She stumbled into the place when she first moved to town, back when rents were arguably cheap but certainly reasonable. Staying put kept her rent from jumping very much, a fact she accepted with great appreciation and relief. It was a fair compromise. The newer buildings were flashier and more comfortable, but they had price tags to match. Never mind that several didn't have anywhere to park. Eric, an occasional member of her circle of friends, lived in a neighborhood where many of those sorts of buildings were popping up. He was more than willing to comment on their impact.

Among the typical stuffing that filled her mailbox was a nondescript and unstamped envelope. It was from the building's management company – or, more accurately, the sole landlady Deborah. She was a small and fiercely independent woman, what Sarah imagined her own grandmother would be like were she a coyote. They had a good rapport from the day Sarah first saw the apartment. Deborah was always willing to try and fix anything that came up from the residents, even the sort of work that a woman of her age would rarely attempt. Sarah could hardly think of a time she called for a handyman and it wasn't Deborah herself that came to fix things.

She immediately felt a rush of guilt. Letters from Deborah were rare, and it was relatively early in the month. *Did I forget to pay rent? I had to have paid, my phone reminded me, I know I went to the site right after...*

It took her an embarrassing amount of time to realize that the mystery could be solved by opening the letter. It was typed; not unheard of from Deborah, but rare. She preferred to write everything out, even the annual rent increases. This had to be something important.

Dear residents,

I hope you're all doing just lovely! I sure have been. These last few years have been wonderful for our little family. So many new faces!

Most of you know me pretty well by now. You know I care about you all, you know I enjoy doing everything I can for you all. You also know I didn't used to be such a gray coyote! So I'm afraid it's just about time for me to hang up my boots and retire. I wish I could keep going for another 50 years, but it's getting so hard to keep up with everyone!

Don't you fret, though! I'm handing over the keys to the folks at Waterknell Management. Yes, it's a big group of folks, but they have a bunch of little families in town. I've heard good things about them, so I'm sure they'll take care of you folks just fine. They'll be moving in a few weeks from now. October 1st! My, is it almost the end of the year already? Anyway, their man Andrew will be taking my office, so I hope you all take a chance to get to know him. He's a fine young hare, but he's sure got some little shoes to fill here!

Hugs and kisses,

Deborah

Deborah always wrote the way she talked.

The news surprised Sarah only because, in the back of her mind, she expected Deborah would never retire. She'd be replacing a lightbulb in one of the hallway sconces, step down off her old green stepladder, take a seat on it, and just pass away quietly then and there. A morbid idea, sure. But she figured that's what she would have wanted to do, to work on her building right up to the end.

Instead, she was retiring.

Is it her health? I didn't know she was in bad shape... is she in bad shape? Or, maybe money? I dunno, I'd probably give up by the time I got to her age. She's what, 73 now? 74? I'd cash out too.

She kept asking herself questions that were better asked to someone else as she rode up the cramped elevator. A hundred-year-old building meant a hundred-year-old elevator, one with a scissor gate blocking its entry. It could've come from the days when elevators had dedicated operators. But then, it felt far too small for that. Riding it with even two other people could get personal.

She stepped out of the elevator and turned the corner. Carl was in the hallway, sitting on a stool outside his apartment door. He wore his usual blue collar uniform, a dirtied sweater from a local college and jeans that were distressed and faded from work rather than fashion. His large paws held pliers, working a small metal sheet gently and methodically. His working life was about wood, but now that he was retired, it was about metal.

21

The timber industry where Carl once worked used to dominate the city. Now, the few mills and factories that survived did so on the backs of shipping interests and the growing ranks of small-scale artisans. Since his retirement, he'd moved towards joining those ranks. He passed the days by making small trinkets for himself and people he knew. Sarah even had one sitting next to her TV. He'd occasionally sell a few, but he didn't care much for the craft fair circuit. He wasn't relying on the money, anyway.

"Evening, Carl," Sarah said as she approached.

"Evening," he said wearily, looking up from his work.

"What're you working on now?"

"Some metal origami." Carl put his work down on his good leg. "Saw a little guide on doing it, figured I'd take a whack at it. Make something different."

Sarah gave it a quick glance. "Seems to be going pretty well."

"Well, wait until it's done, then we'll see how it's going." Sarah wasn't sure if the phrasing was wisdom or just Carl messing around with words.

"That's true. Did you check your mail yet?"

"Yep. Debby's taking the gold watch. Can't blame her, she's been here forever. Longer than I have."

Carl had been in that apartment for a decade. It was a long tenure for that building. He moved in with his wife after the kids went to college; they didn't need their old home, and they could get a good selling price for it. Carl didn't want to mow the lawn every week anyway, the weeds were such a pain in the ass, and his neighbors always gave them hassle for the dumbest things. He'd swear up and down that they just didn't like hyenas.

Sarah knew all this because Carl loved to talk. He especially loved talking with Sarah. She actually listened.

"Guess I gotta be glad for her," Sarah said. "Didn't think she'd retire, but..."

"Probably got bought out," Carl said. "Just the land's probably worth a million or two to some jackass in a suit." He enjoyed being frank.

"She did say it was some local management company. Never heard of 'em, but still."

"Don't mean they're not jackasses."

She paused. "True."

Carl stood up. "Town's got plenty of weird folks, but they're good folks. Working for a living. I swear, though, there's more suits every day. Shame."

In a way, Sarah agreed. She would've gone to New York if she was interested in business. But, despite her tan pants and plaid top, she probably counted as one of those suits. If she was honest with herself.

"Yeah. Lot of random startups popping up, too. One of our product guys just left for a banking thing."

"Well, fuck 'em," Carl said, getting a small laugh out of Sarah. "If he's willing to do something dumb like that, it's his ass. No point taking a dumb risk. Plenty of good ones lying about."

"Definitely."

"Speaking of, you make a move on your boyfriend yet?"

Sarah blushed and laughed. Only Carl or her mom could get away with asking about Sean like that. "No, I-"

"You know the boy likes you!"

"I do! I just... don't think he knows he does."

Carl laughed his hearty, old man laugh. "Well then, I guess I'll have to keep on you about it."

"And I'll keep on you about the origami, then. Wanna see it when it's done."

She opened her apartment door and tossed the junk mail aside, rereading the letter. Her door remained open.

CHAPTER FIVE

Sarah had never experienced a takeover, by any definition. Her personal life was free of any major upheavals. She never worked for any company that got acquired. Things changed, of course, but the news was rarely sudden or unpredictable. She could always prepare for the change.

She couldn't remember hearing of Waterknell Management before. There were so many apartment buildings already in town. Dozens more were going up. Even if she was interested in the detailed machinations of the real estate business she probably couldn't keep track of it all. It was one of a million topics that affected other people, but not her. She never gave it a second thought.

Now that it affected her, she found herself sitting at her desk, trying to research the new company. There were a dozen Waterknells, dotted across the country, making claims to anything from suburban townhouses to commercial towers. It was a strange name to be so generic. None looked like they held very strictly to any geographic area, so Sarah wasn't sure which would be her new landlord come October.

But her job was marketing. She wasn't a devoted practitioner, but she knew what she was doing. And she knew what others were doing. It may take some time to piece it together, but she could read the insides of a marketing campaign, even envision the people who made it. Everyone left their paw print.

Purely from a marketing standpoint, something was fishy about the Waterknells. Browsing across a few sites between work tasks, she started noticing similarities. The website layouts started to match, almost precisely.

She wasn't too surprised – some of her clients used templates just to keep things moving. It could be an artifact of some management software they used; she knew Deborah used something along those lines.

But it was smoke, and the fire started to emerge. The photographs had the same pacing, the same feel. The shots flowed through the rooms the same way, no matter what kind of apartment or office it was. And the descriptions were formatted almost identically. The language changed here and there – competitors hate having identical copy, after all – but they were close enough that they could've come from the same writer. Sarah remembered her efforts from when she did copywriting, how similar her language was between projects.

The floor plans sparked her strongest suspicion. She pulled up three apartments, from three different buildings, side by side. They seemed to share a cookie-cutter sense of architecture. The floor plans weren't precisely the same, but they were close enough.

It was the illustrations that did it. The text was in the same positions, the same visual hierarchy, the same typeface. Sure, they could have all come from the same program, but wouldn't they customize the output? Or they could have come from the same construction firm, but with one building in California and one in Georgia? It was too close for coincidence.

She was willing to entertain the idea that her eyes were fooling her, that she just saw patterns where there weren't any. She trusted Deborah, and if Deborah trusted them, she had no reason not to. Maybe real estate branding had just coalesced like this. None of her clients were in real estate, and it had been years since she looked for an apartment. It wasn't impossible.

It was, however, improbable. And since she had yet another conference call that was moving along fine without her, she kept browsing. Soon she started comparing contact information for each of the different Waterknells. The managers put their name and photo right on the page – a standard trick for small businesses and any company trying to make

26

themselves seem more personable. There weren't many categories that needed a personal touch more than housing.

A building down in San Mateo had as its contact a brown-grey hare. He was a classic real estate suit; confident smile, well-groomed fur, perfectly angled pose. The page gave his name – Andrew Casterwall.

This must be the guy. Seems to check out. Guess he's moving up here.

She continued browsing, this time to a condo tower in Houston. Its contact page also had the manager's name and photo, all laid out the same way. All laid out with the same content. It was Andrew again.

Well. Huh. She took a moment to work through the facts. *I... guess they're not local. They're... they're definitely not local. No way. Man, Carl is gonna be pissed when he finds out.*

She wasn't sure how she felt about the fact. She knew there was strong advocacy for doing everything local, and from time to time she went along with it. But most of her furniture at home came from Ikea. She had no qualms about shopping at the Target downtown.

She could only be upset for Deborah. Apparently, she had been drastically misled. Was Andrew just going around the country, sweeping up properties? If so, what would he do with the building? He certainly wouldn't be hand-writing notes to the residents and fixing the hallway lights himself.

CHAPTER SIX

The questions and worries remained on her mind all the way to Alex's studio. It was just across the river, but those few hundred yards felt like a world away. Downtown was full of impressive, almost foreboding office towers. The east side held its array of old, short warehouses, many of them now empty and dilapidated.

Alex's studio was in that area; one of those warehouses had been converted to studio spaces. They were habitable enough and, more importantly, cheap. They attracted all manner of weasel and coyote on the skids, along with artists like Alex. He was the only otter Sarah ever saw there, and tended to be the best kept of anyone. Some days, that didn't seem like it meant much.

Sarah pushed through the apartment door, sticking in its frame. She was barely two steps in before Alex started offering directions. "Hey Sarah. Real quick, that black cord thing? Third pile from your left, really long, looks like a shoelace, feels like spaghetti? Could you toss that up here, please?"

"I'm fine, thanks, how are you," she replied in deadpan. Despite the sarcasm, she complied with his request.

While Sarah's life could be considered organized chaos at worst, Alex's could best be described as chaotic organization. That cord was in a very precise spot that only he could explain. From atop the ladder in the corner, he could easily see where it was, but amidst the scattered personal effects and "borrowed" art supplies it was difficult for Sarah to work out where anything was.

"Very funny," he said.

"Which third pile?"

"The third – that one." He pointed to the opposite corner and went back to dismantling the work hanging on his wall. It was his most elaborate piece yet, an array of paintings on canvases of varied depth and size. Dark curves bulged like a bubbling swamp off several pieces. Sarah would describe it as a sort of sculpture painting mishmash, for lack of any better words.

She would describe Alex as a mishmash too. He would talk art history and hip-hop rumors in the same breath. He wore a newsboy cap that allowed only a small shock of orange to stick out underneath, combined with a loose-fitting suit jacket, t-shirt, and yoga pants. His socks, as usual, didn't match. Still, he pulled off the look.

Sarah dug and eventually found what she assumed he was looking for. She held it up to the ladder with a quizzical look, and Alex extended his paw to confirm the guess. She tossed the cord to him and went back to organizing the pieces that were already laid out.

"How do you feel about the show?" she asked, sitting on his mattress.

"Not bad, not bad," Alex said. "Got out of the bar for the day, fucking finally."

"They weren't giving you the night off?"

"No, Pete's been a twat. Had to remind him like five times about it, make sure I'm not scheduled for anything. Dumbass probably would've if I didn't remind him Sunday."

"That... would've sucked." It had been so long since Sarah had a job that involved having shifts scheduled that she had virtually forgotten the stresses that went along with it.

"Yeah. Just, like, a lot."

He climbed down from the ladder, carrying wires and other small pieces of mounting, before hopping off with a soft squeak. Sarah was always willing to help him, whether it was delivering his work to a gallery or just listening to his problems. She had to admit that she could rarely ever relate to them. Alex was a proper artist, with works in galleries and everything. In Sarah's mind, it didn't get more "artist" than that. He was free to work on what he found interesting, mostly macabre takes on stock oil paintings. In Sarah's office, any artistic creativity was a matter of committee.

She looked around at the bare brick walls, the tiny kitchen, the sparse mess spread across the floor. It wasn't a good place to live by any stretch, but it was an artist's home, and for that reason alone she liked it.

"Is he still giving you shit about the skirt?" she asked.
"He gives me shit about everything. Always picking on the little guy."

Sarah wasn't unusually tall, but she was taller than him. She didn't wear a skirt as often as he did, though.

"I'm sorry."
He shrugged. "Eh."
"Well, there is that guild thing I mentioned a while back. I mean, could get you a new job."
"I guess."
Sarah paused. "Did you go?"
He groaned. "I just... I dunno. Between work, and trying to put stuff together, it's like..."
"Don't have time?"
"Yeah. Just been too busy."
"Well, I mean... the meetings aren't all that long. Hell, there's free food. You can just go and eat, it's fine."
"Yeah, but..." He stretched for an excuse.

Sarah didn't want to push it this time. She knew how much Alex struggled to get by, how hard it was for any artist to make a living in this town. There were ways to make it easier, she figured, and she wanted Alex to take one of those options. She didn't see any reason for him to do the whole starving artist thing, outside of romanticizing the whole idea.

Or, stubbornness. They were each stubborn in their own way. When they dated, Sarah would persistently argue her case for what she was after until

Alex agreed. He would listen to suggestions, smile his meek smile, and carry on how he wanted anyway.

As far as she knew, his friends never pushed him like she did. But she wanted him to be successful. He was willing to put up with her stumbling through an attempt to learn art; nobody else had the patience. She respected that. It made her want to be more helpful, to pick him up when he was struggling. It didn't quite matter to her that she had almost no understanding of the art world.

Nowhere was that lack of understanding more evident than a gallery show. The one they were preparing for was in the north part of town, in an old converted church. It was a moment of sensory overload for Sarah; the intimidating gothic architecture, combined with the highly conceptual modern works, was just enough to beat on her senses. She could piece together what was going on, but why it was happening? That was beyond her.

So Alex did the talking. It was his domain, after all. The space made his voice double in volume. They dropped his boxes along a blank wall, his work's home for at least the weekend. He immediately scurried off to find a ladder, leaving Sarah to stand awkwardly. She looked around for some way to help. The boxes grabbed her attention, so she started to empty the boxes around her, hoping not to mess up his obtuse system.

She looked around. Mice and badgers wearing scarves and skinny jeans shuffled around, carrying sculptures and ceramics. They moved confidently, weaving around the uncertain Sarah.

I don't belong here.

CHAPTER SEVEN

"Everything okay, Sarah? You're kinda tense."

Kate still wore her suit from work, though the jacket was already loosened up. Out of the entire movie group, she was always the most talkative and energetic, and she was always willing to probe. Often it felt like an investigation. This time, the meerkat seemed genuinely concerned.

They were hitting a small, independent theater on the east side, its marquee featuring what it called "recent classics." This time, it was *No Country for Old Men*, one of Sarah's favorites. There was a dull excitement for the movie within her, buried beneath some unspoken stress.

"I guess. A little." She was buying time, working out for herself where the mood might've truly come from.

"How'd things go with Alex?" Sean asked.

"Oh. It was okay."

"Usual?"

"As usual as he ever is."

"C'mon, details!" Kate said. Her stance perked up fully, in classic meerkat fashion. "How weird was it? See any cool stuff? Did he try to hit on you?"

"No, he was – he's been good about that."

"He still not over things?" Sean asked.

"Seemed like it." She shrugged lightly. "Thought he was months ago, so I hope so by now."

"True."

Sarah and Alex were a light couple; it was more of a casual thing than any serious dating. They were both single, Alex found Sarah attractive, she was willing to give him a try. Inevitably, the romance wasn't very strong. It fizzled out well before Sarah found the movie group, but they were a tight group. They shared.

Kate overshared. Sarah knew more about Kate's personal life than she was interested in ever knowing. She could name most of her boyfriends, even the ones she had never met in person. She knew more gossip about the real estate world than she knew about her own office.

In a way, Kate was a balance to Lee. While she was large in stature and personality, he was a meek and small ferret. He had been standing with the group in the lobby without saying much of anything.

The four made a balanced core group, a kind of four-man band. Many others would join in regularly, but this evening was just them. Sarah was okay with that.

"So, Lee." Kate eagerly broke the silence. "What's new with the whole job situation?"

He shrugged. "Boss is a dick."

"Fair," Sean said.

There was an awkward pause. Nobody volunteered to continue the conversation.

Eventually, Lee continued. "And, like... I guess nobody really needs chemical engineers around here. I've looked; there's not really anything around. It's all coding stuff."

"Sorry," Sean said.

"Not your fault. Just means he thinks he can get away with shit."

"Or," Sarah said, "he could just be a dick naturally." She shrugged to offer the idea. Lee shrugged back, slinking into his jacket.

"Well," Sean said, "if you want to do coding stuff I could help. It sucks that you can't find anything as it is, but I'm sure you could do it if you had to. You're pretty smart."

Lee shrugged again. Sean stopped pressing the issue any further. Sarah wanted to, though; she knew how badly stuck Lee was with his current job. She didn't want any of her friends in that position, but she didn't know the first thing about writing code. It never appealed to her. Even though she wanted to help, she knew she couldn't.

The group made their way into the theater, already debating what would be next week's movie. The movie choice was ultimately Sean's decision, but he picked it knowing full well who would like it. This week was a slow drama for Sarah's sake; the next would probably be a horror movie more to Lee's taste. He seemed to like making sure that everyone knew why they were the movies he picked. It was as if he was reminding his subjects how kind a leader he was.

They sat down as Sean entered the self-congratulatory phase of the conversation.

"Sean, is it okay if I just throw something out there real quick?" Kate asked, sitting a few seats away.
"Proceed," he said, keeping up the playfully haughty tone.
"You're kind of an obnoxious twerp."
Sarah laughed and joined in. "You kinda are, dude."
"I know." Sean nodded confidently.
Kate failed to hold in her laugh. "That's not supposed to be a good thing!"
"Well, hey," Sean said, "I know I'm annoying. I'm okay with that. You guys are the only ones that put up with me, so really it's your fault for sticking around."
"Now, you're not that bad," Sarah said. "There's annoying, and then there's like..."
"I know what you mean. I'm like annoying-lite."
"Still annoying," Lee said.

"We got him to talk!" Sean said with an enthusiastic snark. He always did a small celebration when Lee jumped in without a prompt. "See, being annoying can be helpful."

Sarah enjoyed that about him. He was annoying, but it was a playful annoying. More importantly, Sean was aware of it. When the two of them were alone, he was much more willing to tone it down. He'd even talk about his flaws. It was private, off the record. That seemed to put him at ease.

"Well, you could always try to, like... not be," Kate said, grimacing at her own language.

"It's who I am, though," Sean said. "I'm just gonna be a little annoying, no matter what."

"Naw. You can still be you and just keep that stuff quiet, I guess. I mean, if you know it's going to annoy someone."

"Yeah, but that's not me."

"It's still you," Sarah said. "Just like if Kate shut up, she'd still be Kate."

"And I'd be concerned," Sean said.

"So would I, why am I shutting up here?"

"I don't know," Sarah said, "maybe someone stabbed you in the larynx or something?"

Sarah smiled. She was getting snide. The group had a way of drawing a playful mood out of her.

Kate played along. "Okay, so I've been stabbed in the larynx. I didn't seek medical attention, why?"

"No, I would think you did, and they patch you up, but it's like, you have to heal for a bit."

"What if they gave her one of those voice box things?" Sean loved the hypotheticals. He relished the chance to work something out logically, even if it was one of the ridiculous situations that Sarah came up with as a joke.

"Wait, like Stephen Hawking?" Kate sounded concerned.

"Well, a different voice," he offered. "You could get the navigation lady voice."

"Then she'd be more annoying than you," Sarah said.

"Exactly!"

Meanwhile, Lee sat at the end of their row. He checked his phone periodically, waiting for the show to start. Sarah could see his expression occasionally shift as though holding in a laugh or trying to avoid rolling his eyes.

CHAPTER EIGHT

The sky was already dim when the group entered the theater. It was pitch black and cloudless by the time they made their way across the street to a small, candlelit bar in the middle of a block of storefronts. The space was sparse and warm, lined with oak accents, smelling of beer and grenadine. A sharply-dressed ocelot stood behind the counter; he was changing the record on a turntable.

"This is such a hipster place," Sean whispered.

"Oh, bah," Kate said. "It's comfortable. And Matthew is a wizard with bourbon."

And she had say over the evening. She was absent from the group's events for weeks, her time consumed by a major real estate deal. The deal finally finished, and she wanted to celebrate with her friends. As much as Sean acted as if he ran the show, he would freely concede control on such an occasion.

But it wouldn't prevent him from cracking wise about it.

"Seriously, this is just-"

"It's not your style, I know," Kate said. "I thought you liked to explore?"

"I'm here, aren't I?"

Kate scoffed. "Fine, what is your style? You a dive kinda guy? Snooty wine bar?"

"He's a Red Mast guy, totally," Lee said.

"Hey! Those are fighting words." Sean seemed legitimately offended, surprising Lee.

He recoiled. "Sorry man."

"No, it's..." Sean sighed. "Sorry. I know you were joking." He shuffled his feet. "You're not even that far off, honestly. I guess I like something more... anonymous? I mean, I'd love a sports bar that just didn't do sports. You know?"

"Think so," Sarah said. "More the restaurant, tavern sort of thing?"

"Yeah, I guess." He turned to Lee. "What's your kind of place? We can do that next time."

"Divey. Small, cheap, no frills. And you don't have to."

"We can try it, at least."

"You don't have to." Lee was insistent this time.

Sean paused. Rather than keep arguing, he asked Sarah, "What about you? I know you have a coffee place."

"Which becomes a bar at night."

"Which you never go to. Doesn't count."

Sarah rolled her eyes. "Fine. I guess..."

She looked around. It did feel like a hipster bar, but it felt like it had been there long before "hipster bar" was a thing. It was well-worn but well-maintained, its wooden stools comfortable with showing their age. Using vinyl records for background music felt a bit much, but she was on Kate's side. It felt like a good bar.

"I guess I'd be okay with this, honestly."

"Well good!" Kate claimed a booth with her purse. There were plenty of options available. "First round is on me!"

There was only ever one round. Typically, it was at a place that seemed more like Sean's style – taverns and pubs meant to be unassuming and inoffensive, along with the occasional microbrewery. They made for good venues. Everyone could handle one drink without complaint and could talk without distraction.

Kate wasn't interested in discussing the movie at all. She immediately started on about the deal, and how much work it took, and how great it was going to be for the whole Buckman neighborhood. Everyone else was willing to oblige; they hadn't seen her for at least a month, after all.

She must have made an arrangement with Matthew beforehand. Sarah had only come close to finishing her beer before a second round appeared unprompted.

"I guess we're properly partying at this point?" Sarah asked.

"What, is two in one night too many?" Sean replied.

Sarah gave him a flat look. "I can do, like, three before it's a problem. We just usually keep to one."

"Well, hey, it's a big night!" Kate said. She was one Old Fashioned in and already sounded loose. "I get to celebrate a big deal with my best friends! I love you guys."

"Aww," Sean said. "We love you too."

Kate took it as an invitation to lean on his shoulder, her thin tail wagging slightly. Lee gave Sarah a concerned look, but neither said anything. They knew what was going to happen next: Sean would pat her head with a platonic kindness, completely missing that when Kate said she loved "you guys" she meant him. She had admitted as much, outside of his company.

The group kept things going throughout the evening, each round followed by a fresh one. Matthew seemed to appreciate their presence, engaging in small talk as he came by. Sarah could even see him back behind the bar, chuckling at some of Sean's better jibes. Other than Sarah's group, the place was quiet.

As the night carried on, conversations began to avoid crossing the table. Lee and Sarah discussed movies more than anything. Observations about cinematic techniques, trivia around Kubrick and Carpenter. Sarah felt herself get more talkative with each round. Lee might have been doing the same, or he was just appeasing her constant conversation. Either one was fine. It was idle, friendly chatter, more intellectual than emotional.

The tone on the other side was more romantic. Kate and Sean weren't a couple – Sarah couldn't even think of a time he had a girlfriend – but they were acting as if they had been for ages. At least, Kate was. Her cheeks were flush with liquor and infatuation, her playful kicks under the table occasionally nicked Sarah's leg out of carelessness.

Sarah assumed it was just how she behaved when drunk. She had never seen it before. Some of the loving tones were even lobbed carelessly across the table. They made Lee blush, clearly embarrassed.

They'd either make a great couple or a terrible one. Now, Sean... Sean and I would work. Totally.

She had nothing but a year of social events to base the idea on. Sure, they had movie nights alone, tended to sit next to each other in theaters or at soccer games, and were occasional confidants when the situation demanded it. But Sean never expressed interest. Even here, he didn't seem to be reacting to Kate's attempts. He seemed more groggy than cuddly.

It was nearly midnight when Sarah finally called a cab, five drinks in. She had paid for none of them. Kate made sure of that. She tossed the driver more than enough to cover the fare before they set off and slouched into the back seat. The streetlights blurred.

Must be what it's like to be rich, Sarah thought, gradually, the evening's activities clouding her mind. *Throwing drinks at your friends all night like it's nothing. Must be nice.*

The radio was playing oldies; Styx, The Eagles, and the like. She hated oldies. Having to listen to them felt like a deserved punishment. All her drinking would be a bad idea come morning. Accepting this, she righted herself in the seat, trying to avoid falling asleep.

CHAPTER NINE

Sarah knew that putting herself within inches of a serious hangover was not the way to start a Monday morning. People loved to start their week with meetings, and they loved to drag her into them time and time again.

The actual hangover didn't bother her as much as the knowledge that it was unnecessary. She knew better.

She couldn't call in sick. There was a long meeting starting that morning, one that she had been organizing and preparing for the entire week prior. There was a bit of space between her and the beginning of the meeting, but it wasn't a wide enough window to escape through.

The morning dragged her feet like a ball and chain, making the hike to her desk all the more straining. The coffee was too far to consider. All she wanted to do was sit quietly and wait for the aspirin to kick in.

So of course, Michelle had to be unusually cheerful and bushy-tailed, her blouse blindingly bright. It could have just been the significant difference in moods tilting her perspective, but that didn't leave Sarah feeling any less insulted.

"Good morning! How was your weekend?" Michelle asked in a bouncing high tone as she arrived at her desk.

Sarah held out a paw and tipped it side to side, keeping her head on her desk, not bothering to look up.

Michelle huffed. "Rough, huh?" She inspected Sarah closer. "You do look kinda sick."

"Well, I'm feeling kinda sick, so that lines up."

"You could just take a sick day, you know."

Sarah finally picked her head up slightly. Her ears still lagged on the desk. "Not really. Wallace has their big meeting today. All heads. Can't get out of it."

"Can't work from home?"

"I'd still feel like shit." She leaned back, dropping her weight against the back of the chair. "I'll just grab some coffee and slap myself in the face."

"I can do that for you if it'd help."

"You mean grab coffee, right?" Sarah had moments where she wanted to slap Michelle in the face. She assumed the feeling was mutual.

"Pff, of course!" She trotted off with a slight spring in her step.

Sarah focused on merely trying to focus. She ran down the bullet points that they needed to cover. The list was on her computer, right in front of her, but the screen blurred in front of her eyes.

It wasn't going to be a good morning.

"Alright, here you go." Michelle delivered a mug, along with a few packets of sugar and creamer. "Wasn't sure how you do it."

"Eh. Might as well do black." She took a sip. It woke her up, but not the way she wanted. "Actually, no. No."

Michelle inspected her face again. "Oh... oh jeez. Are you hung over?"

"Well... I've had worse."

She let out equal parts giggle and chuckle. "Must've been a good weekend then! Didn't figure you partied that hard."

"I don't."

Between the aspirin and coffee, Sarah was slowly coming to. She dragged herself to the conference room, blending in with anyone else who resented Monday for the sin of existing.

9 o'clock came and went. She silently prayed that she would have to delay the meeting until another day. She sat across from Ash, a fellow rabbit from sales, and Omar, a red fox from design. Neither of them seemed interested in being there either.

44

The video conference was empty. The team on Wallace's side was never late before.

"I'm giving them five more minutes," Omar said, filling the dead air.

"It's only been five minutes," Ash said.

"Exactly. Give them ten minutes. Then, fuck it. I've got other stuff to do."

"Not to make this any more annoying, but where's Brian?" Sarah asked.

"Do we really want him in this meeting?" Omar asked.

"No. And there shouldn't be any tech parts left anyway. I'll just need an excuse why he's not here."

The video finally lit up. A pair of badgers was on the other side. "Hey guys, sorry we're late," the one on the right said. "It's been a madhouse. End of quarter and all that."

"Been the same here," Omar said. "Think we've all gone mad."

"Good morning to you too, Omar," the other badger deadpanned. "This everyone?"

"I think so," Sarah said. "Don't think there was anyone else on the invite."

"Is Brian around?" the first badger asked. "We may need to run a few things by him."

Omar sighed as he got up. "I'll go get him."

Sarah now had to bide for time. In many meetings, that felt like her primary responsibility. "So, Dan, should we wait for them, or can we get started?"

"Let's wait," the badger on the right said. "Don't want to have to repeat anything."

Sarah did her best to keep her grimace from showing. For as long as they had worked together, Dan was always more focused on moving things along. He usually was what made the group move forward without Sarah's help. She asked him as a gambit, and for the few dire minutes after it failed, small talk became the order of the day.

Omar returned with a tall coyote in tow. "Sorry I'm late, guys," he said. "Guess I didn't see the invite. Hey Dan, hey Allison."

"Hi Brian," they said in unison from the video screen.

"Alright," Sarah said, "we should probably get things moving here. Got lots to cover, lot of things are sort of smashing together at this point."

"'Smashing together.' I like that," Allison said, holding in a laugh.

"Does feel like a car crash sometimes," Ash muttered into her chest.

"Well, before we get rolling," Brian said, "can I just run one thing past everyone? I was checking in with Dan's team on Friday, just want to make sure everyone's good with some details on the tech side."

There shouldn't be any tech stuff left, Sarah repeated to herself, wanting to yell it. Instead, "Right, let's give that a quick minute, then we'll get on to collaterals" came out instead.

She wanted to kick herself. The headache from the hangover was gone, but a new one was taking its place.

By the time the meeting broke for lunch, Sarah had hoped to be discussing distribution. Omar had questions on that point, and she felt they were important. Instead, the subject was probably hours away, as Brian's one thing turned into a zombie, shambling along and refusing to die.

She downed lunch rapidly as if going fast here would make the rest of the day go fast as well. It would not.

Even if meetings were an important part of her job, Sarah never enjoyed them. She doubted anyone did. It was often a pain of boredom, of time consumed that didn't need consuming. They weren't stressful to her, just annoying.

This meeting was especially annoying. Miscommunications came to light while new ones seemed to form before her eyes. She had lost control of the schedule. All she could do was keep Dan and Omar from getting at each other's throats. It wasn't even a question of species animosity – she knew of no bad blood between foxes and badgers – they were just too stubborn about everything.

Eventually, the digressions were too much. "Alright! Alright, alright, alright." Sarah had to raise her voice just to be heard. "Look. It's 4 o'clock here, it's 5 o'clock there, we still have a shitload of stuff to go over. We're done for today. I'm going to go, I'm going to filter all this down to whoever's in charge of what, and I'm going to send an email to each one of you. You tell me what's up, I'll put it together, send it to everyone, and then. Only then, if you want to keep arguing, then you can go for it. Right now, we need to head home."

It was the most she had talked in the entire meeting.

"Can I just-"
"No, Dan, no. We're good. We're done. Please, let's just get back to this tomorrow."

The emails she assigned herself took a long time. She always found it difficult to write while angry, and that meeting left her fuming. The words had to be squeezed out unnaturally. They took on a cynical cheerfulness, as though she were masking her feelings by inverting them.

She left the office almost two hours later, passing by the conference room on her way out. Dan and Omar were still going at it. Clearly, nobody else wanted any part of it.

CHAPTER TEN

Rush hour should have finished by the time Sarah started cutting across downtown. Judging by the lines of cars and the red glow radiating above the streets, that wasn't the case. The glow was only red, no blue mixed in. Most likely, there were no accidents, nothing to reasonably cause the backup.

Though, perhaps it wasn't any worse. Maybe she was taking her work home with her, as she always did, and the sour mood had started to color her view of the traffic. Even mundane levels of traffic were bound to fell torturous. She honked angrily at every SUV and BMW that cut her off. The mildest traffic violation turned into a personal slight.

Her muscles held tight, her chest tensed and ached. She felt sick. The traffic gave her plenty of time to worry about that.

Just as the roads seemed stuffed to the brim with cars, so was her apartment building's parking lot. Cars filled her usual spots, even the convenient spot near the front that nobody ever seemed to claim. She settled for a spot on the street.

None of these nuisances were all that unusual. Some days, traffic was just heavy; sometimes the parking lot just filled up. But they interfered with her routine, and right now, she did not need anything interfering with her routine.

Getting inside provided calm. The mail room was the same old mail room it always was, lined with the same mailboxes, each stuffed with the same junk mail. The same ceiling light glowed yellow inside the same frosted dome. It was boring but consistent.

Sarah grabbed her mail. All junk mail. She sighed in relief; finally, something was back to normal.

As she walked to the elevator, she glanced around at the doors of the smaller, cheaper ground-level apartments. A scattered few had sheets of paper taped to them.

Guess a lot of people didn't pay their rent. Wonder what happened. Or... wait, is that how Deborah handles it? Don't think I've ever seen it.

She never saw any rent notice herself. Even if she had to cut it close, she paid on time. There were few things more important to keep in good standing than a home.

There were more sheets taped to more doors when she arrived on her floor. They covered an entire wall of doors.

Can't be rent. Not this many people. Has to be something else. Maybe something with Waterknell. Probably just how they spread the news.

Waterknell wasn't in charge yet, but logistics can take time. Carl had spotted Andrew roaming the building on several occasions. Crews seemed to be doing inspections, taking stock of the place themselves.

Sarah preferred Deborah's letters. At least that way, she knew people got the message. As it was, she could just run down the hall grabbing every note off of the doors, and nobody would be any the wiser. It would be mean and pointless, but possible. And it would let off some steam.

Her wandering mind stopped in its tracks as she reached her door. It found the sense of fear and guilt it seemed to be seeking out. Her door had a note on it as well. She pulled it down, dropped her purse on her couch, and opened it.

Residents,

We hope you've seen the news that your building is becoming another wonderful Waterknell Management property! This is a historic and unique building that we all share, and we want to do our best to treat it – and you – with care and respect.

Like any transition period, there will be a bit of dust. Our maintenance crew will be doing some guided inspections of the units starting this Wednesday. You won't have to be present, and per state law, we'll remind you the day before we enter your unit. For your own reference, we'll be taking a look at your unit 309 on Friday.

The letter was typed, with the unit number and date stamped in their places, a small and impersonal touch. Still, it was no big deal. Just a maintenance note surrounded by typical corporate speak. The language could be more charming and inviting, but if this was Waterknell's style, then so be it.

Sarah was privately relieved, and then embarrassed that she was so concerned about something so seemingly minor. The note went on further.

We will do our best to keep policies around noise, maintenance requests, rent payments and all the other details close to what you're already used to. These changes are always difficult, and we don't want to make things harder than they need to be.

There are, however, some changes that will need to be made, particularly in regards to your leases. Because of the change of ownership, each resident will need to sign a new lease with Waterknell Management. You'll have to sign by November 1st. We know that many residents are on month-to-month leases, and for those residents, we will continue to extend that option. As these are new leases, they will be brought closer in line with market expectations for this class of building. Your unit type and lease rate information are included below.

Residents who do not wish to sign a new lease with Waterknell will be required to vacate their units by November 1st. If necessary, we will work with residents who may need an additional day or two.

We apologize for any inconvenience, and we hope to have a chance to serve all of you as our latest Waterknell community!

Thanks,
Andrew Casterwall

"The fuck's going on?" Sarah asked nobody. She was used to corporate speak and euphemisms, so the meaning was hardly lost. Still, the entire situation left her uneasy.

She heard Carl's apartment door open. His didn't have a note on it, so he had apparently already read it. "Hey, Carl? Did you check this note out?"

"Yeah, it's fucking bullshit," he said.

"I know. It feels... bad."

"Of course it's bad. It's a goddamn eviction."

She stared at him blankly. "Seriously?" *Evicted? Us?*

"Sure as hell sounds like it. Look." Carl pointed at Sarah's note, still in her paw. "Look at what those motherfuckers are gonna charge us for the place."

Sarah checked the bottom of the note. The combined utility cost was the same, but her rent would be going up nearly $500 a month. That would be a sizable chunk of what she was paying now. The jump was probably less painful for people who had just moved into the building, but for someone like Carl who had been there a decade...

"Did you talk to any of them?" Sarah asked.

"Yup. Andrew swung by. I read the note, nearly swung at him. Bastard's doubling my rent."

"Shit. I'm sorry dude."

"Goddamn out of towers," Carl said, limping down the hall. "Fucking up a perfectly good thing."

It was a good thing. Sarah grabbed her apartment when things were relatively cheap. Deborah was so concerned about the people living there that she barely raised rents when things started picking up. Sure, it meant

52

maintenance fell to the side from time to time, but Sarah found no reason to complain.

Sean had moved more recently, though, and Kate always talked about the real estate market. It wasn't friendly. Those two could certainly handle it, and perhaps Sarah could too, but there was no way Carl could. He couldn't possibly have enough saved up in his retirement fund.

He was right to be angry.

Sarah hoped to find some help or advice she could give. She started half a dozen different sentences in her head before conceding that she had nothing. All she could do is let him vent. As Carl made his way to the elevator, Sarah could hear that he was taking every opportunity to do so.

Sarah brooded instead. The Deadline Cafe was the one place that felt most like home to her, but her own apartment was a strong runner up. She had everything settled from years of living in the apartment. The furniture had been rearranged several times over the years, and it now perfectly fit her routines. Likewise, her routines had come to fit her apartment.

Perhaps that was what she was so attached to. Everything about the place was familiar – the slightly vaulted ceiling, the worn hardwood floor. It was routine, typical, safe. It was what she wanted. Now, even with the walls around her and floor below her, it felt as though everything she enjoyed had all vanished.

Grabbing her laptop, she vanished as well, walking down the street in the cooling September night.

CHAPTER ELEVEN

Sarah never went to the Deadline Cafe at night, when it turned into a bar. She definitely didn't want to drink, not after Sunday night. Though, after the Monday she'd had, the thought did occur to her.

"You guys still do coffee at this hour, right?" she asked the badger behind the counter. Her usual barista was nowhere to be found.

"I guess so," he said. "Nobody really asks."

There was hardly anybody around who could have asked. For as quiet as her usual Sunday afternoon visits were from time to time, the evening seemed completely dead. Yet, there was a small crowd, relaxing over cocktails and glasses of wine, more than could be said about the bar she was at on Sunday.

Sarah was jittery even before touching her latte. She put her laptop on the table and scanned all of the possibilities she had been trying to budget. They were there in case something went wrong, and something had definitely now gone wrong.

She couldn't find any budgets in case she lost her apartment.

"Christ," she muttered to herself. "Why did I not think of this?"

The list of worries looked more like a list of fantasies. The scenarios she had planned for now, in hindsight, seemed ridiculous. Of course she wasn't going to lose her job, of course Sean wasn't going to move in with her, of course...

At least, there was groundwork laid. She had an excellent idea of how her finances moved around, all of it already logged. She had already identified areas of spending that could be improved. Adding another scenario to the list was comparatively easy work.

It was also scary work. She found herself tweaking numbers beyond reality to allow herself to stay where she was. She made optimistic assumptions that she knew deep down were false. Even with all of that fantasy, she didn't feel secure. The belt would be too tight.

She sighed. *I should've saved more. Probably could've bought me another five months. Maybe six. But, no, it's not enough, I'm not month-to-month. I'd have to sign a full year. Maybe I should finally make a move with Sean, get a two bedroom with him. He just moved, though. And... no, there's no way he even would. Sheesh, come on Sarah. You need to be serious here, stop fucking around.*

She couldn't force herself to be optimistic. After hearing from Sean about his hunt, she dreaded going through it herself. There wasn't any other neighborhood that she particularly liked. They were all becoming too flashy, too upscale, too full of themselves. Or, they were neighborhoods so far from the center of town that they were functionally suburban.

She let herself wallow into her coffee for a few minutes, mind wandering aimlessly. Her attention floated to the artwork she would see every week, looking more sinister now in the limited light. The hanging pyramid of wires glowed orange in the dim light.

Nobody here was going to give her a pep talk. She would have to do it herself.

Alright, rabbit. Two things. One. Text Sean. Tell him what's going on, find out whatever he knows, what advice he can give. Hopefully, he can help. Two. Figure out what your options are. Staying is not going to work. Anything cheaper, at least, give it a look.

It was a plan. It was cobbled together and promised nothing, but it was a plan, and Sarah liked having a plan. She quickly sent Sean a text, hardly thinking about what she was saying, then started pulling up every website for finding an apartment she could think of.

Her usual corner was now illuminated by a variety of colors emanating from her screen, the result of her wandering from website to website. The walls absorbed as much as they could to keep the subdued ambiance in the rest of the room. The painting, behind her as usual, was clearly illuminated by her screen; her ears, usually protecting it, fell flat alongside her head.

She decided, as a matter of principle, to ignore any of the buildings that Waterknell managed already. She wasn't going to go through the effort of getting away from them only to fall back into their claws. Besides, considering how much they were going to charge for her current apartment, anything cheaper they were offering had to be a noticeable step down.

Despite that limitation, the news looked good at first glance. There were plenty of apartments around town that she could look into. However, only a handful were less expensive than the rate she was threatened with. Those would still be a jump, and sometimes a large one, but she felt a little better about them. They would be difficult to manage, but they could work.

She had a handful saved when her phone buzzed. Sean had texted his reply. "What are you talking about?"

Sarah, in her mad and mindless rush to make progress, had apparently sent "Apart prob talk?" She could understand why Sean was confused. She wasn't entirely sure what it was supposed to be either.

"Your apartment hunt, can we talk about it sometime? I'm getting kicked from my place," she sent.

Sean's reply came quickly. "Sorry :(Wanna swing by Wednesday after work?"

"Sure," Sarah sent, putting her phone down.

CHAPTER TWELVE

A good week at work was not going to happen. The arguments with Wallace were either dying down or happening outside of her view, but Sarah knew they still existed. Either way, she held on to the hope that the project would clean up without any last-minute madness.

She was focused on her computer screen, typing an email, when Roger gave a knock at her desk.

"Hey, you got a moment?" he said.

Sarah shrugged, knowing she wasn't going to change the outcome.

"Let's grab one of the offices, I got some news for you."

Roger had always been difficult to pin down. Sarah found him hard to trust, but he never did anything to deserve the impression. He was just a fat, aging squirrel who still fidgeted as much as any squirrel did.

He knew how to be precise with his words. "I want to talk" always meant bad news, but never about the person hearing the news. Only when he went with "I'm gonna need to talk for a bit" were you in trouble.

"I got some news" was relatively accurate. It'd be news. Not necessarily good, or bad, or even relevant to the person receiving it.

But it still required a closed door, which Sarah learned only after entering the small office.

"So, what did I do this time?" she asked, trying to lift her own mood. She knew his approach to language, so she knew the joke would be harmless.

"Well, there is the whole... no, I can't," Roger said. "Seriously, though, we're kinda gearing things up for the Q4 work."

Sarah nodded. "Good?"

"I guess," he said with a nervous laugh. "I mean, we've definitely had better, but it doesn't seem like it's the worst."

The worst resulted in layoffs, so she was happy that wasn't going to happen. "Guessing you need something from me, then?"

"Well, maybe." He hesitated. "So, the thing is, Thomas is going to leave."

Sarah hardly reacted. She and Thomas had only interacted once, maybe twice. They tended to cover widely different industries with their work, and besides, Sarah didn't really care to compete with the other marketing managers. They were partners, not enemies.

"All his stuff is gonna get moved around, obviously. Which, he's got a few things frozen, so right now, it's just the HiSense account."

She was a bit surprised that he only ran one campaign, but then, maybe it was a large one. Regardless, it was neutral news – not bad, not good, just a thing that happened. "Okay then," she said flatly, not sure how he expected her to react.

"Well, from what I understand, you've got some free space the next quarter or two?"

Sarah thought for a moment. "Yeah, I guess so. I mean, Wallace Sport is getting into execution mode. Unless Brian keeps fucking with the schedule."

"Oh, is he doing that again?"

She rolled her eyes. "Don't get me started."

"Well, too late."

A polite chuckle. "But, yeah, they're not going to need me all that much at that point. They shouldn't, anyway."

"Good, good." His eyes wandered. "Well, to be fair, Vinish was on that one contract that ended up falling apart, so he's pretty light on stuff too. And Michelle's been saying she has space for a while."

"I can see that. She's been pretty chatty this quarter."

"Heh. Well, yeah, good luck with that I guess."

"It's not a problem."

"Good. But, yeah, losing Thomas means someone's gotta take over his stuff. So Gary and I are gonna have to decide who takes it over. Just wanted to make sure you knew it could be coming up."

"I guess this is where I should be all 'pick me, pick me,' right?" She didn't want to do it, but she could at least pretend she cared that much.

"I mean, if you want," Roger said with a nervous laugh. "This is more just letting you know."

"You think it's going to fall into my lap?"

"I don't know, we haven't really discussed it much yet. Think it's an even chance between you and Vinish."

"Not Michelle?"

"Well, yeah, and Michelle. Of course."

Sarah returned to her desk. Her part of the building felt quieter than usual; she assumed it was just because Michelle had taken the day off. But she couldn't avoid feeling an ominous undercurrent. Strange, considering the news delivered was neutral. Good, potentially.

Maybe things with Wallace were going haywire again. She passed around a handful of emails, then started digging through the internal documentation on HiSense. She didn't want the extra work, ultimately, but she knew her reputation around the office. Roger was probably batting for her, and there was a fair chance he'd win.

The research soon became a necessary way to fill her day. Despite the humming, ever-present panic that marked the end of the quarter, her inbox was quiet. Apartment hunting was only providing so many leads and so much distraction. She needed something to keep her occupied until her dinner with Alex.

CHAPTER THIRTEEN

There were plenty of Portland's neighborhoods that Sarah would feel comfortable moving into. Alex's was not one of them. It would be affordable, almost astoundingly so, but it was cheap for a reason. It was an old industrial area, once a major center of commerce and productivity, now half-abandoned. Some of the warehouses had been converted to other uses. The work was generally cheap and quick, and it showed.

It became a gathering place for many of the city's poor and artistic. There were affordable places to live, even if a few were hardly a step up from a flophouse. The kind of reasonable studio that Alex had required a waiting list the length of which rivaled the most luxurious new condos.

The shops that lined the neighborhood's roads were all somewhat worn down. At least, they felt that way compared to the freshly-renovated downtown shops. Among them was a pizza place, a tight hole in the wall. It wasn't fancy, but it wasn't expensive either. Even though the kangaroo behind the counter and many of the scraggly patrons made her nervous sometimes, Sarah liked the place. It felt honest.

Alex liked it too. He was the one that recommended it when they dated, and even now it served as an occasional base of operations. He never seemed nervous here; many of those scraggly patrons were his neighbors, his friends.

Sarah arrived with a mission. She wanted to vent about the eviction, primarily, but she also wanted to help Alex.

"So, I saw there's a place opening up downtown," she started. "Couple blocks from my office. Gallery kind of thing, I guess."

"Oh?" Alex asked, already sounding slightly dismissive.

"Yeah. It said they were looking for people who had work to sell. You should drop by and talk to them."

"Naw, I couldn't do that."

"You sure? I mean, I know I don't know the whole art scene very well, but I figured you could."

"It's... the whole scene is complicated." Alex took a bite, looking down at the table.

"Well, still. Could even just be another spot to work. Looked like they already had a little studio thing set up."

Alex looked up at the bare vents held together with duct tape. They didn't appear to be an aesthetic choice.

"I dunno. My place is fine."

"You like it there?" She tried to avoid a judgmental tone.

"I guess. Like, it's where I work, and it works." He shrugged. "I don't really think about it, honestly."

"It's inspiration?"

He shook his head. "Not really. I don't think so."

Sarah glanced around, wondering if anything in the pizza place could offer her inspiration. That is, assuming she was looking for it. "Well, maybe it's worth a try, but you don't have to."

"I know."

"It's just... you complain about the place a lot. Let's be honest."

Alex nodded. "It does kinda suck."

"I think the phrase you used was 'damp druggie shithole?'"

Alex smiled and giggled. He had a way of acting like a high school girl who had just set up one particularly mean prank.

Sarah narrowed her eyes. "What? What did..." Her eyes widened as she caught on. "Alex."

He kept laughing quietly. "I was gonna say 'it's my shithole,' but..."

Sarah burst out laughing. "Goddammit, Alex!"

"You were thinking it!"

"No, I wasn't!"

"What's going on over there?" the kangaroo behind the counter called out in a gravely, aggravated voice. "Did Seinfeld show up when I wasn't looking?"

"I'm just fucking with her, Tommy," Alex called back. "Don't worry about it."

"Fine, there you go," he said.

Tommy was a gruff man who would be retired if he wasn't running the pizza place. He had a habit of interacting with customers, especially when they started getting loud. Sometimes, Sarah was grateful that he'd set a rowdy crowd straight; occasionally, it felt like he was mocking the customers instead. No matter the direction his comments were aimed in, it was uncomfortable to hear.

Still, better that than a disinterested barista.

"Come on," Alex said, "you like the jokes. Admit it."

"No, I don't!" Her laughter was slowly subsiding.

"Girls love a guy with a sense of humor, don't they?"

"Would- Seriously. Would you go for a guy just because he was funny? Honestly."

"I guess. I mean, if he was cute, sure."

"Well, duh, of course, you go for a guy if he's cute. I'm saying, sense of humor, nothing else."

"But I didn't say it's just a sense of humor. Like, it helps, it's an add-on, it makes the whole thing better."

Sarah didn't find it odd that she could discuss the relative virtues of potential boyfriends with her former boyfriend. She couldn't do it with any of her other exes, but then, she didn't remain friends with any of her other exes. And none of them were like Alex.

The two spent a few more minutes running through their playful arguments, debating the finer points of attractiveness. Sarah had to admit a disadvantage here. Since they broke up, she hadn't found another boyfriend. She rarely even found herself wanting one. Alex, meanwhile,

65

had both another girlfriend and a boyfriend in the intervening year. Sarah never met either of them. She wondered how she compared.

At this point, they were both single again, spending time together as friends. Sarah found comfort in knowing that they could go through everything they'd gone through and still come out of it okay. She had initially worried that Alex would come to resent her, or that they would drift far apart, or any number of more absurd hesitations.

They had drifted apart, slightly. Alex wasn't interested in the movie group. Sarah continued to go to gallery showings and generally support Alex how she could, but it was much less than she used to.

The conversation stalled, having gotten too ridiculous for either to continue one-upping the other. "So. They're kicking you out, huh?" Alex finally asked.

"Yeah. That's how Carl's taking it, at least. It's not a real eviction, but it's like... Deborah got bought out, they jack up the rent, I don't know if I can afford it."

He nodded. "Man. Didn't think you'd get stuck with that."

"I know, it's kinda crazy."

"I mean, you're like... rich."

Sarah grimaced. "I'm not rich. Like, okay. I've been doing well, sure. But Sean makes, at least, thirty grand more a year than I do. And he doesn't even have student loans. Kate threw five or six rounds at the bar on Sunday night, like it was nothing. They're rich."

"Yeah, but you weren't worried about rent before this."

"I had cheap rent! I was lucky, that's all it was. I'm always lucky. Like, I lucked into my job, it's better than I probably deserve. I got lucky with the rent, and now that's gone, and it's like..."

She looked for a conclusion to her thought and came up empty. Rabbits were supposed to be lucky, so to Sarah, everything was luck. The thought that her success and comfort was the result of any work she put in seemed too distant to be real. Since everything was just luck, she couldn't shake the feeling that she ought to be struggling more. She was doing too well for how much effort she put in.

And here was Alex, always struggling. She always felt guilty about it, as if she had stolen all of his luck and kept it for herself. She wanted to give it back. Being nearby wouldn't help, considering luck isn't a communicable disease. But maybe she could do something for him. She certainly didn't want him to do anything for her. She could take care of herself.

"Well, I hope you end up finding something," Alex eventually said. "It's pretty shitty out there."

"I know. I was looking a bit at work, it's pretty stupid."

"Some of those are probably just jokes."

"They certainly feel like it," Sarah said, frustrated.

"Well, I mean, Darien likes doing that sort of thing."

"What, putting up fake apartment listings?"

Alex nodded with a subtle joy. "Yeah. They're obvious jokes, I think so anyway. Mostly making fun of the high-end shit out there. But sometimes, it's like, I wouldn't be surprised if someone bought it."

Sarah sighed. "That's not exactly going to help."

"Oh, come on. If you weren't hunting you'd find it funny."

"I dunno. Seems kinda mean."

"It's kinda cool. He's just poking the whole stupid thing in the eye. It's what he does. I paint things that scare people, he pisses on capitalism."

"Your stuff's not scary. It's just weird."

Alex smiled. "That's why I like you."

CHAPTER FOURTEEN

Sean lived in one of the new apartments that popped up since Sarah first moved to town. It was flashy and modern, coated in glass and steel, part of a neighborhood that bloomed out of old breweries and factories. Alex's neighborhood was probably destined for the same fate. If Sean's building didn't have so many neighbors of similar style, it would stick out like an ominous spire along the river. Instead, it was one of a bouquet, a cluster that radiated the desires and mindset of the city's newest imports.

It wasn't Sarah's style. She didn't resent the buildings being there, unlike some of her more vocal coworkers. Sure, they could block some lovely views from Forest Park and caused some heavy traffic from time to time, but if people were going to move here anyway, they might as well build what they could. She didn't know of anything that neighborhood was being used for before they started popping up. Maybe her impending rent would be even worse without them.

The inside felt as utilitarian as the outside. The owners, whoever they were, clearly tried to make it more inviting. However, gray carpets and bare concrete pillars weren't "inviting" by Sarah's definition. Seeing the skeleton of the tower, freshly-built and well-engineered, felt more unsettling than seeing the splitting beams and stacks of brick that made up Alex's building. Something so polished, so precise, felt like it had to be hiding something.

She liked what Sean had done with his little slice of the building. His personality better matched the technical, perfected feel. He had built a shrine to the future in his apartment; computers and consoles sitting like sculptures on tall desks, monitors and TVs positioned like electronic paintings.

His selection of furniture was more random, a collection cobbled together by chance. Each piece looked either vintage or bargain, no two pieces matching, even fewer fitting together in style. It reminded her of the back part of the Deadline Cafe. She had wanted to do the same with her own decor, but she already had all the furniture she needed.

"Think you could stand a place like this?" Sean asked, laying on his bed. His apartment was a studio, leaving few other places to sit. Despite his best efforts to create the illusion of a bedroom, the fact was inescapable.

"It's worth a try, at least," Sarah said, wandering around the space. "Is the management all that bad?"

"They're fine. Far as I can tell. I only had one other place back home, so I don't have much reference."

"Roger. Kinda doubt they're as good as Deborah, anyway."

"She's the one that's booting you?"

"Not really. She sold, the new guys are raising rates."

"Gotcha. Heard they were pretty bad about that here, initially. The management changed maybe... two months after I moved in? Something like that."

"Pretty recent."

"Yeah. They've been okay so far. Don't have any of the community stuff anymore, though. Used to be like, something going on every other night. Now it's pretty quiet."

Sarah shrugged. "Quiet's good, honestly."

"I thought you liked to know your neighbors?"

"I like Carl. Carl's interesting."

"Thought you were like that with everyone."

"Nope. Just him. The people in the apartment next to me, I still don't know their names."

He sat up. "Well, I don't know any of my neighbors' names, so, welcome home!"

Sarah laughed, just nervous enough for her to notice. "Are the other apartments pretty similar? Far as you know?"

"Far as I know. They're all just copies," Sean said, gesturing at the walls. "I saw one a couple floors up before I moved in, was exactly the same as this. The one bedroom is funky, though. And huge."

"And way too much. I did some digging at work." She sat at one of the few chairs not situated in front of a computer. "Besides, this place is bigger than mine."

"You're kidding. Your place is definitely bigger."

"Five eighty-eight. This is six twenty, according to the site."

"Well, damn." He looked around. "Where'd all my space go?"

"Your computers are taking it all up. You should clearly get rid of those."

"Evil woman." He reached to grab a pillow. "Move over there, I don't wanna hit anything valuable."

"You'd miss anyway."

Sean put on fake gravitas. "Madam, I accept your challenge."

Sarah enjoyed teasing Sean. It was easy. "Well, hey, if I do wind up living around here you'll be able to bother me a lot more."

"So why would you want to live here? I'm annoying, we've agreed on this."

"It's an endearing kind of annoying. Otherwise, none of us would put up with you." Sean chuckled in agreement. "Besides, you're not that bad."

"Thank you. I've been trying."

Sarah blinked. He sounded surprisingly earnest. "Wait. Really?"

Sean dithered, as though he had shared too much. "Jessie's been biting at me lately about it. Guess I've been pissing him off too much."

"He's on your team?"

"Yep. Can't really avoid him."

"Well, I mean, it's just one opinion. You don't have to get along with everyone."

Sean pointed. "You do, though."

"Not really. Michelle hates me."

"I mean, the people you have to manage."

Sarah thought. "Eh, even they don't really like me. I don't think they hate me, but still."

"Well, either way, he's right. I should probably cut it down a little bit."

Sarah dropped onto the bed, laying next to Sean. "It's fine. It's just part of who you are."

"I guess."

"I mean, if you want to change, then sure, change. Just, don't do it just because one person doesn't like you. Go with what's in your heart."

Sean rolled over, looking at Sarah with a flat expression. "What are you, my mom?"

Sarah deserved it. She didn't know where the sappy sentiment came from. "Dude. No. You're older than me."

Sean grinned. "Okay. Sister?"

The grin alone was enough to get Sarah giggling. "God, I hope not. That'd be awful."

"Hey, you see me at Thanksgiving every year. That's a family thing."

"Only because my parents won't fly out here. They make me go back there for Christmas."

"How are the folks, by the way? Usual?"

"Far as I know," she said with a sigh. "Told mom about the apartment thing, she just gave me the whole 'you're a grown woman, you can figure it out' thing. Says that for everything."

"Oh well."

"Yeah. Your mom the same way?"

Sean hesitated. "Probably."

Sarah didn't know why she asked. He sounded uncomfortable, and it wasn't something she could help with anyway.

They talked idly for hours. By the time Sarah left, it was well past when she planned to have dinner. She grabbed some Chinese on the way home – Buddha's Delight, like she routinely had in her college days.

Those days were predictable. She always knew what to do next, what was coming next. The apartment she shared with an old classmate stayed the same year after year, no surprises or instability. Her boyfriend Zach was always available, right until he got his dream job in Belfast. Even that came with enough warning that Sarah was ready for it.

For whatever reason, as the rain started to fall from the dark gray sky, those days came into her head. They seemed so far away now. Sean and Zach were different animals, but they felt so much alike.

She went to sleep, relaxed. If luck were on her side, things would be relaxed in the office as well.

CHAPTER FIFTEEN

Initially, her luck seemed to hold out. She arrived at the office to find a cease-fire between Dan and Omar. Things could finally flow and finish up with much less interference. Wallace should finish on time, exactly as Sarah had hoped.

She sipped her coffee calmly, expecting a decent day.

"So."

Michelle wasn't bright or bubbly today. Her face hung flat, the corner of her mouth pulled back with just a hint of a sneer. Her tail dragged close behind her, lifeless. Sarah guessed she was either plotting something or resented something.

"So?" Sarah asked, confused, bending an ear forward. She put down her coffee.

"Got a chance to catch up with Roger," she said. "Guess we're battling now."

"One way to look at it."

"You're not?"

Sarah leaned back in her chair. "I mean, if it was something either of us could do anything about, sure. But from what Roger said, he and Gary just have to work out who's gonna get it."

"Right. And you really don't think they're going to watch us from here on to decide?"

Sarah shrugged. "We've been here for years, if they're gonna base it on the next couple weeks, then they're idiots. They're not going to."

"But you don't know that."

"I don't really care," she said, spinning back to face her computer.

Michelle sat down, sliding her chair closer to Sarah's desk. "Well then, tell Roger that. Get yourself out of the running. Leave it to someone who needs it."

Needs it? Sarah thought. She turned back around to face Michelle, her ears folded back. "I'm not going to tell my boss that I don't care about my job. I mean, even if that's not what I say, I'm sure that's how he's going to take it."

"Just say you're not interested in this project. Make it really clear, really specific."

She looked narrowly at Michelle. "Why are you so insistent that I drop on this?"

"Why do you keep insisting not to?"

Sarah grimaced, uncertain of the answer herself. "They're going to give it to you anyway."

"How do you know?"

"I haven't done a thing in the tech sector. You have. You'd know it better than me. Besides, you're the senior."

"Exactly, they'll give the app company to the kid."

Sarah groaned. "Goddammit, you know what I meant. You've been here longer. You're better at this than I am. I barely have any apps on my phone as it is. Your kids probably know more about this stuff than I do."

"I don't let Oliver touch it," Michelle said proudly. "He always gets himself into trouble with a computer. He's just about broken his tablet, he put so much crap on the thing."

"There, exactly." She tried to sound encouraging. "You've got a subject matter expert in your freakin' home. You got this."

Michelle turned to face her computer, seeming to process the thought. Sarah turned as well, confident that the matter was dropped. She didn't want to keep arguing if she didn't have to.

"So are you gonna tell Roger you don't want to do it?"

Sarah hung her head and bit her lip. "If they know what they're doing, they'll give the account to the best person for it. That's not me. That's either you or Vinish and frankly, I think they'd pick you over him. But, if they want to give it to me, then fine, I'll take it. That's the job."

"They'll give it to you." She sounded defeated.

"You don't know that! We're not the ones making the decision, they are. And they're not even deciding until October. Unless you go and, like, burn the place down and run off to a Mexican resort, you're going to be fine. They're going to give it to you."

"Then why not give it up? Get it off your mind?"

"It's not going to matter. It's not."

With that, Sarah walked off to another meeting. She knew she didn't want Thomas' project that badly, and she had even less interest in brown-nosing upper management. It would keep her workload reasonable, at least, and having something in the works might protect her in case anything started going south. But which project she had next, be it Thomas' or one that arrived next quarter, didn't matter.

But she didn't want to lose to a wolf. Rabbits always lost to wolves. The idea was drilled into her head her entire life, and it tinted how she saw the world. She had slowly learned not to be afraid of them, but it took conscious effort to actually fight back against one.

Fighting was scary. Fighting forced her to take a stand on something, which inevitably meant being against someone else. It made her attack and defend and try not to come out bloodied in one way or another, whether matted fur or bruised ego.

She spent the meeting calming down instead of paying attention. She knew it wasn't a large fight, but it still hit her adrenaline. Afterwards, she loitered in the office and waited until Michelle was away from her desk. The opportunity opening, she grabbed her purse and made her way out the door.

CHAPTER SIXTEEN

It was rare for Sarah to have a chance to eat lunch in peace and quiet, and even rarer for her to take advantage of it. Her job was one of constant activity, whether being busy or simply appearing to be. The last weeks of the quarter were the worst. To take any sort of downtime in the midst of all the chaos and noise was bizarre, almost irresponsible, but she knew she had to give her mind a break.

She never had an enemy at work before. Most of the people she worked with over the years were kind at best and passive-aggressive at worst. They were annoying and got in the way, but there was no animosity. There wouldn't be a fight unless she picked it. Which she never did. It was never worth it.

Sarah walked to no particular destination, intending only to release and clarify her thoughts. As practice, she forced herself to take in the architecture around her. She had passed the buildings a dozen times before but never paid any attention to them.

The closest buildings, all glass and concrete, towered over her. The buildings off in the distance felt less imposing only because they were far away. As she walked towards them, they stretched up, making their presence known to her.

She stopped at a crosswalk, shielding herself from the chill winds, and looked at the citadel that sat catty-corner to her. It was a bank building, sleek and barren, white concrete spires framing it on every side. She figured it was taller than the building Sean worked out of, on the other end of downtown. It was more intimidating, for sure. Its concrete blocks demanded obedience.

Architecture never interested Sarah, and that showed no signs of changing. Her focus was a means of distraction – away from the office, away from the apartment, away from the cooling weather. That would be an uphill battle. Every office building reminded her of her own, no matter how different it was. She tried to divert her thoughts to her friends, but that lead her back to conversations with Sean and Alex, and thus the apartment.

She was desperate for something to focus on. The people? There were many around for the lunch hour. Many of them branched out from the government buildings, wearing suits or buttoned-up blouses. Michelle would be dressed down compared to them. There were pockets of students carrying backpacks and programmers wearing their hoodie-and-jeans uniform. The students probably envied the secure success of the programmers, and the programmers probably envied the adventurous freedom of the students. Sarah envied both.

There were those she pitied. One shambled towards her, wearing a blanket as a cape, tail matted and dragging, interested in nothing around him. Sarah hastily shuffled past when they crossed. He probably asked her for change, but she didn't pay any attention. She gave to charities each year to help people like him; surely, she had done her duty. The warming flush of guilt reminded her that she was lying.

She had far less need for help, but she knew it wasn't coming to her either. There were plenty of politics at the office that she had managed to stay out of so far. They had a way of emerging when something was on the line, and most of her coworkers had their allegiances and alliances. Michelle was definitely working to find designers and sales staff that would support her campaign. She didn't have much of a head start, from what little Sarah had gathered. All of the marketing managers had a more or less even reputation.

Another gust of wind. She was sick of the cold at this point. The parking garage she happened to be next to had a small deli in its ground floor that she ducked inside. It was small and secluded, barely a row of tables constituting its dining area. The floor was well-worn linoleum, the tables draped with basic tablecloths, the chairs seemingly ripped from a convention center. It was bland, without a doubt.

She went with a Mediterranean pasta salad. Something familiar and comfortable. It was nothing special, hardly worth the walk, but the exercise gave her space. That was all she needed. The stress started to dissipate, slowly dripping from her shoulders. She watched more workers walk past the window, most of them in blue collar outfits – a dozen other Carls, or at least, likely ones. They all had some task to complete, some labor to endure, some place to go back to.

So did Sarah. She didn't want to go back to the office, though. She didn't want to go to the handful of meetings that she still had to handle that day. She didn't want to deal with Michelle's sneer. She didn't want to write another email, no matter how valuable it supposedly would be. She didn't want the lingering frustrations, and the fear that they would pop up again out of nowhere, a jack-in-the-box built to surprise and spite her.

She pulled a pen out of her purse, grabbed an extra napkin, and started to doodle.

CHAPTER SEVENTEEN

"Why be fatalistic, though?"

Sarah was laying on Alex's mattress, staring up at the barren ceiling. It wasn't comfortable, feeling like a rigid block of foam compared to her own. She could feel a notch beneath her lower back; Alex probably cut it out himself for his tail. Not somewhere she wanted to spend her Saturday, but she needed to get out of her apartment. It didn't really matter where she went.

Her apartment hunt wasn't going well. She had options – including one she was scheduled to visit later – but they were limited. The good ones all seemed to vanish before she had an opportunity to see them.

"I'm not being fatalistic," she said. "It's more, I'm trying to be honest with this. It sucks now, it's probably gonna suck more, and I don't know how I'm going to take care of it."

"Well, you could always ask your friend Sean. He always seems to know everything."

"Alex. Don't start."

He was leaning against the kitchen counter, half of his attention pointed out the window. There was an idle crane outside, a few blocks away.

"I mean, it sounds like he pays attention to this stuff. And you're more like him anyway, he'd be better at helping."

"I don't think I want help right now. Think I just want to vent."

"Okay, vent." He came over and sat on the edge of the bed.

Sarah sighed, not positive where to begin. "I dunno. I guess it's just too sudden. Like, one day Deborah's retiring, the next I'm getting evicted. I mean, maybe I'd be okay with it if I saw it coming, but... Like, the folks like Carl, they're getting really fucked over. If I'm having this much trouble finding something, how the hell is he going to get by?" She knew she was exaggerating her situation.

"You'll find something," Alex said. "Might be a little smaller than what you've got, may have to go out to Milwaukee or something, but I mean, it's out there."

"Yeah, I guess. It's just..."

"You want something like what you have now."

"I want what I have now."

"Well, that's not an option, apparently."

Sarah sighed, continuing to stare blankly upwards. She didn't like to vent. She liked to solve problems, whether by her own work or by organizing others. She accomplished things that way.

The whole visit was a stalling tactic. She knew it. It would give her something to do other than obsessing about finding a new place. The fact that she could get a hit of nostalgia for an old relationship seemed like a nice bonus.

Alex dropped himself on the mattress next to her, his tail fitting neatly into the groove. "Well, you know what you have to do."

"I know, I know. I have to find an apartment, I have to actually get there before they keep vanishing..."

"Right."

"And I have to just hope, I guess."

"And let yourself accept that this is going on. You're not going to escape this."

Another sigh. "I know."

"And it's not going to be perfect."

The reminder seemed to bother her more than anything else. "That doesn't mean I have to settle for something crappy."

"No, but you said it yourself. You're only going to be satisfied with what you have now."

Sarah nodded, frustrated. Alex figured her out pretty well over the years, better than she had figured him out. Some days, he could make a valid argument for knowing her better than she knew herself.

"I know. It just sucks." Her voice was weakening from defeat.

"Yeah, it does. Sucks for all of us." He started staring up at the ceiling as well. "Apparently Ravi had to leave the building a few weeks ago. Said he was moving back with his folks, but someone apparently saw him sleeping in his car out towards 82nd."

"Shit." Sarah hadn't met Ravi, but she couldn't imagine living out of her car.

"Yeah. It's getting to be pretty hard for anyone who isn't rich. Story of the world, huh."

"I thought you said I was rich."

"Well," he said dryly, "are you struggling, or just moping?"

"You don't have to be so blunt about it." She tried to keep the annoyance out of her voice. She didn't want to be annoyed with Alex; they were too good, too old of friends.

"I'm just saying. If you need to vent, vent. I'm always here to listen. Just, have some perspective is all. I know it's really hard and annoying and all that, but it's not the end of the world. You'll get through this just fine."

"Yeah, I guess."

"I mean, you always talk about rabbit's luck. How you always manage to land on your feet."

"Been a long time since I've been tossed like this, though."

He hopped up to his feet. "Well, now you get to practice your landings."

Sarah watched him wander back to the kitchen counter. He started putting away dishes that were left to dry, his tail wagging slightly. Despite the persistent hum of pipes, she swore she could hear him whistling.

"Hey. Alex. Serious question."
"Yeah?"

"How the fuck are you so cheerful?"

He burst out laughing, bending over, almost dropping the glass he had in his paw.

"I'm serious! You were just lecturing me about how everything sucks, your friends are living in cars, and now you're fucking whistling. I don't get it."

Alex gave himself a moment to regain his composure. "I don't know. Guess it just doesn't do me any good to dwell on it so much. Like, if I was doing the sort of stuff Darien does, then yeah I'd think about how shitty everything is. It'd be good fuel." He gestured towards his corner of canvases and half-finished works. "But with my whole thing, it's like, I'll get home, let myself be angry, throw some paint around, and then just make something from that. Just let the anger be on there, then I don't have to hold onto it."

She looked at his paintings. Many of them were clearly half-finished, their splashes of color unblended and haphazard. Maroon and black splashes showed up repeatedly, seeming to flow across neighboring canvases. Several of them looked like they could be deemed complete, despite their blurry detail. They all felt sinister.

"Seems to work pretty well," she said.

"Thanks." He exchanged the blank canvas on his easel for a half-painted one. "But then people look at them, and they're like 'there's such raw anger and emotion, must be this dark and mysterious artist.'"

Sarah laughed at the suggestion.

"Exactly! Like, they're expecting this dark and brooding figure, and then they get this weird otter, and they're just like 'what's wrong with you?' Like, yeah, I act cheerful, I put all the bullshit over there."

"Wish I could do that. Just throw the anger somewhere else."

"You have something to be angry about, though. It's fair."

She grimaced. "Well, no, not really. I mean, Michelle and I have been getting at each other lately, I just can't seem to leave it at the office. And the whole thing Monday? I was pissed before I even got home. All the way home, I was just ready to bite someone."

"Hey, some people are into that."

She gave him a bitter stare. "I mean, I've been unhappy plenty of times, but it's been forever since I've been straight-up pissed. Forgot how to manage it."

"I hope the venting helps, at least. Like I said, I'm here to listen."

Sarah nodded. "And if the painting isn't enough, I'll listen too."

"I'll be fine."

Sarah winced slightly. She knew even as she said it that it'd be hard for her to just listen. She always felt compelled to do something. He deserved to have his problems solved, she figured, and eventually she'd find a way to solve them.

Not now, though. Right now, she had her own problems to solve.

CHAPTER EIGHTEEN

Sarah pulled onto a Laurelhurst side street, one lined with trees and surrounded by even more of them. The neighborhood felt like it had been carved out of a grove, the one clearing of a forest taken over by civilization.

She was off to see an apartment. It wasn't on Craigslist or anywhere else she looked; it came to her through one of Kate's coworkers. The backchannels seemed to be her best hope of finding anything.

The complex was a short horseshoe of townhouses, the opening facing the street to let traffic in. The building looked relatively new — 50s or 60s perhaps, certainly newer than the turn-of-the-century places in her old neighborhood. Nothing about it was flashy or ultra-modern. It showed the scuffs and dents of age, no different than the freestanding houses that surrounded it.

Despite those scuffs, the facades were clean and robust. The trees and grass that sat on the outside of the horseshoe were tightly manicured and well kept. There weren't even any weeds. She would have a yard if she lived here, but judging by the consistency and the openness, she wouldn't have to take care of it.

"Have to say, you take good care of the place," she said.
"Well, thank you. We pride ourselves on a first impression."

Sarah had only met Greg moments ago, so she had to do a rapid assessment. He was a red fox, probably mid-40s. He wore a plain button-down shirt, fresh sneakers, and jeans as crisp as if they were dress slacks. He obviously wasn't the one caring for the lawn.

As he walked, his tail hung loosely, his ears perked straight up. It was a gait of approachability; signs of eagerness, no signs of aggression. It was something Sarah remembered from a sales class in college. Gradually, as the salesman needs to assert control, the ears move forward, the tail up and lightly swaying, the stance subtly leaning forward. Ready to pounce. Her professor claimed the tail was the most important part.

Maybe that was why there weren't many rabbits in sales.

"So," he started as he unlocked the door, "this is our standard one-bedroom unit. It's a little thinner than the two-bedrooms that we have, of course." He gestured around the living room, at the stairway almost touching the front door, at the kitchen towards the back. "Has all the usuals you'd expect. Kitchen has fresh cabinets, good angle for the sunlight..."

Greg wandered around the place, rattling off his well-rehearsed speech. He hardly seemed interested in whether or not Sarah was following or even paying attention. Perhaps he was going along for the sheer joy of it.

"It's just you moving in? No kids, no boyfriend?" he asked as he started up the narrow stairs.

Sarah was still examining the kitchen, and even though there was nobody else with them, she paused to make sure he was talking to her.

"Yep, just me."

She went back to examining. The cabinets didn't seem like anything noteworthy.

"Well, should be plenty of space to stretch your legs, then."

"Feels like it."

She did her best to make a mental note of everything that seemed interesting: the shade offered by the trees, the geometry of the rooms, the evidence of a heating system, the cable and electrical outlets. The she made a mental note to bring an actual notepad next time. She had forgotten how many details went into a home.

"How are the neighbors?" Sarah asked, walking up the stairs behind Greg.

"Pretty quiet."

Sarah heard something in his tone that made her suspicious. "What kind of residents are we talking about? Lot of families, lot of students?"

"Not many students," he said.

"Alright. Families?"

Greg's ears fell back slightly as they entered the empty bedroom. "There are a couple families. Mostly new families, want to take advantage of the schools and the park right there." He pointed across the street; the park was a block away, but Sarah got the idea. "So, every two bedroom home is taken up by one of them."

"Can't really blame them. Guess that means a lot of little kids, though."

As if on cue, she heard a young coyote howling and crying nearby. It sounded as if it came from the other side of the wall.

Greg laughed nervously and shuffled his weight around. "Yeah, there are a couple, obviously. But, you know, it's not all that bad. Just part of apartment life, really. I'm sure you have kids and kits making noise where you are now."

Sarah gave it a brief thought. "I don't know. I didn't really think about it, but either my neighbors don't have kids or I just never hear them."

"Well, you're in Alphabet, right? So that's not too surprising. Doesn't have the best of schools. This is definitely a better area if you're going to have kids."

The schools weren't a selling point. Sarah wasn't planning to have kids anytime soon. "Anyway. Andrea said this was six hundred and... eighty square feet, was it?"

"Yep, six eighty. Pretty good size, though of course, it's split two floors. Still, good for the price, certainly."

Sarah nodded. He was telling the truth there. "Better than what I'm facing now. Utilities?"

"There, cable and internet, that's on you."

"Typical."

"Electric goes through PGE, everything else we roll up. Usually adds about fifty or sixty to the rent."

A little more complicated than Sarah was used to, but nothing impossible. "Alright. And she said this was available October 1st?"

Greg inhaled, his ears leaning slightly forward. Salesman time. "Well, this one was spoken for on Thursday, so this is gone I'm afraid. But we do have one on the north side, exact same layout, exact same price, that one's available November 15th. You can get in early on that."

Sarah's ears started pointing backward. She noticed her paw clenched tight. "I was told there was one available next month."

"Well, that would've been this one. When did she say it was still available?"

"I called early yesterday." Her voice was flat, almost condescending.

"Oh, huh. I don't think I had the signed agreement filed until noon. Might be why she still thought it was available. Were you really hoping to move in that soon?"

"Yeah. It's... I really want to get moving soon."

"Well, I mean, it's a pretty busy market these days, you gotta hop on what you can!" He flashed a cheesy grin. "There is that one in mid-November, you can claim that now and be set."

"Can't do that."

"It's not that far off. Just, what, two months? Less than."

"I'm not gonna have a home in two months," she said with a faint growl. "I have to get out of there by Halloween or I'm fucked."

Greg released his salesman pose. "Well, I'm sorry. I know you had your heart set on this one."

She didn't. It was just okay, not much more. She probably wouldn't mind living there – quiet, right off Burnside, right by a park – and the occasional screaming infant wouldn't be the worst thing to deal with. But she couldn't stand the run-around she was getting.

"Well, I mean, I was told yesterday this place would still be available. And you knew since Thursday that it wasn't. And... look. We're wasting our time."

"I'm sorry."

Sarah stammered. "I talked with Andrea yesterday, and you knew this wasn't available then. If you had just told her, we wouldn't be bothering. So, thank you for the tour, I'm not interested."

With that, she walked back to her car, unescorted. She glanced at the townhouses as she passed them, their scuffs and scars seeming to stand out even more. For as perfect as the lawn was, the parking lot looked almost dilapidated, as if the weeds had been pushed over there instead.

She got into her car and slammed the door, harder than usual, hard enough for her to notice. "Fucking idiot," she mumbled to herself as she started the car.

CHAPTER NINETEEN

A rabbit sat in a coffee shop, tense and tired, her ears stiff and vertical while her body slumped into an old wooden chair. A cup of coffee sat on the table beside her, a spring of mint painted into its foam. She was yet to touch it.

The apartment hunt was dragging along. She knew for months, intellectually, that the housing market was tight. Dozens, maybe hundreds, were moving into town every day. Every construction crane she saw, every scaffolded facade, all an attempt to keep up with the deluge.

Despite that, she had only just started to understand the emotional toll it took. The days were flying by quickly now. She had to move out in forty days. So she had to find a new place in under forty days. If she went so much as an hour without doing something about it, she felt guilty. She would be falling behind, and that hour would've been the one that made everything okay. The strain was building up.

She knew it wasn't rational, that she was setting a dangerous expectation for herself. It was the kind of self-flagellation she noticed herself doing at work, that constant self-induced pressure to do everything better. It was starting to follow her everywhere. At least the Deadline had better coffee.

And it was quiet. Nestled in the back corner, she only shared the space with two others. One, a young squirrel in basic jeans and t-shirt, headphones isolating him from the outside world. He was obviously there for the wi-fi; with how rarely he touched his cup, he probably only bought it out of a sense of obligation.

Sarah wondered what he did. A student, perhaps, writing an essay or dissertation or procrastinating on one he should be doing. Perhaps he was working remotely, catching up on emails or writing code.

Could be freelancing, Sarah thought. She tried to avoid staring while paying attention to him. *That must be interesting. Work whenever you want, wherever it's comfortable. Never have to deal with Michelle or Roger or anyone like that. Probably a lot of meetings, sure, but whatever. I have that already. Hell, I could do my job from the apartment as it is.*

The apartment. Her mind had a way of pushing her back to her task. But Craigslist wasn't worth repeatedly refreshing. The housing problems were equal parts high demand and low supply, the worst of both worlds.

She gave a look to her other neighbor in the space, also poking idly at a laptop. He was an ordinary-looking coyote, maybe a little older than Sarah. He still wore a windbreaker despite the cafe being comfortably warm. He slouched, his ears and face drooping in equal measure, as though coffee had no effect on him.

He looked familiar. Maybe he was a regular that Sarah had never noticed before. She was usually too tied up in her own mind to focus on anyone else around her. Maybe he just had that kind of face, his eyes and snout and mouth all positioned in a recognizable and average position.

There was something strangely handsome about someone so instantly familiar. Sarah didn't find many guys who piqued her interest, and she could never ask them out anyway. Even many of her friends assumed that she was constantly ready and eager for sex, just because she was a rabbit. An offer from her to hang out would always be met with false connotations.

So she glanced from across the room with a slight unease. Now wasn't the time to look for a boyfriend, and even if it were, Sean was her first pick. A random coyote, even if he were attractive, wouldn't be better than someone she knew well.

Besides, rabbits and coyotes were not expected to get along. Sarah had been taught that coyotes were dangerous; not cruel or evil, necessarily, but they would harm rabbits without a care. Her mother reminded her about it consistently. It was just the natural order of things, something a grown-up rabbit had to know and watch out for.

Yet, Sarah had learned that of wolves and foxes as well, and she spent all day at the office surrounded by them. Sure, Michelle was annoying and her sneers could occasionally become scary, but she wasn't dangerous. Omar was friendly when he wasn't agitated. Maybe the warnings were overblown.

Maybe I could talk to him. Just say "hey, have I seen you before?" and he'll say "no" and that'll be that. At least I tried. And if he wants to keep talking, then okay.

She was staring. The coyote noticed, making brief eye contact before immediately looking back to his screen. Sarah blushed and did the same. She wasn't going to look at anyone, now.

Her attention was completely ripped away from the apartment hunt, so much so that she lost her place among the listings she was scanning.

Well. I need to talk to Sean. If I'm gonna hit on anyone, then fuck it, I'm gonna hit on him.

CHAPTER TWENTY

It took Sean a moment to let Sarah in when she arrived at his building. She stood outside in a calm September night, watching. Luxury cars rolled past, thin mothers in yoga pants ran on the sidewalk with their babies in strollers. A shopping cart rattled some blocks away; the transients mostly stayed on the neighborhood's perimeter, as if they knew these people weren't going to be any help.

"Sorry about that," Sean said. "Forgot to grab my keys."

"You're like, two floors up. You can leave the door unlocked for a minute."

"Now, that's crazy talk," he said with a playful smile.

Sarah didn't feel like teasing back. The effects of her apartment visit the day before were still lingering on her mind, weighing down her shoulders and ears. Worse, she felt like she had somehow cheated on Sean. This, despite doing nothing with the coyote and not even being Sean's girlfriend to begin with.

The inevitable march toward Monday wasn't helping either. Another day of dealing with Michelle. Now that Davro Auto, her other major account, was picking up again, it would probably be another day of dealing with slow meetings.

"No Lee this week," Sean said from the kitchen side of the room.

"Big surprise."

"So what're we thinking, something light, something dark? Still gotta get you to watch *Spaceballs*."

"Eh. I'm actually thinking Kubrick."

"You're always thinking Kubrick." Sarah glared, in no mood for teasing. "Okay. *Clockwork Orange?*"

"Too creepy. What about *2001*, that around?"

"Going that mellow, huh?"

He handed over a beer – a lighter one this time, after what happened at Kate's party – and dropped himself on the couch next to Sarah. As he sat, his tail fell into Sarah's lap with a careless awkwardness.

"Ooof. Hello," she said, surprised.

"Oh, jeez, sorry." Sean laughed at himself and swung his tail to the other side.

"No, no, that was fine. Do it again." She tried to make it sound like a tease, but she didn't mind having his tail in her lap. Though, that wasn't the sort of thing she wanted to tell him.

"I'll be sure to." He corrected his position and grabbed the remote. "How'd that apartment turn out, by the way? Look good?"

"Yeah, looked great. Wouldn't be that thrilled about the east side, but whatever."

"Well, congrats."

"Thanks. Apparently someone already claimed it on Thursday."

Sean offered a quizzical look. "Seriously?"

"Yep. And they're so disorganized that I still did all the tour crap even though they knew I wouldn't be able to move in."

"Well, fuck 'em."

"Yeah. Gonna growl a little at Kate about it."

"It's not her fault."

"I know, I know. I just need to growl at somebody."

"Fair enough. Want a hug?" He sounded halfway between sarcastic and sincere.

"Sure."

Sean's approach was a friendly hug, the kind meant merely to show empathy. It was loose, kept the head distant, and included a few back pats for good measure. Sarah's was stronger, the hug a child gives their

100

returning parent at the airport. She held him tight, putting her head on his shoulder, breaking abruptly when it felt like it had gone on too long.

"You smacked me with your ear, by the way," Sean said.
"Good. We're even."

These movie nights, personal and quiet in their apartments, were starting to feel awkward. The rest of the group seemed uninterested in stopping by lately, leaving just Sean and Sarah to themselves. Sean always looked anxious as a result, as if he didn't want to be left alone with her. So they sat on opposite ends of the couch, pretending they were in different seats. It was easier to do here than at Sarah's place. Her couch was more of a loveseat, but Sean's was a respectable size.

Despite any awkwardness, she insisted on having these movie nights. She wanted to be closer to Sean as much as she could. A bit of discomfort wasn't going to stop her. She knew she couldn't work up the nerve to say anything when the rest of the group was around, but perhaps she could muster the courage when they were left alone.

No luck so far, though. The hug was the most she could manage. A victory, sure, but she felt how they were two very different kinds of hugs. She kept her disappointment hidden.

They had both seen *2001* before, so Sarah's interest in the plot was minimal. She found herself thinking about cliches instead, analyzing the film and the tropes it gave birth to. There were so many parodies of HAL by now.

She also thought of the cliche of the couple in the theater. The guy stretches and puts his arm around the girl's shoulder. She thought about the time Zach tried it on her. She hated the move, how cringe-inducing the whole image felt, how awkward it made the moment.

Yet, she thought about doing it to Sean. Just as a joke, she'd say. Just to spook him a little bit. It probably would startle him; he was engrossed in the plot, absorbing every detail, even though he had seen it before.

No, that's just... that's dumb. That's probably the worst way to try and hit on him. He's not even gonna think it's a joke, he's just gonna think I'm weird. He totally wouldn't trust me to not be, like, insane.

Sarah looked across the couch. Sean's attention was still mostly consumed by the movie, although he glanced quickly at Sarah during the occasional slow plot moment. They said nothing. He had his laptop with him, squeezed protectively between his body and the armrest.

Does he actually trust me? Maybe that's why he gets kinda weird when it's just us. He's expecting me to play a trick or something. Or it's the whole... rabbit thing. Wonder how I could get him past that. I mean yeah, I'd want to sleep with him, but-

A deadbolt released behind them. Sean immediately jumped up and turned around, only returning his attention to the movie after they heard his neighbor's door swing open and slam shut.

Man, forget trusting me. Does he trust anyone?

CHAPTER TWENTY-ONE

Since Portland was steadily moving from being powered by timber and art and towards programmers and office workers, the regular get-togethers that popped up followed suit. Sarah could go every week to some event that had free food and professional mingling. This Monday was the largest, gathering a full cross-section of the city's new guard. Executives and would-be executives rambled endlessly about trends, programmers hovered over the pizza and beer, recruiters stalked the crowds like feral predators.

Few people cared about what Sarah did. It wasn't a powerful enough role and there wasn't any shortage of people doing it. So she mingled, quietly, floating among the crowds that seemed to dominate the hall.

She would go every month if it were worth doing. It could be something to do, a routine to uphold. The free food wouldn't hurt. There were presentations each time, locals with some idea or supposed insight. Now and then they were interesting. Sometimes the people were interesting too. Mostly, it was a way to be around conversation without needing to participate in it.

There was a reason to participate this time. One of the presentations would come from a former fine artist, a sculptor who was now in charge of design at some small startup that Sarah had never heard of before. The company would probably be gone in a year or two, she figured. But his story already happened, and it was his story she was interested in. She wanted Alex to have a similar one.

The crowd was massive and difficult to navigate. Sarah didn't know what the speaker, Johann, looked like. Not even his species. It would be useless to try and track him down, so she stood near the food and waited, watching the name tags of every man that walked past. There were quite a few to observe.

The atmosphere was different now that she had an objective. As people appeared, they sorted themselves into groups. Sarah tried to analyze them quickly, assigning demographics to each of them. The men in suits were ruled out; even after entering the business world, Johann would probably keep the artist's sense of fashion. That largely ruled out the guys in hoodies or company t-shirts as well, though he could have migrated to that style. Perhaps if one had a detail that struck her as artistic, then she could make an assumption.

She stood in the corner, surveying the landscape. There was no aimless wandering; the rabbit had a mission.

As did a cougar, apparently, since she pushed her way straight to a distracted Sarah. "Hey there!" she said. "Nice to see some more women around here!"

"Yeah, hi!" Sarah offered a paw to shake. She had been to enough of these events to know the customs, and a quick fake smile always helped in her work. "Sarah Madsen, nice to meet you."

"Vickie Crittenden, nice to meet you too!"

"So, what're you working on?" Typical small talk. She kept glancing around for Johann.

"Well, I'm a technical recruiter, which keeps me busy lately." A typical answer. "You?"

"I'm a marketing manager at a TV agency downtown."

"Oh? What's that involve?" Her tone immediately went from hopeful to polite. Despite Sarah's tomboy fashion sense, expected of a female programmer, she was not the intended prey.

She used the opportunity to go on at length about her work, evolving from small talk to venting complaints. Soon she was holding Vickie socially hostage. It was always hard to break out of a conversation at these events, and Sarah decided to take advantage of the fact. It was mean, perhaps, but ultimately a harmless trick to play.

Vickie had to know the song and dance herself. It was part of her job. She repeatedly broke eye contact to look around the room. Once Sarah paused, Vickie grabbed a nearby leopard and glanced at his name tag. "Sarah, have you met Johann yet?"

Rabbit's luck. "I haven't, no. Johann, nice to meet you."

They shook. "Nice to meet you, Sarah was it?" He had a thick German accent and a solid handshake.

Vickie was already a step away. "I'm gonna run off, mingle a little more. Good talking to you!" She bolted off, leaving no room for a reply.

"I didn't interrupt, did I?" Johann asked, glancing at the escaping cougar.

"No, no, she was trying to run away for a while. But anyway, you're presenting tonight, aren't you?"

"Yes. A bit nervous, honestly." Hesitation fell between each word. Either he was telling the truth or he was still working on his English.

"Bah, don't worry. It's not that hard." Sarah had never presented to this crowd before, but it didn't seem too tough. "I'm actually glad I ran into you, kinda wanted to ask about your background a bit."

"Oh, well thank you. Are you an artist as well?"

"I'm... not really. I'm still getting my feet wet there."

"Ah, I see."

"But, my friend Alex has been an artist for a while, and he's mentioned wanting to take the sort of route that you did. Going from art to design and all that."

"Well, that's good to hear. It's pretty hard to just be an artist anymore. Especially in this town. I'm glad I made the move when I did. Is she around, by any chance?"

"He, and no, he had to work."

"Oh, I'm sorry."

"Alright!" A voice cried out from the other end of the hall. "We're gonna get started in about five minutes!"

"You probably need to get going," Sarah said.

"Looks like. Here."

Johann dug into the back pocket of his khakis, pulling out a cluster of business cards. He handed one to Sarah. She hadn't had a business card of her own in years; holding one felt like holding an antique.

"Could you pass that along to Alex?" he asked. "He can get a hold of me, I'd be happy to help him out."
"Absolutely." She smiled.

Johann made his way to the other end of the hall. Sarah slipped his card into her pocket and grabbed another beer. There were plenty to go around.

She rarely sat through the presentations. Even at a professional level, taken as a snapshot of local marketing trends, she was never all that interested. But it was only polite to take a seat and stay through Johann's presentation. He had helped her out. Since his presentation was first, it wasn't much of an obligation.

The hope was that he would say something about his personal story. She assumed it would be a good fit for the audience, a story of evolving into the fast-paced tech world that people here seemed to idolize. It might be an overwrought tale, but it would make people feel good.

Instead, he gave a pitch. His background barely came up; instead, the focus was on his company and how they claimed they would change the world. There were graphs, charts, projections. Bland photos of happy, suited foxes and beavers. Perhaps it was interesting to somebody there, but not to Sarah.

She waited until he finished, politely clapped, then headed for the door.

CHAPTER TWENTY-TWO

On paper, Sarah's Tuesday was occupied by meetings on a dozen different topics, all bland and slow as ever. She had to play the politics and show up despite the boredom. She had to make herself visible and sell herself if she was going to win out over Michelle. Maybe Gary and Roger had made their decision already, but maybe not. Best to be safe.

It felt dirty. It felt like the kind of behavior that made work unbearable and never made a situation any better. It felt like shameless selfishness, the inflating of egos already plenty large.

Perhaps it was. Maybe she should give up the banal fight and worry about something more important.

There had to be something with more impact than sitting in a conference room listening to Roger wander through the leads that sales nearly had closed. None of them were guarantees. Lately, they were more likely to fall through than complete. But, in the interest of preparation, they had to carry on as if the leads were all sure things.

"Got one more thing here," Roger said, flipping through his slide deck. "This is sort of cloak and dagger, kinda early on, but Lawrence and Andre might be pulling through some big projects. These could be Q1, Q2, Q-not-next-one, but it's worth the prep time."

He started stepping through the projects, any of which could potentially be Sarah's work. Or, they could be her coworkers' responsibility, or just as easily nobody's. Roger had a way of getting ahead of himself.

The seven sat around an oblong table. Roger claimed the head seat. The cougar, Vinish, sat near the screens on the wall, watching the slides attentively. Chris, a stout beaver, sat disinterested next to him, the departing fox Thomas on the end. Michelle and Jessica surrounded Sarah on the other side.

"Now, a bunch of these are travel, so Jessica, you're pretty much a lock for these if you have the bandwidth. Hate to volunteer you, but, y'know."

"It's okay," the badger said.

"Sarah, if any athletic projects come through, they're on you."

"Roger," she said.

"Hmm?"

It took a moment for Sarah to realize the confusion. "Oh, I mean, I got it."

"Oh. Alright. Anyway, we can't really give the tech to Thomas anymore, so we'll have to play those as they happen. So, y'know, blame him for that." He chuckled lightly.

"Boo!" Michelle joined in.

"Speaking of," Vinish said, "how are we settling the existing projects? Have we made any decisions there?" He kept his ears perked like a fox's, always showing interest in what Roger had to say.

"Well there's just the one, right?" Thomas asked. "Everything else is already on Chris's plate."

"Yeah, I got it," Chris said.

"Well good," Roger said, "but I still need to work with Gary on that last one. Unfortunately, Thomas, you're a bit of a specialist, so it's gonna hurt to see you go."

"I'm sorry, I'm sorry." He clearly wasn't.

"Anyway, we'll have that figured out by the end of the week."

"Is this when we start making our stump speeches?" Michelle asked, bouncing slightly in her chair. "Elect me, elect me!"

"Go right ahead," Roger said, laughing his nervous laugh. "Just don't go forming parties. Although, actually, we will have a little party for Tom's last day, just a heads-up."

Sarah assumed Roger was being polite with his jokes. The two talked about the office politics in the past and how much they both disliked them. He hated how much he had played the game throughout his career. It got him where he was, but he'd readily admit the toll it took on him.

Nothing Sarah did was politics, as far as she was concerned. She always assumed she was straightforward and fair, but there was the occasional comment accusing her of being deceptive or aggressively independent. She brushed it off as stereotyping. Rabbits are supposed to be tricksters, after all.

She found a gap between meetings and worked her way over to Thomas's desk. He sat, looking halfway distracted, seemingly plotting his next cunning move. He was already leaving his dress shirt untucked, his grey-flecked red fur a little less precisely groomed. He had clearly stopped caring.

They grabbed a private office. "Guessing you're on the short list, huh?" he asked before Sarah could get the door closed.

"That's what Roger said, at least."

"Figured. Wonder how short the list is, I've already had a couple people come talk."

"Michelle and Vinish, I'm guessing?"

"Yeah. Vinish only came by once, Michelle's been here non-stop. She's gunning for it."

"I know." She leaned back in the chair. "She's mentioned being eager for it."

"Yeah, she seems to think Roger likes it if you're all enthusiastic and bubbly and shit."

"Would explain a lot."

"I know. Plus, she could use a good launch. Hasn't had one in a while. Guess that's why she's so gung-ho about this in particular."

"Right. Don't know how much it's gonna matter, though."

"It's not," Thomas said with a small sigh. "Gary doesn't really care about who does what. He just throws darts, far as I can tell."

Sarah felt compelled to defend their VP, but he was right. She hadn't talked to Gary in at least a year, not even by email.

"That's kinda why I wanted to talk. If they throw it at me, I don't want to fuck it up."

His ears started falling back. "I don't think you'd fuck it up. It's pretty hard to at this point."

"Really?" She could see a hint of uncertainty.

"I mean, I think so. But the guys on the HiSense side sounded really disappointed when I said I was leaving, and they've gotten kinda... difficult, I guess? Like, they're changing things before the freeze."

"Nothing new. You heard what happened with Wallace, right?"

"Yeah, Omar's in deep shit for that."

"Not Brian?"

Thomas shook his head. "Course not. He went to school with half of engineering management."

She wasn't surprised to hear that, but it was news to her. Sarah wasn't interested in the office gossip, especially not among the engineering department.

"Either way, I should be fine. Worst case I end up drinking more."

"Join the club." Thomas laughed to himself. "Feel kinda bad for her, though."

"Michelle?"

"Yeah. I mean, she's really gunning for this, and it's not going to matter. Place isn't gonna be around in a year or two anyway."

"Bit pessimistic." She brushed off the idea.

"Eh, who knows. I just wouldn't get invested with any of this. Gary's probably already decided. He'll just pick whoever he likes and make it hard for everyone else." His nose wrinkled.

"Guessing he doesn't like you anymore."

"Nope. Did for a while, not anymore. Little frustrating." His voice belied the understatement.

"Should probably keep my head down, then. Don't give him a reason to dislike me."

"That'll work. I wouldn't worry about it, though, it's not something you can really control. Besides, I've already got it all written up. Like, notebooks of this stuff. We can talk if you really want, though."

Sarah opted not to. Instead, she debated how she would carry on. Staying the course seemed like the best option; if Thomas were right, playing the politics would be futile to begin with, whether short-term or long-term. If he were wrong, though, she would be at a disadvantage.

While Michelle wandered from meeting to meeting, campaigning all the while, Sarah learned what she could about Johann. Persuading Alex was a more important campaign.

CHAPTER TWENTY-THREE

The more time Sarah spent in her apartment, the more it seemed to compress her. The frustration of knowing she would lose it started to grate on her, turning every creak and groan of the floor into a bitter shriek.

She started to avoid going straight home after work. Often that just meant a longer drive or finding an errand to run en route. She didn't have errands that night, but she knew Alex was working his bar job – one of his side jobs to make ends meet – so she headed in that direction instead.

It was a quiet Tuesday night. Only handful of older men sat at the bar, leaning into their drinks. They all seemed to make their clothing appear shaggy and ill-fitting, whether they wore a reasonable blue suit or a distressed painter's overalls. Only Alex and the bartender were working; maybe someone was working the kitchen, but that was probably Alex's job as well.

Sarah sat in a corner booth, the table covered with carved initials. A smell of smoke and hops radiated from the surrounding walls. When Alex sat down to join her, she handed over Johann's business card.

"What's this?" he asked.

"It's a business card, it's used to share contact information, but that's not important right now."

Alex rolled his eyes. "Very funny."

"Thanks," Sarah said with a smile. "Anyway, he used to be a sculptor, did mixed media stuff. Close to what you're doing."

"Used to?"

"Well, yeah, he does design stuff now. Sounded like it's going really well for him. Figured he might be worth talking to, could help your career out a bit."

"Why?"

Sarah hesitated. "You mentioned that the art stuff hasn't been going that great, so..."

"So..."

"I just thought, y'know, there are options. Don't want you feeling stuck or anything. I know you don't like where you are with things." She didn't want to identify the job Alex was most vocal about. He was working it right then.

"It's... yeah." He let out a faint squeak. He always did it when he was nervous. Sarah found it cute. "I just don't wanna be one of those guys."

"Alex." She leaned forward onto the table, ears forward, looking square into his eyes. "You are not those guys. You are the opposite of those guys. You couldn't be those guys if you wanted to."

He broke eye contact. "Then why give me this?"

"Because... I mean, you don't have to be one of those startup bros. I wouldn't want you to be."

"They're the ones who get the jobs."

Sarah didn't have an argument. "Alex, you can do this. I just want things to be a little easier for you, that's all."

"I know, I know. I'll think about it."

She wanted to push him further in the hope that she could convince him to commit. But she could tell that he wasn't enjoying the evening, and her presence wasn't helping. He didn't need any more pressure.

He went back to work, leaving her to look around idly and sip at her beer. The walls were dark, covered with indecipherable and vulgar scribbles. The floor was concrete painted dark to match the walls. It was her prototype of a dive bar, the kind of place that made her hold her purse a little closer to her body.

Her glances fell to Alex again, bussing the lone table that had any evidence of customers. His head and tail hung with boredom. She noticed his outfit, a simple black waitress's uniform. It fit him unusually well. She waited until he came closer so they could talk in more hushed tones.

"Should I be going with 'she' now?" Sarah asked.

"Hmm?"

She gestured. "The skirt."

"Oh," Alex said. "I don't really know. Don't think it matters right now. Been kinda feeling in between with things." He sounded disappointed with the fact.

"Roger that." She sipped her beer. "Kinda feels like we're all in between stuff."

Alex nodded, looking around. "That's how it's supposed to work, right? One thing changes, another settles down, it's like... can't imagine having things just never change."

"I know. Almost feels like I've been at my job too long. Like that's supposed to have changed by now."

"Four years is pretty crazy. You gotta be bored."

Sarah thought for a moment. "I am, honestly. A little bit. But I mean, waiting tables is what, a year at most? Not very consistent."

"Yeah. Baristas last a bit longer if you have that hipster shit going for you. Or if you do Starbucks, easy to stick around there."

"You would never work at Starbucks."

"Neither would you. You wouldn't put up with it." He was right. "Can't get away with anything."

"You get away with the skirt here, I'm guessing."

"Boss hates it," he said with a slight smile. "But whatever. Girls get tips." He added a mock curtsey.

Sarah let out a small laugh. "Cute. I don't wanna get lecturing, though, but maybe you should care a little?"

"You mean, what? Stop wearing the skirts?"

"No, no, no. Skirts are fine. You're adorable in them. I'm just saying, y'know, if you tried to show you cared you wouldn't have to job hop so much. And I know you hate that."

"I guess."

"I mean, yeah, change is good and all, but maybe some stability would be good for you. Or at least, if you change, make it something that pushes you forward. I hate to see you just treading water." She paused. "Well, not-bad choice of words, sorry."

Alex squeaked again. "I know. It's hard, though. Half the places I worked lately have closed. This place is probably gonna close, the rate it's going. And everything that's popping up, they don't want me."

"That's why I'm trying to help."

"I know, I know. I just... I'll figure out what I want to do."

"Alright." She stopped herself from pushing again, opting to head home instead.

She wanted to trust that Alex would do something to help himself, but she doubted it. Maybe going to that event wasn't worth it. But if it helped him, even just a little bit, it had to be worthwhile. There had to be something that would pay him better, use more of his talents, let him wear the skirts. The city was growing and changing too much for there not to be an option. She just had to find it.

CHAPTER TWENTY-FOUR

When Sarah needed a confidant, it meant that she needed Sean. Alex could provide wisdom, and there was value in that, but Sean provided advice and a stronger, more sympathetic ear.

"Thanks again for dropping by," she said as she let him into the building, wheeling his bike to his side.

"Not a problem. Was just gonna watch TV and poke around the internet all night anyway."

"I would say that sounds lonely, but that's probably what I would be doing."

"There you go. We can be lonely together."

Sarah stammered.

"That kinda makes it sound like a relationship, huh."

"I was gonna say. That sounds like my parents."

It took some effort to get Sean's bike into the small elevator, but they managed. It left the two of them standing close, enough to make Sarah equal parts anxious and happy.

Carl was sitting on his stool, as always, a few wires of brass in his paws and lap. His head hung; tired, perhaps, or just disappointed with the state of things.

"Hey, Carl," Sarah said with a hint of a whisper. "How're you holding up?"

"Oh, I'm holding, I suppose."

He hardly looked up from bending the wires. They were coming together in a sort of French braid. The curves were imprecise and the wires dotted with tool marks, but it was a more impressive effort than Sarah could've mustered.

"I take it you're hunting down a new place," he said.

"Yeah, it's a bit of a pain."

"Don't I know it." He stepped off his stool and limped toward his door. "Benny's thinking I may wanna go to a retirement home, near where he's living."

"Seriously?" Sean asked. "You don't seem to need it."

"Well, I am retired, after all. But that don't mean I need the home. 'Less they're gonna give me the whole home, then I'd go along with it, but that ain't happening. Paula's not on board with it either. Doesn't want me going down there."

"He's in Arizona, right?" Sarah asked.

"New Mexico. Close enough for horseshoes."

"Roger. Gotta be hot as hell down there."

"Don't know how the boy stands it. But then, people can't seem to stand our shitty weather. Always figured it'd keep people out of town, but fat lotta good that's doing us."

"Well," Sean said, "I mean, it doesn't really matter if you spend all your time indoors."

"It does when you're waiting for a bus."

"True. Or on a bike."

Carl examined the bike Sean had with him. It looked durable and well-kept, the green paint only just starting to crack and peel off. "You must be some kinda madman."

Sean laughed. "A bit, yeah."

Carl gave Sarah a fatherly nudge. "See, this is what I mean. You need a lunatic like him, liven things up a bit."

"I'm busy enough," she said. "I'll hit on him later."

"There ya go." He started towards his apartment, using the door frame for a moment of support. "Now, I'm gonna take care of some food, but you two lovebirds need anything, you holler."

Sarah opened her apartment door, letting Sean roll his bike in first.

"Okay," he said, "I lost track of when you were joking."

She chuckled. "Who said I was?"

Sean smiled back. "Evil woman."

She grabbed her laptop and dropped herself on the couch. Sean sat next to her a moment later, being mindful of his tail.

"Let's just keep to business," he said. "Otherwise, we'll be bullshitting all night."

"And what's wrong with that?"

Sean gave a brief look at her face. "Since when are you so cheery?"

"Well, that shit I was talking about with HiSense? Sounding more like I don't need to push for it or anything."

"Congratulations."

"Thanks. Don't know if I'm gonna get it or not, but it's not in my control at least."

"Figured that would freak you out a bit."

"It totally does," she said flatly. "I'm gonna be freaking out until that's decided."

"Would you rather freak out about that or the apartment?"

"I'd rather not freak out about either."

"Then you'll end up freaking out about both. You lose, good day sir," he said with a mock seriousness that made Sarah burst out laughing.

"Fine, Wonka."

She pulled up some of her spreadsheets. They had been private until this point, and it showed. Sean had to ask about all of the labels.

"Alright. Let's talk priorities, then. What do you absolutely need?"

Sarah didn't have a document for that, so she had to think. "Well. Obviously, I have to be able to actually afford it."

"Right."

"Have to be able to get to work easily. Or at least, like, no crazy commute."

"Definitely no Vancouver."

She exhaled, shaking her head. "Man, I couldn't imagine dealing with that every day."

"I know. That all?"

"I guess, I don't want to lose much space. Little smaller's fine, but, y'know."

"Location?"

"In the city, ideally. Just not somewhere sketchy."

Sean got up and grabbed his laptop as if he had an idea. "Define sketchy."

Sarah thought. "Like... I don't know."

"Like, is Eliot sketchy? The stuff right above Broadway?"

"That's like... medium sketchy."

"Medium sketchy? What is it, a curry?"

"I don't know. Stop messing with me." She was exasperated.

"Fine, fine. St. Johns?"

"Don't think I've ever been up that way."

"Me neither. Just keeps coming up when people talk about getting priced out, that's where a lot seem to end up."

She noticed he was searching for something on his laptop, and so refrained from answering. He would probably find it soon enough.

"What're you looking for?" she asked when her curiosity overrode her patience.

"Okay." Sean kept looking at his screen. "When you say 'a sketchy neighborhood,' what are you worried will happen if you lived there?"

Sarah thought. "Well, I don't want my car broken into, for one."

"Right." He started panning around a map made of red and green shapes. "So, we look up crime data. Figure out where that happens. Did this before I moved, looked for somewhere without a lot of bike theft."

"And you ended up in the Pearl?"

"Better than here. Look."

Sure enough, Sarah's apartment was square in the middle of a red block. Bikes were being stolen all around her without her ever noticing.

"Wow. So, what about break-ins?"

"Right. Theft from auto." He had definitely done this before.

Her neighborhood turned yellow; the occasional case, but nothing serious. She knew it was a natural danger no matter where she lived, and she was relieved that she hadn't made it worse for herself without realizing it.

She looked at the downtown blocks. A bright stop sign red. Yet she parked her car there every day without a second thought. The garage wasn't secured from pedestrians. Anyone could walk up and do whatever they wanted. There were security cameras, sure, but did they even work?

21st Ave was red as well. Sure, it felt a little rough compared to the polished 23rd nearby, but she never considered it sketchy. The whole area, virtually a tourist destination, was a real risk, and all of it right outside her door.

"I'm assuming yellow is, like, city average."

"Basically." He scrolled through the other crimes on the list. "Yeah, this neighborhood is pretty average. Except drug use. Must be a hookup here."

"Don't look at me."

"Of course not." It didn't sound teasing. "I have been smelling pot around my building lately."

"Wouldn't surprise me."

"Yeah?"

"Yeah. The sales guys are pretty open about it, and they're total bros. They'd live somewhere flashy, maybe it's them."

Sean shrugged. "Hey, I've smoked pot. Not at home, but..."

"Oh." Sarah didn't know that. "I mean, that's fine, just-"

"No, it's alright, I know what you mean. It's a nice place and all, but I'm kinda not liking it much anymore."

"Really?"

He nodded, more to himself than in confirmation. "Yeah. It's starting to feel a little overpriced. And people are getting annoying."

"Thought you liked being annoying."

"Yes, me," he said with a smile. "Not other people. Feels like they're all rich assholes. Almost feel guilty being there."

"Shame."

Sean had managed to put a name to why Sarah ultimately didn't try moving into his building. It was too upper-class, too distant from the rest of the city. It was its own privileged world.

"Can sorta see why you like Carl, honestly. Seems pretty down to earth."

Sarah glanced out of her open apartment door. "Yeah, he's a good guy. Really likes giving advice, though. Which is kinda... I don't know."

"Rabbit does what rabbit wants?"

Sarah rolled her eyes. "I'm not that stereotypical. You know me."

"I do. You haven't even tried to have sex with me! It's a miracle!"

She laughed. "And you haven't tried to steal anything! It's a miracle!"

He cringed. "Fair, fair."

"He does keep asking when I'm gonna ask you out. Every time I mention you, he asks."

Sean chuckled. "Yep. My grandpa would've been the same way."

I'm not gonna ask about that. Not the time.

"So," Sarah said, "what do we think?"

"Well, you live here, you like it here, you should stay here." Sarah glared. "I mean, the neighborhood. If you can."

"And back in reality?"

"You never know! I mean, it's possible. But, other than that, seems like there are some good parts of Hosford to look at."

"Not too far from Alex's place."

"Really?"

"Yeah. He's closer to the river, though." Those blocks were redder.

"Cool. But, last I heard they're working on cleaning that and Buckman up a fair bit. So, might not be quite what you want."

"Worth a try."

CHAPTER TWENTY-FIVE

Rabbit's luck.

The entire apartment search focused on a particular set of details. One bedroom or larger, cheaper than her impending rent increase, no less than four hundred square feet. They were her boundaries. Putting the search into Craigslist was nearly muscle memory.

This time, she was careless. She forgot to set the maximum rent. As a result, she was inundated with options. The new Pearl District towers lit up, dozens of impractical options making themselves known.

Her own neighborhood lit up as well. She had assumed most of the buildings nearby were already full, if only because there was so much activity on the streets. And the buildings were older, full of modest apartments with character and vintage details. They were the real-life doppelgängers for the popular image of Portland.

They had openings, they were just more expensive than what Sarah was looking for. On inspection, it made sense: they were two-bedroom apartments. Two bedrooms had to be more expensive than what she had looked at. If they weren't, something was wrong.

Sean's comments earlier in the week hung in her head. Maybe he would live somewhere like this. Maybe, if he wanted out of his apartment, he would be willing to move into hers. It'd keep his rent down and get him away from his annoying neighbors. The whole relationship thing would be a convenient bonus.

The idea had never crossed her mind, but now she was sending an email to the manager of a nearby building.

She had stumbled into a great idea. Rabbit's luck.

The work week over, Sarah drove a few blocks off her usual route to wind up at Sinclair Manor. The foggy afternoon had all but subsided, leaving just enough to coat the building in a kind of English charm. It had the look of a manor, or at least, an attempt at one. The exterior had stately details, with statuettes and flourishes around the door. Without them, the building would probably look like any other turn-of-the-century building.

The neighborhood architecture was diverse. The building's neighbor was larger and newer, resplendent in bold art deco details. Around the corner was a shamelessly new building, low and geometric, an everyman's Frank Lloyd Wright. Somehow, the trio looked natural, like it had always been that way.

"Ah, you must be Sarah! Come on in, darling."

A middle-aged otter greeted her with a soft Southern accent. He was nowhere as sleek as Alex, much stronger and more masculine, but he had the same unflappable cheerfulness about him.

"I'm Henry. You're here to check out the two bedroom?"
"That's the plan," Sarah said. "Unless you're fresh out of those."
"No, no, we've got good supply."

The lobby tried to be stately as well. Old wingback chairs and flourished wooden benches made up the waiting room. The building was probably sold as a luxury place when it was new. Now, it didn't resemble any of the places marketed as luxury apartments. The lighting was too yellow and incandescent, the walls more brick than concrete. It felt surprisingly like her current building.

Except the elevator. That was a reasonable size.

"So, what's the availability?" she asked as they stepped into the elevator.

"Well, the one I'm gonna walk you through, that's good October 1st. Pretty much cleaned up."

"Quick."

"I know. Did just get notice on another one, that'll be the first week of November."

"So that's out."

"Need a place sooner?"

"November 1st at the latest."

"Oh, don't worry hun," he said with a sudden cheer. "I can get it bumped up a couple days if it's really needed. Might have to step over a cleaning crew, that's all."

Sarah nodded, hopeful.

"Give your old place notice already?"

"Naw, not really. New owners. They're pricing me out, gotta be out by November."

"Jeez hun, I'm sorry. It's been coming up a lot lately, one of my friends got his rent bumped up well over a hundred bucks. Crazy talk."

Sarah's bump was more than that, but she wasn't going to be the one-upping type. "Well, from the sounds of it, this should help me avoid that."

"Absolutely!" Henry unlocked the apartment door, motioning Sarah in. "The Sinclair's actually under a little co-op we have running. Bunch of us that have these old places around town. We try to share stuff, keep the places affordable. Does mean I'm not always around, but you'd be sick of my face pretty soon anyway!"

A co-op of apartment managers, Sarah thought. *So goddamn Portland.*

"That's pretty awesome," she said, taking some steps around the apartment. "Must make these places go fast, though."

"Oh, don't it. We've got a waiting list on studios these days."

A studio would make more sense. It would be cheaper, possibly cheaper than splitting a place. She always assumed she could fit herself into a

125

smaller place with just a little bit of cleverness. It'd be a reason to get rid of some junk, at any rate.

Two bedrooms, on the other hand, was plenty of space. More than she'd need alone, more than enough to share with someone else. There was only one bathroom, which she could see being a concern, but nothing else set off any alarms.

She pulled out her phone to take some photos of the apartment from various angles, then started typing notes.

"You came prepared."

"A bit." She put her phone away. "How's the noise situation? You mentioned a family was moving out of one of these?"

"Yep, a couple of families, couple of kids. Not gonna lie, this is definitely an older building, there's a bit of noise. Mostly trucks and the like. But you know how it is, floorboards creak, pipes hiss, you can't get away from all of it."

Sarah was impressed with his honesty. She was impressed with Henry in general; he was friendly and humble, almost disinterested in selling. He didn't have to sell her on the place anyway. If Sean were willing to move in with her, she would take it. The whole deal was creeping into the "too good to be true" realm.

"Got someone moving in with you?"

"Hopefully," Sarah said. "Got a friend who's looking to get out of his place. We might try to swing this, just gotta talk to him."

"Well, wonderful! Let's head back to the office, I'll get you some info on the building and the co-op. You go talk to your buddy, and if we're all good, we're all good."

"Roger that. I'll definitely run into him over the weekend, so it shouldn't be that long."

"Alright then. Just, you know, these things like to fly off the shelves. So, no rush, but don't be waiting."

Sarah didn't intend to wait. She was already typing a text to Sean by the time she got into the car.

"Hey. You serious about moving? Found a 2BR."

She moved her car back to her building. As she parked, she could feel her phone ringing. Sean's number.

"Hello?"
"Hey, Sarah. What's going on?"

She was still sitting in her car, papers from the apartment strewn about the passenger seat. The engine was already off, making for a warm and comfortable phone booth.

"I've been scouting out apartments. Stumbled into finding out about a two bedroom near where I am already. So much like my current place." Her voice was already bouncing with excitement while she did the same in the driver's seat. "Really good manager and everything. It's awesome."

"Congrats."

"Thanks. I mean, it's a little more expensive than the plan. It's two bedrooms and all that. So I'm a little freaked out, but like, we could split it and it'd actually be way cheap."

"Yeah, cool." He sounded distracted, distant.

"You alright, man?"

There was a pause. "Yeah, yeah. I just... I dunno. Work was kinda shitty today."

"You wanna talk about it?"

"Eh. Don't worry about it."

She was going to worry anyway.

"It's just stupid stuff, no big deal."

"Alright, I figured. Anyway, you don't have to decide right away. If you don't want to split a place with me, that's cool, I just figured I'd let you know about it."

"Right, right." His voice strained as if he were rolling over. "I assume it's an older kind of place?"

"Yep. Totally like my current one." Her excitement returned immediately.

"Right. I probably have to come take a look, huh?"

"If you want to."

"Be pretty stupid not to."

"Hasn't stopped you before." She gambled on a tease. Maybe it could lift his spirits.

"I guess." No luck.

Okay, this is strange. "Well, alright. You think about it, we'll talk on Sunday, okay?"

"Sure."

Sarah could imagine him slumped on the couch, sprawled out, his tail hanging off the side. It didn't line up with how she had ever seen him before. He sounded exhausted past any sort of physical strain she could imagine. Whatever was preoccupying him had to be serious.

She gathered up the apartment papers. The hunt had kept her preoccupied since it started, but now it had to compete with whatever got into Sean's head. Whatever it was, Sarah had to find out. She wouldn't be able to help otherwise.

CHAPTER TWENTY-SIX

She woke up around 7 am to a text. "Pizza?"

Alex was never up this early. Or, rather, this late. When he worked the bar, he would be out until 3 or 4 in the morning and immediately go to sleep. It made dating him awkward; Sarah had always been a straightforward 9-to-5-er.

Sarah appreciated the days he had off. They could almost be an ordinary couple. She didn't expect a marketing manager and an artist to be a traditional couple – that was part of what drew her to him – but surely, even the weirdest couples went on dates.

"Sure, lunch?" It would give her enough time to wake up, and she wanted to keep the afternoon for herself. As excited as she was for Sinclair Manor, having a backup was essential. She wanted to be a sensible rabbit.

"1:30," he responded. He wasn't one to send long text messages in the first place, but there was a sense of curtness about these. Or was it Sean on her mind again?

She wondered if the two were connected. It was such a long shot, but then, having two of her most cheerful friends in what seemed like sour moods at the same time was also unlikely.

Maybe she was just reading too much into it.

She grabbed her old, beat-up jeans and a t-shirt loose enough that it almost hid her tail. She dressed casually for work, but this was too laid back. It'd never fly in the office. It was strictly a laundry day type of outfit. Not that it mattered; Alex never cared what she wore.

As much as she tried to deny it, she did care what he wore. If she was going to date someone so flowing in gender that it would impress David Bowie, she had to accept that he would cross-dress. She wouldn't be able to stop him anyway. He was too stubborn.

But it embarrassed her, ever so slightly. They joked that he could make a better girl than she could if he tried. But she was the girl, and he was the guy. She wasn't interested in changing that, but if Alex was going around being so feminine, people might think she was. She never wanted people to get the wrong idea.

Alex was already at the pizza place when Sarah arrived. He sat in the far back, but the orange tuft on his head was visible from the door. He was still dressed in his waitress's outfit – that, or he had taken to wearing it off the clock. Either option seemed likely.

He didn't have food with him, but he sat staring at the table as though studying the pizza that should be there. He was startled when Sarah approached and sat down across from him.

"You look like hell, dude," she said after he calmed down.
"And you look like a dude, so." His voice was flat and beaten down.
She leaned forward, ears up and attentive. "What's going on?"
The pause felt like a year. Measurably long, but surmountable. "I got fired."

Sarah bit her lower lip, trying to avoid saying anything. She knew what happened. His boss was sick of him being so weird. His stubborn indifference finally caught up with him. It wouldn't be the first time she had to console him after such an event.

She gave Alex a pat on the shoulder. "Do you wanna talk about it?"
"Not really."

"It was the skirt thing, wasn't it?" Alex glared at her, confirming her suspicions. "Sorry."

"It's so fucking dumb. But, whatever. He was an idiot anyway."

She looked for the most consoling words she could find. *What would I want him to say if I got fired?* "Well... I know you'll find something else."

"Like hell I will."

"You can. I know you can. Look." She nudged his head up to look into his eyes. They were bloodshot. "I believe in you. You will be fine."

Alex leaned away from Sarah, into the back of his chair. He slumped like a corpse.

"Jesus. Did you sleep?"

"I drank."

Her heart sank. He still smoked pot – she couldn't get him to quit that – but he stopped drinking when they were dating. He drank a lot those days, enough that it worried Sarah. That was the first thing she encouraged him to change, positive that it would be good for him and his art. It didn't affect his work, but he did admit to feeling better.

"Shit. Alex."

"I know, I know."

"Look. Whatever you need me to do, I'll do it. If I have to visit every night, I'll do it. Whatever." She wasn't convinced she was telling the truth.

Alex didn't look like he was buying it either. "I'll figure it out. I'll sleep this off, throw it all at the paintings. Maybe then I'll fucking sell one."

"You've had sales lately, haven't you?"

"Just Kevin's run of prints. Not worth much."

"It's something." If she couldn't offer help, she could try to offer a positive perspective.

"Not enough."

"Well... okay. Let's think about this."

"I don't want to." He slowly pulled himself up, leaning on the table once more.

Sarah could see the options already. Maybe something would pan out with Johann. Maybe there was some opening at her office that he'd be a fit

131

for. She could spare some reputation and put in a good word for him. But, none of the options would work if he wasn't interested.

"Alright, how about this. I'll come by your place on... say, next Saturday. You get your rest, you relax until then. I'll bring the supplies I still have, we'll start going through the lessons again."

"Don't," he mumbled. "I mean... I'm in no shape for it."

"That's what I mean. Give it a week. And I'll pay in full, then and there."

"You don't have to pay."

"You could use the money."

"You're not paying."

Sarah sighed, with a small grumble. "I'm at least paying for lunch."

She went to the counter before he could protest. Tommy knew their regular order – peppers and onions for her, anchovies for him – and had it ready as she arrived.

"Figured that was your bum," he said, jerking his head in Alex's direction.

"He's a bit recognizable."

"Just make sure he doesn't puke over there, got it?"

"Don't worry, he's not gonna puke." She paused, expecting to be instantly proven wrong. When nothing came from his direction, she turned to see Alex's head resting on the table. "See, out like a light. He's fine."

"There you go. Just make sure you take him home, don't want any kinda situation here, y'know?"

She couldn't tell if it was a request or a threat, so she took it to heart regardless. The smell of food woke Alex up gradually, but he remained an inch from sleeping through the entire meal.

They walked slowly back to his apartment, Sarah supporting his weight when he needed it. She made sure he was on his bed, tail tucked in the groove, before she left.

The walk back to her car was brisk. Alex lived in a sketchy neighborhood, a dark red for car break-ins. She didn't need the weekend to get worse.

CHAPTER TWENTY-SEVEN

Sarah made a point to arrive at the theater first that Sunday. She hoped to catch Kate or Lee before Sean got there. Anyone else from the group would be fine, but they were less likely to know what was going on.

Her best case was seeing Kate first. Whatever Kate knew, she would share. Lee would be harder to extract anything from. She didn't want Sean to get there first, forcing her to go into that conversation unprepared.

She stood outside the theater, leaning against the wall, repeatedly checking her phone. She felt conspicuous, out of place. At least the smokers had a reason to be standing idly outside.

Lee arrived first. His jacket seemed a size too big for him, making him look like an even smaller ferret than he was.

"Hey, Lee." Sarah gave him a nod but left it at that. He always seemed to prefer that.

He leaned against the same wall, a movie poster hanging between them. "How've you been?" he responded after a small pause.

"Been okay. Apartment hunting." She kept her voice light and disengaged like Lee always did.

"I heard. Sticking with one bedroom?"

It was already more conversation than she expected to get out of him all night. Her voice started picking up energy.

"If I can. I mean, studios are getting pricey."

"It's not so bad. If you're good with not having a lot of stuff, it's actually pretty nice."

"I guess that's what you have?"

"Yep. Never saw a need for anything bigger."

"Nice. I could stand to downsize." She looked out at the street. "Of course, I say that, but I've been looking at sharing a two bedroom with Sean. Would probably be more space."

"Really? Surprised he'd go for that."

"Well, we talked Friday. He's thinking about it. We'll see what happens."

Lee looked up and down the street as though he were going to cross it. "Wouldn't really count on it. I don't think he likes being left alone with anyone. When it's just the two of us, he gets kinda weird. I mean, different weird than usual."

"I was gonna say."

Lee laughed. Lee almost never laughed. "I dunno. He's a good guy and all. Just doesn't like people, I guess."

"We hang out, though."

"Well yeah, there's these things."

"No, I mean, just the two of us." She looked at Lee. He seemed surprised by the news. "Not that often, but, yeah. When we need someone to talk to, I guess. And we still do those home movie nights."

"Huh." He looked at his feet. "Guess it's just me he doesn't like."

"C'mon, he doesn't... not like you." She didn't know how Sean actually felt about anyone in the group, but she had to be consoling somehow. "You're just always quiet."

"Yeah, 'cause Kate won't shut the fuck up."

Sarah burst out laughing. "Oh, God. Yeah."

Lee was smiling. He seemed to move about more. Either his energy was picking up or the temperature was getting to him. He certainly seemed more interested in conversation.

"I don't know how you get a word in with her, seriously. It's tough. But, I mean, I usually don't have anything to add anyway."

"I'm sure you do."

"Maybe," he said. "I don't wanna be that guy, though. Like, Sean's that guy. He likes the attention, likes to take charge. And that's cool and all, I just don't want to deal with that."

"I know what you mean. It's, like, my least favorite part of being an adult."

"Yep." He sighed. "Guess that's what extroverts are like."

"Maybe." Sarah wasn't sure where she fell. Forced extrovert, maybe? "But when have you ever heard of an extroverted programmer?"

Lee chuckled. "Agreed. And Kate's kinda quiet for a realtor. My folks bought a house couple years ago, I helped out. Had to be around realtors a whole lot. Dear God."

"Yeah. Meanwhile, we're in the back, just like, 'chill it out you two.' They're oddly alike."

"I know. Wonder when they're gonna fuck already."

Sarah's ears perked up. She pushed herself off the wall. "What?"

Lee looked confused. "Yeah. Like, everything she says is just flirting with him. She's told me once, she only really comes to these things to hit on him."

"Wow. I knew she did it occasionally, but like, I didn't know Sean was on board with it."

"I don't know. Might be."

She leaned back against the wall, dropping her weight against the bricks. "I just... I can't see them actually dating."

"He does play coy with the whole thing."

"I don't think he even realizes it. Like, I could probably go right up to him and be like 'I wanna go out with you' and he'd say 'but we're already out' or something. It'd completely go over his head."

"Don't tell me you have a crush on him too."

Sarah's eyes narrowed. "Don't tell me you have a crush on him."

Lee thought for a moment. "Naw. He's not my type. Didn't even figure he was your type. He's nothing like Alex."

"When did you meet Alex?"

Lee was the newest regular in the group. He only arrived in May, after Alex stopped coming with Sarah. At least, she thought that was how the timeline went.

"I tried her art classes."

"Oh, it's 'him' now. Actually, wait. When did you last see him?"

Lee shrugged. "Couple months ago? When she- he did that mural in the lobby at work."

"That was your place? Nice. But, yeah. He's going with male. Started wearing the skirts again, though, so who knows."

"Well, that's what I mean. Could you imagine Sean in a skirt?"

Sarah tried. She started laughing to herself. "You're right."

"Exactly. So if Alex is your type, and Sean's not like Alex, then..."

"Alex was my type, though. I don't know if he still is. Think my type changed."

Lee nodded. "Fair enough. Wonder what Sean's type is."

"A computer?" She realized how relaxed she was with Lee now. Her snark was showing.

Lee embraced it. "Robosexual, then?"

"Well, that's what he cares about, isn't it?"

Lee glanced down the street. "You could ask him."

Sean rode up close, gliding to the two of them before braking sharply. His bike looked beaten up. The rear tire had a rough gray line cut along it, the handlebars scraped up. The frame didn't seem bent so it couldn't have been an accident. His helmet and satchels were in as good a shape as always. She was surprised to see any damage at all; if there was anything that competed with computers for Sean's affection, it was his bike.

He swung off the seat with the face of a cyclist nearly killed by a driver. "Hey, guys."

"Man, you okay?" Sarah asked. "Someone almost hit you?"

"Don't wanna talk about it."

"Dude, seriously. You look like hell," Lee said. "What happened?"

Sean grumbled, tearing his helmet off his head. "Jeremy stole my bike."

"The fuck?"

Sarah had never met Jeremy. She assumed he was a coworker though Sean had never mentioned him before. Regardless, it was clearly an attempted theft, but Sean seemed no less slighted.

"Yeah. We don't lock them up when they're in the office since we got the cards and all that. So, I start heading out Friday, he's wheeling my bike out. And he doesn't even have a bike. Just hops on and fucking bolts. I had to run him down, finally caught him at a light. Almost beat the shit out of him."

"Jesus," Sarah said. "Why the fuck would he steal your bike?"

"Because he's a fucking asshole. And he probably figured he was getting fired soon anyway, so it's like, take the raccoon's shit, he fucking deserves it."

"Sean," she insisted, "that's not what-"

"I know, I know. It's just..." He paused and exhaled. "I'm gonna go see if there's anywhere inside I can put this. I got, like, three new locks now but I still don't wanna risk it. I'll be right back."

He rolled his bike into the theater. Lee and Sarah stood outside quietly, exchanging confused stares. She couldn't possibly ask about the apartment tonight. It would have to wait.

CHAPTER TWENTY-EIGHT

She offered to check in with him on Monday. Officially, it was so that he could have someone to talk to outside of his office, someone more distant to whatever relationship he and Jeremy had. If he brought up the apartment idea, then she'd go along with it. If not, it could wait. She wasn't going to bring it up first.

Their offices weren't especially close, but they were both downtown. They could easily meet for lunch. Sarah tried to be as accommodating as possible, picking a Greek restaurant close enough to Sean's office that he could just walk there.

He brought his bike regardless. She found him standing next to it outside. It was chained up like a wild beast, all three locks in use at the least. He still looked strained and nervous, but the pressure seemed reduced. His tail moved slightly, no longer dead weight behind him.

"There's a table that looks right out here," he said as an introduction.
"Sounds like a good idea." She let him lead as they went inside. "How're you holding up?"
"Well, Jeremy got fired."
"Good."
"Yeah. Honestly, I don't know how he ever got the job, but like, whatever. I'm okay, he's gone, fuck him."
"Attaboy."

Sarah knew the conversation would be light. Sean looked right past her as they ate. He had taken the seat facing the window and kept most of his focus on his bike. He was eating slower than she remembered and was as quiet as Lee normally was. Still, she could see him trying to smile. That was all she expected and all she needed.

"I'm sorry," he eventually said. "I haven't thought about the apartment at all."

"That's totally fair. You're kinda preoccupied."

"Yeah." He dug idly at his salad. "He actually said, when he was getting thrown out today? He said I deserved it."

"Well, he's wrong. And an asshole."

"I know. But, like, he didn't say why."

"I really doubt it's because you're a raccoon."

"Yeah. He's a leopard, and like, if there's anything there it's news to me. And, I mean, I barely ever worked with him."

Sarah thought for a moment. "You beat him out for a promotion or something?"

"Never been promoted. Doesn't happen much, really. If you wanna move up, you change jobs."

"Really?"

"Yeah. But I mean, it doesn't matter. I don't think so anyway. Just don't want him showing up at my door one night."

"With an ax? Screaming 'here's Johnny!'?" She meant it at a joke but got no reaction.

"Yeah, exactly."

"Shit. Is he really that crazy?"

"Maybe," Sean said, hesitating. "I don't know. I did see him browsing gun forums at work one time. And he always gave this one girl in support shit 'cause she's from California."

"You're from California."

"He never knew." He thought as he took his next bite. "I don't think he knew, at least. He acted like I was a local, but maybe he found out. Maybe that's what it was."

"Pretty stupid reason, if it is."

"Only one that makes any sense."

"How did someone like him get the job anyway? He sounds like some people I've interviewed, I always tell them to fuck off. They're not good to have around."

"Agreed. But we're desperate. We're not flashy and trendy anymore. I mean, it wasn't trendy when I started there, but whatever. Most of the devs that move here just want a San Francisco they can afford. That showoff startup stuff. And I mean, if you want to do that, fine, but I couldn't. Not again."

"Yeah, me neither. But we've been losing a bunch of people to that."

"Exactly. So, we just end up taking the first person who can do a fizzbuzz."

"I... assume that's hard?"

Sean shook his head. "It's super simple."

"Oh." She laughed to herself. "Yeah, that makes sense, once I actually think about what you said."

Sean smiled. "I thought the whole point of your job was listening to people?"

"No, no. Occasionally I yell at them too." She was testing the waters, seeing if his mood really was picking up.

"Man, I want your job."

Better than nothing. "See, I told you this would help. You're back to your old annoying self."

He pointed his fork at her with a jab. "I can be more annoying. You watch."

There he is. "Roger that."

There was more silence between them, and that was fine with Sarah. Sean was still glancing out the window regularly, but he also glanced at Sarah. She did her best to avoid eye contact, knowing that it would make it harder for her to bite her tongue. She wanted to hold to her promise. *Let him bring it up. Don't bring it up.*

"So, anyway. You wanted to talk about the apartment."

"If you want to." She tried to contain her energy. It felt rude to be so eager about something right now, considering the mood of the day.

"Well, I mean, I don't know. I've got some time tonight, at least. If you wanna pick me up, I'll give it a look. It's worth a shot."

143

"Henry said he can't do Mondays. Has to help out with one of the other buildings."

"Oh well. Tomorrow?"

"That should work. I'll give him a call tomorrow morning."

They finished and walked out. Sean unchained his bike slowly. Sarah sat in her car, watching him walk his bike back to his office. She wasn't eager to get back to work either, but once Sean got out of view, she started the engine and pulled away from the curb. There wasn't anything else to be done right now. Yet she knew she would try to think of something. She wouldn't be able to help it.

CHAPTER TWENTY-NINE

Sarah got out of her car and walked from the parking garage. She tired enough to notice it. It was a loss of energy that pulled her shoulders down but kept her stable on her feet. Talking to Sean was good for him, she hoped, but it sapped her.

She dropped herself into her chair like an overstuffed sack, dropping her purse on the end of her desk. She didn't bother taking her jacket off. That would be too much effort, and besides, autumn was catching up to her. She was already sniffling every time she came inside.

Her ears drooped lop-like along her head. They muffled the office, giving her some semblance of peace, some small space to reenergize in. Thankfully, Michelle wasn't around to ruin it. At a meeting, probably. Sarah had her own soon, but it was nothing to worry about right now.

She closed her eyes. Her mind was running too fast to fully embrace the calm and quiet, but the thoughts were muted enough that she could feel relaxed. Just for a moment.

"Hey, Sarah?"

She opened her eyes. Roger's interruption was a nuisance, and a worse one than usual. She spun around slowly, looking up at the jittering squirrel. He had a folder in one paw and a coffee cup in the other.

"What's up?" she said.
"Oh, the usual. You busy right now?"
"No, just a little tired. Been a bit stressful lately."

"I hear that. Do you mind if we grab an office? I want to talk for a bit."

She took her jacket off, pulled herself out of her chair, and followed him across the office. *"I want to talk for a bit?" That's a new one. Wonder what's going on here.*

Roger gently closed the door. "Alright, so, this kinda sucks, but bear with me here." He was apologizing before he even hit the chair.

"Bearing," Sarah said, holding a tired yet optimistic tone.

"Right, so. You remember the meeting we had, where we had all those deals in the pipeline and things were looking up and maybe we'd be okay?" He was hesitating as he rambled, looking around for the right words to use.

"Yeah. I was there." *Don't ask about any of them, though. Was half asleep.*

"Well, Lawrence, the guy who was working on all of those? The hot-shot sales guy that everyone was like 'Lawrence is gonna be great! It'll be so awesome!' Yeah, they arrested him this morning."

That woke Sarah up. Her ears regained their upright stance. "You're kidding."

"I know! A sales guy being all sketchy and stuff." He laughed nervously to himself. "But yeah, the rumor is, none of those deals were real. A whole ton of fraud and embezzlement and all that good stuff."

She laughed quietly. Humor seemed like the only direction to go. "I wish I had met the guy. Then I could be all like, 'sounds like something he would do' or something."

Roger laughed again. His fidgeting was picking up. "I have met him actually, and yeah, this didn't actually surprise me that much. The whole, making up the leads entirely for fake expenses, that was a bit of a surprise. Like, lying, sure, but stealing, whoa buddy."

Sarah let out a nervous laugh. She wished she had her jacket on; the chill of impending bad news was approaching. "Well, that sounds kinda bad."

"Yeah, a little bit. Um, bad enough that, apparently, we're gonna have to lay some people off."

Sarah's brown fur had to be going white. The timing couldn't be worse. She knew any apartment she looked at would do income verification. If she got laid off, no income. No income, no new apartment. No new apartment, no choice but get screwed over by Waterknell.

146

"Look," she said meekly, "whatever I can do, with the position I'm in-"

"Calm down, Sarah!" His ease made her uneasy. "It's okay. I mean, it sucks, but it's okay." He pulled a piece of paper – not pink, thankfully – out of his folder. "The good news is, we're able to pay severance for whoever decides to leave."

"Decides?"

Roger sat up in a more confident pose. "Yeah. So, obviously I can't be like 'this guy screwed us over, you're fired,' like that's a shitty thing to do. So I'm going down my list, talking to all the marketing managers and whatnot, and I'm just trying to find someone who's already thinking about leaving. Figured, start with you."

Her ears stood up crooked. "Someone told you I was thinking about leaving?" She had, but not seriously. She certainly hadn't told anyone about it; this sort of situation seemed inevitable if she did.

"Well, no, but I know, 'cause I'm all omniscient and such." The jokes had to be his way of keeping calm. "But no, no, you were just the first I ran into. I'm gonna have to ask everyone, at least until two folks agree to it."

"Wow, two?"

"Yeah, and it might hit a couple other departments. He took a couple million."

Sarah's eyes flashed wide. "Well, hey, if you're gonna con, con."

"I know, couple million sounds nice." He coughed and shuffled himself into his best impression of a stoic professional. "The severance isn't a couple million, of course, it's just two months. Which is nice and all, I mean, you could absolutely get a new job in two months. Plenty of companies moving into town."

"Yeah. Honestly, I'm surprised there's severance at all."

"Well, don't say I never did anything for you."

Uh... okay? "So, what does this mean with Thomas' stuff? I mean, the whole thing with HiSense?"

"Right, that. That's still happening, and it's like, if you and Michelle take the deal, then Vinish gets it kinda by default. Same if you and Vinish leave, like, that's how it'll go all around. We'll figure out how the rest of it gets shuffled when we know who's out."

"Figured. And what if nobody takes it?"

"Then we take you all to an island, give you some weapons- no, no. Then Gary and I have to pick who goes."

Sarah could tell he didn't want to do it. She couldn't blame him. "Well, I don't think I have a decision right now."

"Oh, of course not, take however long you need to. It's a big decision and all that. But, it is first come first serve on this. So, you know, no rush or anything, but decide quick."

His parting words hung in her mind during her next meeting. "No rush." It seemed more of a wish than a suggestion. There were too many deadlines, too many people demanding an answer. There was always a rush.

CHAPTER THIRTY

Michelle was definitely still in the building. Her jacket was draped over the back of her chair, her purse leaning on the seat. Yet Sarah couldn't find her. She wasn't at her desk, or in an office with Roger, or in a meeting room with her clients.

Sarah wasn't looking for her so much as she was looking for someone else who had heard the news. She could talk to Vinish or Jessica, but Michelle was the best option. As much as Sarah didn't like her, she knew her.

"Is Michelle around?" she asked Nick, a beaver that sat behind her.
"Think she went to call someone. Sounded kinda worried. Hope it wasn't her kid."
Sarah nodded. It was the most she had ever talked to him.

She stuffed her laptop into her bag and carried it to the elevators. She could use a bit of space to think through her options. She wanted to head to a coffee shop, either the Deadline or something like it. Downtown only had Starbucks. It would have to do.

Michelle was in the lobby, on the phone, pacing. She had definitely gotten the news. Sarah paused to consider if she should talk to her, or at least, indicate that she was willing to. Maybe it would help for the two of them to talk. At this point, she couldn't consider the two of them enemies anymore.

She thought better of it. Michelle could use her privacy, and besides, Sarah worked best in a coffee shop. She walked the few blocks to Washington Street, trying to clear her head in the process.

Her budget was on her laptop at home. She cursed herself for never emailing it to herself or doing anything else that would give her access to it now. She thought she could stretch two months' severance further than just two months, but how much further? If Thomas were right, she would need to stretch it as far as she could.

She sat at a bar along the window, a clean sheet of false granite that fit well with the small, identical metal tables. Virtually every tower downtown had a Starbucks like this or, failing that, some stand that tried to come close.

"Sarah, latte with mint?" the skunk barista called out.

She never liked that they did that. Somehow, her name and drink felt too personal to be shouting across a small room. Especially at this level of afternoon commotion, with just enough space for conversation to bubble up and just enough people to pick up on it.

She swirled her cup idly, watching cars pass by. The coffee and mint chased each other into her nostrils. *I can't do it. I'd be unemployed. I guess that's not too bad, really. Happens to everyone. Just, not right now. I don't need this right now.* She took a sip, giving herself a pause. *Is there going to be anything out there for me anyway? People just want programmers, from the looks of it. At least, that's what I keep hearing. Maybe Sean could teach me?*

The idea wasn't very appealing. Sean always had his share of horror stories about his coworkers. Jeremy and the bike theft was just the latest and most surprising.

I don't have to put up with shit like that where I am now. She picked her head up and laughed to herself. *Wait. I'm dealing with that shit right now. Goddammit, Lawrence.*

She opened her work laptop and pulled up a blank page, giving it two columns: "stay" and "go". Classic, basic decision-making. She wasn't going to do any analytical weighing or anything elaborate that she did for her clients. This was just for her.

Alright. First off, do not make that Clash joke to yourself. You can do better than that. So. Why would I want to stay put? Well, pay's decent. I have a bit of reputation at this point, that's pretty valuable. I don't hate anyone. It would mean I don't have to change anything. Michelle's a little annoying, though, guess she's more in the "go" column...

"Christopher, flat white?" The barista's cry rose above the hum of conversation and stole her attention. Sarah considered a different coffee shop, or just claiming a room back at the office.

Right. Focus. Why should I leave? Hmm. Severance is nice, really surprised by that. If I can get something before that runs out, then I win. Hooray. But, that's if.

She watched as a group of foxes in suits walked past. They looked relaxed, comfortable, as though they never had to worry about finding their next job. They probably didn't.

Maybe it's time to move on, though. Like, four years. Not a ton, dad's been in his job since I was in middle school. Still, decent amount of time. I'd probably be junior there too. I mean, I'm junior where I am. Unless moving gets me a promotion in the process. That's how programmers do it, apparently.

She stopped typing and opened a web browser. The entire decision ultimately came down to whether or not she could find her next job. She didn't want the stress of a job hunt. Looking for her new apartment was bad enough. But she felt compelled to look. No matter what, things were going to change soon anyway.

It was getting close to her last meeting of the day. She wasn't going to get anything more than a cursory glance at job listings, but that was better than nothing.

As she packed up her computer, the barista called out one last time. "Paula, mocha, no whip?"

Her ear perked slightly. For a split-second, she thought it could've been Carl's daughter. He had been talking about her a lot lately. It wasn't her – a raccoon, not a hyena, picked up the drink – but the idea still sat in her head. Paula didn't sound like the type to come downtown, much less to some corporate coffee shop in a mostly anonymous office tower.

Though, Sarah didn't quite think she was the type either.

CHAPTER THIRTY-ONE

There was cake.

Cupcakes, more accurately, and plenty of them. Someone picked them up from a small, twee bakery on the other side of downtown. All they made were those cupcakes. Sarah heard that they just opened a third store.

It was Thomas's last day. Congratulations and well-wishes were dished out to him steadily. The office kitchen was stuffed full of the marketing staff, mingling and taking advantage of the excuse to avoid work.

Or, they were just there for the cake.

They needed a celebration. Spirits were low. Rumors of layoffs had spread, leaving a trail of uncertainty in their wake. The worries would one-up each other until someone was convinced the entire company was shutting down. It ended there not because it sounded implausible, but because it could go no further.

The marketing managers all knew what the story was by now. They knew their jobs were safe, as long as someone else didn't want theirs. Still, that created tension. Nobody knew who would or wouldn't want their job, so nobody knew if they were safe. They only knew it wouldn't be random, that it was more Mexican standoff than Russian roulette.

Sarah overheard a tired male voice a few feet away. "Hell, I've already started packing up."
"Can't blame you."

She didn't know their names, but she recognized them as designers. She took a glance at the man speaking, his leopard-spotted arms gesturing weakly as he talked about expecting the pink slip any moment now.

Chris approached her from the other side and joined in leaning against the window. She was hesitant to talk to the beaver, but there was never any other way to escape a standoff.

"How're things holding for you?" she asked.

"Alright. Not sure what I'll do next."

"Same." She took a bite of her cupcake and idly watched the crowd.

"Fiona's nudging me to go for it. Wants me to go learn to program, she's like 'if you can't code nobody's gonna want you' and all that."

"Sheesh. That's harsh."

"She can be," he shrugged. "But, I mean, she's right."

"I guess. There's a little bit of stuff out there. I've been looking."

"Everyone has, probably."

"Not Michelle." She spotted her on the other side of the room. She didn't look worried.

"True. Where'd you find people were hiring?"

"Well..." she tried to remember. "Think there was only one or two that actually wanted marketing managers. But there were others that seemed kinda similar. I don't know, though, I didn't really look into it."

"That's what I've seen. There's stuff and all, it's just different." He sighed out his words.

"Different's not that bad."

"Sure, sure." He took a bite. "It's just hard to jump from one kind of job to another, you know? They can probably find someone who's better at it. Or some cheap kid out of college."

"Probably. But it's still worth trying."

She was surprised to listen to her own words. *Since when was I optimistic with all this?*

Chris spoke through another bite. "Gonna do one of those coding camps?"

"Hmm? Eh, I don't know. Don't know if they're any good."

154

"Me neither. But Fiona keeps suggesting it constantly, she seems to think it's a good idea."

"Constantly?"

"Yeah. Like, at least once a week. She hasn't even done one herself, she just keeps insisting they're a good idea for me."

"Man. Sounds kinda pushy."

"A bit, yeah."

Sarah nodded. "But, yeah, guess I'll ask Sean about it at least. He does coding, should know more about them than I do."

"He your boyfriend?"

She bit her tongue. "No. Not really."

Roger waved his arms and tail until the room quieted down. "Alright, alright. You've all had your fun. Now, if you don't mind, I'm going to say a couple words real quick. That good with everyone?"

A mumbled "yes" surfaced from the crowd.

"Great. So, I always like to embarrass people a little when they leave. I kinda hope it'll keep other people from leaving too." He laughed nervously. "But yeah, Thomas has been with us for... six years now, is it? Six years. Man. Time kinda flies, huh? Anyway, he's done wonders for us, especially with tech companies, and those have been super important lately. Lot of them popping up and spending. So I guess this is the worst time to lose you, right? It's fine, it's fine, you're already dead to us."

Thomas smiled throughout, cringing at every joke. Roger's sense of humor was the sort of dark deadpan that not everyone likes.

"Anyway, Thomas, I'm sure you've got something great coming next, so best of luck with all that."

"Thanks."

"Where are you off to?" Michelle asked over the crowd's heads.

"Denver, actually. Have some old friends in the biotech space, they want me to come help out. Plus, the skiing's great."

"Yeah, lot more of it than just Mt. Hood," Roger said, straining to be enthusiastic.

155

He's moving out of town? Hmm. Wonder what kind of place he had. Never mentioned a house, so... Maybe. Worth a try.

"And I'm sure you won't miss the rain either," Roger continued. "Well, there's still some cake, there's drinks, so, yeah."

Sarah pushed herself through the crowd, trying to intercept Thomas. He beat her to the exit, but she got his attention shortly after.

"Congrats on getting out of here, man," she said.

"Oh, thanks. And I guess, maybe the same to you?"

"We'll see. At least you got to do it on your own terms."

He laughed to himself. "Yeah, I feel kinda dumb bailing now. If I knew that was coming, I would've just waited. Jumped on the layoff instead."

"We couldn't have known, really. Just kinda happened all of a sudden."

"Should've known, though. Feels like the ship's been sinking since I got here. Figured if I didn't get out now I was gonna get pushed out."

"Like I might."

"Yep." He looked around at the desks, emptied by the partygoers. His ears sagged. "Wonder if it was worth it to even give a shit."

"You or me?"

"Both, I guess. Didn't do me a whole lotta good."

"Kept you around for six years. Got you that Denver job."

"They would've hit me up anyway. Oh well. Good practice for next time."

The conversation stalled. They reached Thomas's desk, which he had already started clearing out. She sat on a neighboring desk.

"So, if you don't mind me asking, what kind of place are you leaving behind?"

"What do you mean?"

"I'm looking for a new apartment."

"Good luck there."

"I know. Just thought I'd ask."

"Right. It's nothing all that great, honestly. Little place on the east side, nothing fancy."

"I live in a, like, hundred-year-old building. Everything's fancier."

"Well, maybe you would like it. Getting priced out?"

"More or less. You?"

"Not really. Denver is a little cheaper, and I can make a little more. It's a startup and all, but there's no real bullshit over there."

She could respect that. He was yet another coworker to leave for yet another startup, but biotech sounded important and useful. She had heard stories of offices with full arcades, walls of coffees and candies, and multiple fully stocked kegs, all to support a company that did... well, she was never sure. Some of them sounded like they did nothing.

She didn't want to take the layoff. There was too much going on, and even if she did find something new, there was no guarantee it'd be any better. Her job wasn't great, but it could easily be worse.

The same was true of her apartment. Her place wasn't great, but she had seen much worse on Craigslist. Getting Thomas' place would be a shot so long that she tried to ignore the idea. The Sinclair Manor apartment was the only one she found that seemed like it would be feasible. The one she was planning to visit that evening.

The one she had meant to call back earlier in the day.

"Shit," she mumbled, jogging back to her desk.

She sat down and grabbed her phone. With her neighbors still milling about the party, the corner was quiet and calm. There wasn't any need to duck into a room for privacy.

The phone rang repeatedly. Her foot tapped rapidly. As it started thumping, she heard someone on the other end pick up.

"Sorry about the hold, Sinclair Manor, how can I help you?"

"Henry? Hey, it's Sarah. I saw the two bedroom on Friday? Finally had a chance to talk to my friend about it, can we swing by later today?" She wasn't giving him a chance to get a word in.

"Oh, hi Sarah! Nice to hear from you. Now, that apartment, unfortunately, someone just grabbed it out from under ya. Cleared it a couple hours ago."

"Well. If you don't mind me saying so, crap." Henry was so polite that she felt bad even mildly swearing at him.

"I know, I'm sorry. It happens sometimes."

"You said you had a second one, though, right? The one opening in November?"

"Gone too, I'm afraid. Unless their credit check doesn't pan out, but I'd be a little surprised."

"Don't suppose you have any others available? One bedrooms? Studio?"

She could hear him shuffling some papers. "Nope, afraid not. I haven't gotten any notices, at least. If they're headed out, they sure haven't told me."

"Oh... man." Her resolve to swear was running out.

"Don't know if anyone in the co-op has anything, actually. Pretty tight time."

"Well, could you send me anything you hear about? You should have my email already."

"Yeah, I can definitely do that for ya. Really sorry we didn't have anything, though!"

"Oh, no worries, I've got time."

She hung up and tossed her phone on her desk.

"Fuck!"

She sat still for minutes, only the distant party and her thumping foot making any noise. "No rush." Henry said it on Friday and both options were gone by Tuesday. Roger said it on Monday; maybe she was already out of options.

Thomas walked past, carrying his box of personal effects. "Y'know, you can just bail early."

She looked up. "Yeah, I know. Just have to talk to a friend first. Take care, enjoy Denver."

"Thanks. Enjoy Portland."

Sarah assumed there was subtext, but since Thomas had already turned in his badge and left, it would have to remain an assumption.

She grabbed her phone and started texting Sean. "No go tonight. Both places are gone already."

Sean's reply was nearly immediate. "Sucks :(you sure?"

"Yeah, all full. Sorry to get your hopes up :("

She pulled up her stay-or-go file. She hadn't written down many factors; each column only had two listed. The "go" column had "the severance package" and "no more dealing with Michelle". The "stay" column had "not unemployed" and "wouldn't need to change anything".

Her phone buzzed. Sean had replied. "No worries, 2 br seemed crazy."

She put her phone down, failing to think of a meaningful reply. *Really? Thought he was on board with it. Guess not. Or is he just being nice here, like "eh, who cares?" Could see him doing that. Could also see him just, like... he didn't like the idea but he went along with it because I asked. That's probably it. Crap. I shouldn't have roped him into the whole idea in the first place. I'm coming on too hard.*

She switched to the web browser and looked for updates on apartments. She moved her hunt back to only one bedroom options; the two bedroom dream now seemed impossible. She could've done the search from home, but some kind of gravity kept her in her chair. Even if she could leave earlier, somehow it didn't feel right. She always left at 5.

Roger walked down the aisle, eating a cupcake. "Y'know, you can just bail early." He had a more sympathetic tone than when Thomas said it.

"I know, I know. Just needed a little air."

"Fair enough." He started to walk off.

"Hey. Roger."

"Yeah?"

She ushered him closer. "The layoffs thing. Did anyone take you up on it yet?"

"Nope, nobody's said anything. Why, you going to take it?"

"Just curious, is all. I don't think I will."

"Alright. Well, I mean, I'm not gonna think any less of you if you do, so." He laughed his typical nervous laugh.

"If I'm gone, I won't care what you think."

"That is true, yeah. Thomas was happy to, uh... to say a lot of things when we did the exit interview."

She chuckled briefly. "I can imagine."

"Yeah, can't really take it personally or anything. Plus he had some pretty good points, so it's not like he was a mean ol' fox or anything."

"Right." She looked back at her screen and waited for Roger to leave.

"Yeah, so, let me know when you decide, okay?" he said after a long awkward pause.

"Rog- okay."

That was enough of a nudge to make her get up and leave the office. Before she closed her computer, she switched back to her stay-or-go file. She added a third entry to the "go" column: "no more dealing with Roger." She tried to think of something to add to the "stay" column, just to balance it out. She couldn't come up with anything.

CHAPTER THIRTY-TWO

A hyena stood outside an apartment building. She was on the shorter side, probably mid-30s, dressed like she had just finished her evening run. She was leaning on the wall alongside the front door, phone up in conversation. The call was enough distraction that she barely noticed when Sarah entered.

Sarah barely noticed her, too. Her usual back door was locked and being replaced. She wasn't familiar enough with who might be loitering in the front to recognize anyone. The hyena was probably just a neighbor she hadn't seen before. There were plenty of those. She could've also been someone looking to get in so they could break into apartments. Sean would've suggested that possibility. But the hyena looked too friendly, was dressed too cleanly. She couldn't possibly be trouble.

The hyena followed her wordlessly into the elevator. Sarah's mind started to change when she got out and realized the hyena was still following her. She had nowhere to sneak around or break away, so she found herself walking faster, just enough to create distance without being obvious about it. She had her keys in her paw long before she made it to her door at the end of the hall.

"Hey, Sarah, you alright?" Carl called from inside his apartment. The door was half open and missing the wire sculpture that decorated it.

"Yeah, why?" She only then noticed she was low on breath.

"You just look a little stressed, that's all."

"Oh. I guess. Had a weird day with work. Do I really look that bad though?"

Carl limped to the door and opened it the rest of the way. "Well, I could see it from inside, so it must be bad."

"It's fine, it's fine. You, though, you look really tired."

If Sarah looked bad, Carl looked horrible. His eyes were dark and heavy, his fur grayer than usual, his limp more pronounced. He leaned on a cane for support.

"Hey dad!" the hyena called from down the hall.

"Oh, hi Paula!" Carl took some steps over to hug his daughter, allowing Sarah to flush with embarrassment outside of his view. "Did you get here okay?"

"Yeah, and I was just about to call when the rabbit let me in." She extended a paw. "Hi, I'm Paula."

"Sarah. Sorry I kinda ran up here. Wasn't sure you were, y'know, you."

"Oh, don't worry about it! I'd be worried about strangers too."

Sarah nodded. "So what's going on?"

As Sarah asked, she glanced inside Carl's apartment. There were cardboard boxes stacked neatly in corners. His workbench, facing out the living room window, was empty.

"Well, since I gotta get out of here eventually, I'm just biting the bullet, getting it over with. Pack it up and hit the road."

Her shoulders sunk. "Man. I'm really sorry."

"Well, you're not the suit that bought this place out! And I know damn well you're not gonna stick around and give those assholes the satisfaction-"

"Dad..." Paula interrupted.

"Hey, I'm an old man. I'm allowed to be a bitter old man. Otherwise, that wouldn't be a thing, now would it?"

"I'm guessing you're staying with her, then?"

"Just for a little while," Paula said.

"She's got a place, over in Ladd's. Got a room she rents out sometimes. Letting her old man crash there free of charge for a while. Like a daughter ought to."

"And I'll be a good landlord, promise."

"Well, you're up against your mother on that one, so good luck."

"So, hey, I might still see you around at least," Sarah said. "Guess you can still do the craft fair in October."

"Can't do much working," Carl said, "but I should be good to sell a little bit. Might do one of the holiday ones if I have to, but we'll see what happens with all that."

"But," Paula said, "after that, can't make any promises. I can only afford to keep you around until February."

"Covering your rent with that room?" Sarah asked.

"Yeah, but shhh! The owner doesn't allow it."

Sarah blinked. "Wow. Can't imagine doing that. Having strangers around the building, much less in the apartment? That sounds insane."

Paula shrugged. "I gotta do something to afford the place. Besides, you get ratings and all that. It's not much worse than bringing some guy home from the bar, I'm sure you've done that."

"Oh, she's got a guy as it is," Carl said.

"I don't-" Sarah cut herself off sharply. "Sean and I are not dating," she insisted, "we're just friends."

"Right, right," Paula said with a smirk.

"Oh, come on," Sarah said, insulted. "Like you can't just be friends with a guy without fucking him."

"Ladies?" Carl tried to get in between the two.

"No, I mean..." Sarah let out a grumbling sigh. "I'm not yelling at you, really, it's just I hear that shit way too much. Just because I'm a straight girl, and he's a straight guy, that doesn't mean we have to be a couple. I already know he's not interested, and that's fine! But then everyone expects me to just fuck everything that moves because hey, rabbit! And I know that's not what you're saying, it's just..." She was tense and shaking. She looked at the floor, trying to regain her composure. "I'm annoyed, I'm tired, I'm pissed that you're leaving, and I just need some fucking peace."

Silence. Sarah's body sunk, ashamed of her outburst.

"Sarah?" Carl said with a fatherly calm. She looked up. "I'm gonna tell you this like you're my daughter. Like you and Paula are sisters."

"Yeah?"

"Calm your shit down." Paula laughed in surprise. "I mean it. You're getting wound up like a pig's tail over this. I know you don't like what's going on, and I agree. But this isn't the end of the world. You'll move somewhere else, you'll get new neighbors. Things will keep changing and moving right along."

"I know, I know. It's just a lot of things changing all at once. It's too much."

"Well, then, deal with the too much. It ain't gonna run away, so you can't run away either. It's what I told Ben all the damn time, you can't run away." He shook his head. "Dumb boy kept running away. Look where it got him."

"Yeah." Sarah shuffled her feet, trying to calm herself. "So I guess this is goodbye then, right? I mean, I don't really know what else to do here."

"You could help with some boxes," Paula said. "If you don't mind, we could use the help."

Sarah exhaled deeply. "Sure."

CHAPTER THIRTY-THREE

Alex's apartment building was easily visible from the office. The warehouse it was built from stood out over its flat neighbors. When Sarah dated him, it was a source of comfort, knowing that her boyfriend was right across the river.

In the year since they broke up, cranes started appearing, threatening its dominance. One was positioned between her office and his apartment, slowly stacking floors on top of a garage along the river. The bright blue tarps made it impossible to ignore.

From afar it was visually noisy, but up close, it was audibly noisy as well. Saws, drills, jackhammers, all manner of construction tools were making their presence known.

"It's not always this bad," Alex said, pacing around his studio, glancing at the heavy Saturday traffic in the distance. "But, yeah, it's a pain in the ass."

Sarah sat on his bed, trying to keep the construction from consuming her hearing. "Do they stop at night so you can sleep, at least?"

"Sometimes. But, this technically isn't residential, so it's like, they don't have to care."

The building did have what the owners of newer buildings would describe as an industrial charm. Its bricks were exposed not so much as a stylistic choice than as a result of age and occasional neglect. A newer building would use them as a final layer over thick concrete, thick enough to keep out the shouting and barking. Not the case here.

Sarah didn't want to be in his studio. Yet she had to support Alex. If he would refuse financial help, then she would support him emotionally.

She was grateful she didn't live here. Hopefully, there would be some apartment somewhere that she could move into. Something that would keep her from settling for this. Or worse.

She watched Alex, in his sweatpants and tight t-shirt. She pitied him. She pitied everyone who lived here, all out of necessity rather than desire. Even the homeless recovery apartments, the scarce few that managed to be funded, were nicer than this.

"We really gotta get you out of here, man."
Alex sighed. "I dunno."
"It's just kinda..."
"It's shit, I know. But I know there's nothing out there."
She wanted to disagree, but she hadn't found anything for herself. "There's nothing for where you are right now, sure. But, I mean, there's nothing keeping you from... improving, I guess?"
He stood at an unfinished canvas, a blur of warm and dark colors suggesting a sunset. "Well, I think I've been improving."
"Did you get another sale?"
He hesitated. "No. Not yet."
"Well, I don't want to say you're not improving, but you should be selling a lot more."
"I know, I know." He sighed. "Maybe I'm not improving. I don't know. Not like I'm trained in this stuff or anything."
"That doesn't matter."

She didn't know if that was true. She didn't know the art market or the community that supported it. She only knew the bits and pieces she picked up at galleries. There were fewer of those opportunities lately.

166

Alex stood at his canvas. He held a brush, uncolored with paint, and shuffled his feet. Sarah tried to think of some advice to offer. It didn't look like he was going to make any progress on the painting.

"There's got to be a way to, like, market you. Like, you as a concept. The whole idea of Alex Molloy, otter artist. Make it so it's not about whatever you're painting or making or whatever."

Alex gave her a silent, skeptical look.

"I mean, you keep saying, people think your stuff is too weird."

"Well, look at it."

He gestured at one of his finished pieces that leaned against the wall. It was a pastoral nature scene at first glance, something that would fit in Bob Ross' portfolio, but its color was bolder, more aggressive. The barren trees felt more dead than in winter hibernation. A bit of green made the shed in the middle of the scene look like it was rotting. The mountains were on fire, the foreground not far behind. It looked as if the world was going to hell.

"So? You do a good job of it. Like, there's a lot of detail there, it gets the idea across. But I mean, what are you thinking about when you do it?"

"Mostly just..." He grumbled, rather than finish the sentence.

"Well, okay, it's not really about that. It's more about you. Alex. This adorable guy, girl, otter, thing. Like..."

"Like what Christian does."

She paused. "I don't think I know him."

"He's an asshole." Alex dabbed his brush with yellow paint and started working the canvas.

"Okay, so, he's got a brand. His brand is, he's an asshole. Not one you want, but-"

He turned around. "No, I mean, he always makes this big fucking deal of himself. Like he's so great and important. And people eat it up just 'cause his mom's got money. He's not working to survive, he's not gonna die with his blue jeans on like the rest of us." He paused before returning to the canvas. "He's not an artist, he's just a rich prick."

"Well, who else is going to make a big deal about you? You have to put in some effort there."

"Like anyone would care."

"Alex," she pleaded, "trust me. This is what I do all day. I've gotten people to care about the most stupid shit. They will care about you. We just have to figure out what works for you. What it is about you that people are going to care about."

He squeaked. "I... no. I don't want to."

"You're going to have to."

Alex put down his brush and paced around the tight studio. Sarah watched silently, hoping he was coming around to the idea.

"What do you say?" she eventually asked.

He slumped against his refrigerator, looking at his bare feet. "We'll talk about it later."

"Alright. You sure you don't want to work on it real quick, before Friday?"

"I'm sure."

Sarah got up and approached Alex, offering him a hug. He walked away instead, preferring the window. He watched the garage under renovation. A jackhammer loudly ripped up the sidewalk around it.

"Have you heard what's going in there yet?" she asked.

"Restaurant, bar, something like that. Supposed to have a hundred taps or something crazy."

"Sounds nice."

Alex twitched. Sarah immediately realized what the construction really meant. Whatever was going there would be far too expensive for him to ever visit, and it would bring more rich tourists into the immediate area. It was an invasion of his territory, and she had sided with the invaders.

She started towards the door. "Alright, I'll see you on Friday. Just, please? Give it a little thought? I'm always willing to help if you want it."

"Yeah," Alex said, still staring out the window.

Sarah grabbed her purse and struggled for one last word of encouragement. Rather than push harder with an idea he was never going to accept, she quietly left and made her way home.

CHAPTER THIRTY-FOUR

"Kate, you can't park there."
"Since when?"

It was an unusual week for home movies. Kate had joined Sean at Sarah's apartment. Sarah waited outside the building to let them both in. Sean biked in, as always. Kate drove there and parked in the parking lot, taking one of the front spaces that were always open.

"Well, I mean, you shouldn't have parked there ever, technically."
Kate laughed it off as she got out of the car. "It's fine, it's fine. Never gotten in trouble for it before, not like I'm gonna get towed now."
"Yeah, but I mean, you're my guest. I'd catch shit for anything you do wrong. And Waterknell's being total assholes about the whole thing. They put up a thing threatening fines now. Even though they're not really in charge, they're totally in charge. It's so dumb."
"Jeez, that can't be legal."
"I have no idea. 'Disruption penalties,' they're calling it."
"Since when?"
"Couple days ago."
"Shit, is it still okay if I bring my bike in?" Sean asked.
"That's fine, apparently."
"Are they even enforcing that?" Kate asked, indignant. "Like, you didn't sign the new lease, right? It's not on any contracts."
"No, but they're still doing it."
"Well shit, sue them! There's got to be housing laws they're breaking."
Sarah shrugged. "Eh. I'd rather just get out of here and never have to deal with their shit again."
"Come on, this is such an easy case to win!"

171

"But then I'd have to deal with all that crap."

"Sheesh, fine! I'll move the car." She turned around with a grumble. "Go ahead and be passive about shit."

Sarah couldn't find a retort. She could rhetorically ask *what could I do about it anyway?* But she knew Kate's answer, and she wasn't willing to take it. She didn't know housing law at all, and Waterknell probably had a large legal team on its payroll. She would be in the right, but she wouldn't win, so why would she try?

"Congrats, you got to yell at Kate," Sean said.

"It's such a dumb thing," Sarah said.

"Dumb thing to fight over, too."

"I know." She watched Kate move her car, grimacing behind the steering wheel. "Kinda surprised I haven't yelled at her before, to be honest."

"Yeah. You didn't get the joy of getting her to stop talking during the movies. She used to be terrible with that."

"She still does it."

"Yeah. She was worse until Dave flipped at her. You met Dave, right?"

"Nope. Don't think so."

Sean nodded. "Yeah. They... did not get along."

Kate stepped out of her car, now parked on the street. She slammed the door and joined the other two as they went inside.

"Sorry about that," Sarah said. "Just don't want either of us dealing with that crap."

"Well then, do something about it!"

Sarah sighed. She didn't want to have the conversation.

"I'll keep on her about it," Sean said. "It'll be fine."

They squeezed into the elevator. Sean kept his bike with him, making it hard for all three to fit.

"Anyway, how's Alex been?" Sean asked. "Is he doing the Friday Art Walk this month?"

Sarah nodded. "He's been alright, I guess. Seemed a little stressed, between his job stuff and the construction going on nearby. Kinda pissing him off."

"Where's that?" Kate asked.

"Central Eastside. One of the warehouses. Sounded like they're turning it into a giant bar."

"Oh, yeah!" Kate bounced slightly. "That's the Thousand Mile. Heard a lot about it, gonna have their own microbrewery there and everything. We should check it out once it's open!"

They made it to Sarah's door. Carl's former apartment was empty, door wide open. She could see a car go past through the empty living room's window.

"Eh, I dunno."

"What don't you know now?" Sean asked. "Besides everything?"

Sarah rolled her eyes. "Nice to see you too."

"Okay," Kate said, confused. "Anyway, I was thinking of going once it opens up. Sounded pretty cool."

"Yeah, I'd be for it," Sean said. He looked at Sarah; she glared back at him. "Don't think Sarah's all that interested."

"It's just," Sarah said, "that's right where Alex lives. I don't want to be one of those hipster assholes making his life harder for no reason."

"Doesn't mean you can't enjoy yourself a little," Kate said.

"I guess that's fair, though," Sean said. "It's really gonna suck for him when it opens. Can't imagine his place is all that quiet as it is."

"Well, yeah, but it's gonna be annoying no matter what," Kate argued. "Us three going isn't a big deal compared to all that."

"I guess," Sarah said. "I'd just feel guilty."

"But there's nothing to feel guilty about."

"There is, though!"

Sarah's ears stood up. She put a foot back, ready to defend from an attack. Her front leg twitched and bounced rapidly.

"The last thing he needs is for me to start making his situation worse," she continued. "I'm supposed to be helping him."

Kate smirked. "You still have a crush on him."

Sarah stammered.

"I knew it! You totally do."

"That's not the fucking point! And no, I don't. I moved on. But that doesn't mean I can be so callous about the whole thing."

"I'm not being callous, the city's just growing like that. Half the places I've repped were busted warehouses or parking lots or... freakin' crackhouses. It's happening, people just need to deal with it."

"That's being callous! That's the exact fucking thing! You could at least try to pretend to give a shit!"

"Ladies!" Sean yelled. "Are we watching a movie or not?"

"Not if she's being an angry bitch," Kate said, pointing at Sarah.

She scoffed. "Oh, fuck you! You're being the heartless bitch. Have some fucking compassion, the rest of us have to deal with this bullshit. You're just getting rich off it."

"I'm not-"

Kate stumbled for words. Giving up, she growled at Sarah and took off down the hall. She found the stairway and slammed the door behind her.

Sarah was breathing loudly. Soon she started to feel herself calm down, her ears going limp. The rest of her body followed. She stumbled to her couch and dropped herself onto it. She still had a scowl on her face, but her eyes were watering.

Sean stood over her, looking down with disappointment. "Just so you know, Dave wasn't that mean about it."

"Fuck off," Sarah said weakly.

He shook his head and wheeled his bike down the hall.

Sarah started at the ceiling, letting the guilt bury her. She pulled her legs in, turned to stare at the blank TV, and quietly cried to herself.

CHAPTER THIRTY-FIVE

Come Monday, she had a hard time remembering anything that happened on Friday. Everything around her felt alien. The names of people and companies didn't seem like words. Her mind was clouded and beaten up.

Sarah dwelled on the argument with Kate. It was so out of character that she struggled to visualize what happened. Most of the argument was a blur, but her regret immediately afterward was clear as ever.

It would take a lot of coffee to wake her up.

She ran into Michelle while getting her second cup. "Hey Sarah!" she said with her usual enthusiasm.

Sarah didn't respond, outside of a quick and neutral nod. She kept walking back to her desk, Michelle following behind. It took a moment for Sarah to recognize the face and work out what was going on.

Michelle gave her a closer look after she sat. "Ah. You have a fun weekend again?"

"It was not fun," Sarah mumbled.

"Oh, sorry. Worried about the whole layoff thing?" She was nearly whispering, either to keep the news secret or to protect Sarah's non-existent hangover.

"Fuck." She held her forehead. "I haven't even thought about it."

"Really? I thought you'd be all for it."

Was I? I was putting together that list, I have it somewhere. Did I just- I completely forgot about finishing it. For fuck's sake.

"I'm not sure," Sarah said. "I don't think I'd be able to. What about you?"

"I'm staying. Definitely."

Sarah leaned back. "Figured."

"Yeah." Michelle sat at her desk. "It'd be great to spend more time with the boys, but they need their mom to work. That's more important to them. But I was tempted, with that severance."

"I was surprised they even offered it."

"I know! It'd be nice to take a couple months off, be with the boys for Christmas and all that, then start somewhere new next year. But, like, what if I don't find anything? It's too risky."

"You would find something if you looked."

"So would you. That's what I was like 'well, Sarah's out then!' You could just kick back, don't have to worry about anything. I saw you leaving on Friday, I figured you were already done with the place!"

Sarah laughed to herself. "Maybe I should've. I was kinda considering it."

"Well, I know Chris is staying, Roger told me that much. Vinish is probably gonna stay."

"He's totally gonna stay. Too loyal."

"I know. Haven't seen Jess, though. She was kinda freaking out about it last week."

"She always freaks out about stuff."

"Yeah, that's true."

Sarah leaned back in her chair with a sigh. "So they're probably gonna just pick names out of a hat."

"If you don't take it."

She looked at Michelle. She had an enthusiastic smile, more than her usual Monday cheerfulness. A sinister smell, more bitter than coffee, started to reach Sarah's head. Maybe Michelle was trying to pull something. Maybe it was just that she was a wolf. Sarah wasn't thinking well enough to judge.

"I'll find Roger," she said. "Talk to him about it, find out what's going on."

176

She stalled on following through. There was a meeting soon, so talking to Roger now might make the conversation too short. His afternoon was filled with scattered meetings; there was a half hour here or there, but even then, pinning him down would be difficult.

It felt like a trap. She couldn't remember which way she was leaning, and in her groggy confusion, she couldn't remember where she made her notes. Michelle was pushing her to leave, she knew it, but she couldn't figure out why.

This is why I stayed out of the politics. Now I can't trust anyone. Can't imagine how Sean does it all the time.

She sat in the meeting, listening to the conference call, feeling unneeded as always. Instead of paying attention she scheduled the meeting with Roger and started going over the debate in her mind. She wanted to go in with some idea of what she was about to do.

He was standing outside the meeting room when she finished. He looked calm and slightly disappointed. "Hey, Sarah. Want to just use this room, then?"

"Long as it's not booked. I thought you were busy right now."

"No, no," he said, taking a seat. "I've just been blocking bits of my calendar so people don't schedule me for anything."

"Sounds smart. So, how was your weekend?" More stalling.

"Umm, shitty." He laughed a little.

"Yeah, mine was kinda the same."

"So, it sounds like Michelle is staying."

"I know, we just talked about it. Sounds like Chris is staying too."

"Yeah, he is. Which is cool and all, just-" He shook his head quickly. "This is what you wanted to talk about, right? I didn't even ask."

"Well, it's kinda preoccupying me," she said dryly. "All of us, really."

"Oh, I know. I'm sorry about it."

"Not your fault. What about Vinish and Jess? They staying?"

"I... do not know yet," he said, thinking. "Kinda hoping one of them does, though, cause if not..."

"Yeah, I know."

"Gonna be a bit of a mess if people don't go for it."

"Hopefully not a mess for whoever takes it."

"Well, that's why there's the whole severance thing."

"True, that does make it a little easier."

A pause. "So, is this where you tell me that you're taking it?" He smiled, eyes wide in hope.

Sarah stalled. The lack of income would make the apartment hunt impossible. There was no guarantee she could find a new job anytime soon. She would have to stop going to the movies with Sean to save money. She had to say no.

"Yeah. I'll take it."

"Alright, well, thank you," Roger said. "And thank you for letting me know, this is gonna help a lot. Umm, so, we can keep you around until the end of the month, so we'll take care of..."

Sarah stopped paying attention.

Did I just quit? I just quit. Fuck.

"...So, yeah, I really appreciate it."

She did her best to remove the shock from her face. "Well, you're welcome."

"Got something planned for after you leave?"

"Honestly? Not really."

"Well, I hope it works out well."

"That makes two of us." She put on a fake smile. "But, I mean, I think it'll end up being the right decision."

She didn't believe her own lie. Roger didn't seem to believe it either.

She went back to her desk and loudly dropped herself in the chair. Michelle noticed her and spun around.

"So, did you take it?" she asked.

"Yep. Don't know why, but I guess I did."

Michelle nodded. "Bored, maybe?"

"Maybe."

"Well, I'm sure you could be doing something more interesting. You're still young, go enjoy it! Do something exciting with yourself!"

"I've had enough excitement lately," she mumbled.

Sarah picked up her phone and started to text Sean. He was always the first person she went to in situations like this, when something happened that made her need guidance. He would have advice or, at least, an ear to lend. But she couldn't send it. Not after what happened the day before. She was on her own here.

Instead, she tossed her phone onto her desk and dug through her computer, looking for the decision document she made. Maybe she had already decided to go and, in her distracted state, simply forgot about it. But the lists were evenly split.

Well, shit. Guess I just wanted to do something.

She looked around, listening to the idle din of conversation. She watched Michelle loudly drink yet another soda. This was what she was giving up, a noisy den of distracting chatter and pointless meetings. Not her own personal hell, but perhaps her purgatory.

Can't really blame myself, then. Just wish I actually thought about it first.

CHAPTER THIRTY-SIX

The Friday art walks were always busy. Sarah always had to park blocks away from where Alex set up. His spot was in the corner of an old mechanic's shop, now used for all manner of art event and exhibits. It wasn't exactly prime real estate. But then, everything in the Pearl was prime real estate to somebody.

The only spot she could find was on the other side of the district, close to Sean's building. She walked her way through the neighborhood, passing by the dozens of established galleries that were participating. They all looked too expensive to browse, crisp and minimalist rooms decorated with paintings and the people who could afford them. They looked like they belonged in magazines.

The crowds spilled onto the sidewalks and roads. The walk was a monthly ritual for the city's well-heeled animals, and so they came out in spades. Cougars in finely-tailored suits, wolves in sophisticated dresses, lynxes in stylish casual wear, all emerging from cars that couldn't be bought at dealerships. Sarah could only name the most ostentatious ones, the Lotuses and Maseratis that desperately demanded attention.

She was a far cry from all that. Her Subaru was inconspicuous, stereotypical. With her windbreaker and jeans, she better resembled the tourists that mixed up the scene. She could tell them at a glance. They dressed in casual, luggage-friendly clothes and carried various shopping bags, Powell's always among them. They were enamored with everything around them. She was well past that phase herself, having lived in town for years, yet she felt more like one of them than any of the natives.

See, I'm not rich. These people are rich. They can afford to have those cars and all that fancy crap. They can actually buy stuff here. Like, no way am I spending a grand on a painting. Can barely spend a grand on rent. I don't know why Alex thinks I'm this well off.

She glanced passively at what art she could see from the sidewalk. Her mind was more occupied by Alex. She hoped he had calmed down, that he tossed any resentment he had onto a canvas, and that when she found him, he would be as sociable as usual.

Instead, she found him at his booth, sitting in a stiff plastic chair, legs and arms crossed, wearing a scowl on his face. The garage had plenty of traffic in and out, but his corner was virtually empty.

"Alex, you okay?"
"I'm fine," he said flatly.
Sarah sighed. "I know you're lying."
"I'm busy."
"Alex." She put a paw on his shoulder and put on her best motherly voice. "Please. I just want to help."
He pointed to the opposite end of the garage. A noisy crowd had swarmed one of the tables. "That's Christian. Fuckers put him right there."

Sarah couldn't see what was happening, but she could hear it. It sounded like a performance, with Christian's soft and confident voice narrating what he was doing and the crowd applauding afterward. Even with her hearing, the garage echoed too much for her to hear the details.

"Did you know he was going to be there?"
"No. Someone must be trying to piss me off, though."
She kept watching Christian. "Why? Do the organizers know you two have a thing?"
"They should." His voice weakened.
Sarah turned around and looked him in the eyes. "Did you tell them? Yes or no."
Alex looked away and squeaked in response.

182

"Goddammit Alex. Nobody's gonna know there's a problem if you don't do anything."

"They should know."

"How are they going to find out if you don't speak up?"

He stayed silent for a moment, glaring at Sarah. "He's not even a good artist. My stuff's better than his, and I'm not even that good."

"Your stuff's good."

"Then why don't you buy any?"

She hesitated. "I can't afford to. I mean, you're pricing things right as far as I can tell, I just... can't. I mean, if you had prints or something, then sure."

"It's not worth it. Did one run, barely made anything." He shuffled in his seat. "Maybe I should just do cheap stuff."

"Dude, look at these people. They're rich. They buy brands."

Alex glared. "Don't start."

"Dude, you know this shit already. This is a luxury market. Christian's doing stuff to get his name known, and now his name is selling. Doesn't matter if his art's shit, nobody can tell. Half these people have no taste anyway."

Alex coughed out a laugh. "True."

Sarah pulled up a nearby plastic chair and sat next to him, leaning forward. He crossed his arms and legs tighter in response, sliding his chair back. It squeaked sharply.

"You can do that," she said, trying to emphasize a kind voice. "You just have to find what makes you, you."

He sighed. "I don't want to talk about this."

"Dude, I'm just trying to help." She could hear herself getting louder. "Look, I know you can do this. You're good at painting, you've got a personality. You just have to try."

"I am trying." He squeezed his arms tighter.

"Well, honestly, it doesn't look like it. Like, where's your personality in all this?" She gestured at his table, a plain display that other vendors had taken to styling their own ways. "You can't just sit around, hoping for something to happen. You've gotta claim people's attention, market yourself. That's what Christian's good at. He pulls people in. Whatever he's doing, he's earning that crowd."

"He's just doing bullshit."

"Bullshit works! I've had so many clients who were happy because I gave them bullshit. If that's what the crowd wants, and that's what he's giving them, then fuck, he deserves to have a crowd."

"I deserve a crowd," Alex said, his voice angry and weary.

Sarah started fidgeting and speaking rapidly. "Not... not really. I mean, if you're not going to put in that effort, then... And I know you can, it's just... I mean, you can't be surprised if people aren't gonna-"

"Get out."

"Alex, I'm just trying to help-"

"Out!"

He jumped up and pushed back his chair, almost knocking it over. His squeaky scream echoed in the garage. It stole much of the crowd's attention, the first thing to break their focus.

"Stop fucking telling me what to do!"

"I'm not telling you what to do!"

"Out!" His eyes were welling up.

Sarah stood up, taking deep breaths. "Dude, I'm sorry," she insisted.

Alex didn't react. He glared silently at her, frozen in place until she hung her head and started walking away. The crowd noise slowly picked up behind her as she left the building.

Fucking hell. Please tell me he'll listen. He needs it.

She made her way back to her car, winding through the grid of streets, grumbling to herself. The October wind blew with a sharp chill.

184

CHAPTER THIRTY-SEVEN

A rabbit sat in a coffee shop, her head hung, leering at the table before her. The table was round, save for a small flat surface that allowed two to join together. Some designer thought of that, just like some designer thought about every detail of the decor: the wingback chairs, the plush couches, the recovered wood tables.

They fit well with the customers, a crowd of the upwardly mobile and the already well off. The cafe radiated the kind of Pacific Northwest character and individuality that could only be mass produced.

Sarah refused to consider herself a hipster. She had opinions on coffee, she preferred places like the Deadline Cafe, but she wasn't so uptight that she wouldn't go to a Starbucks. It wasn't as though there were choices. Those were the only options downtown, and she spent much of the last four years downtown.

She felt like she could be a hipster, though. If she wanted to. She could be her image of one, at least – living in the heart of the city, biking everywhere, buying overly fancy and twee housewares. She already wore the uniform; a plaid shirt, khaki pants, and a dark peacoat.

All the apartments she liked were what she assumed hipsters would like. They had character and charm or were manufactured to that end. They were quintessential Portland, and not one of them was available.

So she went to the suburbs, to see what the atmosphere really was like. What were the sights, who were the people, how was the coffee? More importantly, would there be anywhere to live?

It was well over a year since she came out to Hillsboro. Everything she ever needed was already nearby. She didn't need to leave the city, nor did she want to.

The atmosphere was positive, yet uncomfortable. Nothing around her felt especially new. Sean's building would be just as out of place here than in most parts of Portland. But nothing looked old either. She had passed several strip malls and rows of houses that appeared unchanged since they cropped up mid-century.

Glaring out the window that faced the throughway, in the middle distance between fast food restaurants and fog-covered mountains, she could see cranes. A half-dozen, maybe. Not a lot, but then, not every site needed one. She drove past several sites on her way that didn't have any. Those buildings, short and simple, pushed out of the ground like weeds.

They were all townhouses and apartment buildings, except for the occasional storefront intended for yet another chain store. If Sarah was going to live out here, that was the sort of place she would end up with.

She tried to see her routines play out here. Once she had her new job, she would drive to work in the mornings, come home in the evenings, go to the nearest coffee shop on the weekends. The same as it ever was. Where she lived didn't matter. Where her next job would be didn't matter.

Besides, so many companies were leaving downtown, from what she could tell. Maybe the suburbs were the sensible decision. Maybe this was a lucky opportunity; move now, before everyone tried to get out of the city and come out here. Kate would have some idea if that were going to happen, but she was one of the last people Sarah wanted to talk to.

That list kept getting longer.

She inhaled the smell of her latte, overburdened with mint, and focused on an apartment building. It sat on the other side of a grocery store, obscured only slightly. She tried to imagine herself living there.

She would sit in a big, plush recliner, watching the evening news. She would go to that "all natural" grocery store in front of it. She wouldn't mind that it was a bit expensive. She would look out through the balcony door every morning, watching the neighbors pile their kids into SUVs and drive them to school. She would get an SUV, have a kid, and join them someday.

She would change. She would be an entirely different person.

She would loathe it.

Come on, Sarah. What the hell are you doing? What's gotten into you?

Her eyes burned. For as little sleep as she got the night before, it felt like she didn't get any at all. Her body held tense. She resisted the urge to scream at a young wolf being dragged in by his mother, babbling loudly and making a mess of everything in his reach.

If they fucking come over here, I swear...

She wanted to be alone. Alone was safe. Quiet. It was peace and calm and warmth away from the autumn mist. Alone also meant staying in her apartment, and from the moment she woke up she knew that wasn't an option.

There was the Deadline Cafe. It was full of local art and considerate patrons. It was honest and modest, and she didn't think she deserved it anymore. The Cafe was for the natives, people stumbling through their young adulthood, others reminiscing about the good old days. People who created something. Who contributed to the world. People like Alex.

Her computer was with her, prepared to send him an email. The draft window was open, his email was marked as the receiver, but everything else was empty. There were ideas of what to say, some emotions to try to convey. But the words wouldn't come together.

Goddammit. Come on. You can do this.

Sarah knew – or, at least, hoped – that Sean would talk. He always made her feel better. It was late enough in the morning that he would be awake.

She pulled out her phone. "Alex hates me," she sent.

Immediately, she felt guilty bringing him into the situation. He'd been having his own problems lately, and she wasn't helping him enough with them. He didn't need to be dragged into helping her feel better about her mistakes.

Really hope he doesn't still hate me. Wouldn't blame him if he does.

Her phone rang.

"Hello?" Her voice was hushed and restrained, as though she took the call in a museum.

"Hey, Sarah. Just got your text. What happened?"

She hesitated for what felt like hours. Tears were already forming. She couldn't cry; not in public, not alone. It would be too embarrassing.

"I've been trying to help him, I keep trying to get him to go to that guild thing, and I just... I yelled because he wouldn't. And now he hates me."

"Well... wow. That sucks."

"I know."

"You're not drinking, are you? You sound kinda..."

"No. Just coffee. I'm fine. I just can't believe I fucked up that badly."

"I can kinda believe it."

The impulse to cry overrode her embarrassment. She buried her face in her paws.

188

"How long have you been telling him to go?" Sean continued.

"Months? Years? I don't know."

"He's never gone?"

"He won't! I just keep trying, and he won't put in the effort."

"It's okay, Sarah. Breathe."

"I am breathing."

"Good. First, go apologize. I'm sure you meant well and all that, but seriously, if you were a bitch to him then you were a bitch."

"This was full-on cunt territory." She noticed movement; a hyena sitting nearby glared at her before moving away. Sarah glared back as best as she could. *She's offended by that? Really?*

"Yeah, it probably was. How pissed was he?"

"I don't remember. We both yelled a lot. And he's never yelled like that, so like, is he gonna kill me next time he sees me? Maybe, I don't know. We never fought like this when we were going out. And even when we did we'd just give it a day and things were fine."

"Right. This is gonna take more than a day."

"Well, yeah."

"I mean, apologize and all that, but you might just need to let it blow over."

Sarah leaned back in the wooden chair and stared at the ceiling. The crying stopped, but between the lectures from Sean and the height of the ceiling, she had never felt so small.

"I don't know if I can. Been thinking about it all morning. Plus I have to be at that gallery thing next week. He probably still needs me for that. So, like, I can't avoid him entirely."

"Then you've got a week to patch things up with him."

"It's Wednesday."

Sean hesitated. "Okay. So, you have four days to make him not want to kill you."

"Nice vote of confidence."

"Well, you know your relationship better than I do. Are four days going to be enough?"

189

"I don't know. It might not be enough. Or maybe he's over it already for all I know. He told me he just takes whatever's pissing him off and throws it at his art. Just does that for everything, then he's fine."

"So he might be calmed down already."

"But I've never seen him this angry. About anything." Her voice started to strain again. "Sean, what did I do?"

"You- breathe. Breathe, Sarah. You tried to do good. You tried."

"I know."

"Look. What else are you up to today? Apartment hunting?"

She looked at the apartments past the grocery store. "A little. A little job hunting."

"Job hunting?"

"I took the layoff." She dropped the news as if Sean already knew.

"Oh. Alright." He didn't sound surprised. "Well, do you want me to come over and look too? Just to keep you company. I can bike over, it's not that bad out."

"I'm not at home. Out in Hillsboro. Probably too far to bike."

"Thinking of living out there?"

"Think I have to." She sighed over her cup. "I'd hate it, but I don't have any other option."

"There's got to be options."

"There's nothing!" she shouted over the folk music in the background. "It's all taken, or it's shit, or it's too expensive. It's been like that all month, it's gonna be like that in November, and December, and-"

"Look, I will drag you places if I have to."

"That's not gonna help."

"If it keeps you from dwelling and bitching, then yeah, it will help."

"It won't solve the problem."

"Of course not. You have to solve it yourself. You have to go do something, Sarah. It's not gonna sort itself out for you."

She hung her head and slumped in her chair. She took a sip of her coffee, only the third time since she ordered it.

"Kinda surprised you called," she said.

"Had to. You're my friend."

"That surprises me too."

"Why?"

"Because I've been such an asshole lately. Figured you'd just want to yell at me, if anything."

"Well, if you're acting like an asshole I gotta tell you that."

"I guess." She exhaled loudly. "So, we're really okay?"

"Yeah. Look, we're all allowed to give each other shit. I know you do it because you care, I'm the same way. Just, you know, don't be mean with it. That's all. I mean, hell, I've been bad about giving people crap lately."

"You're not the one ruining friendships. Let alone three in a week."

"Who?"

"You, Kate, Alex."

"Kate's not mad at you."

Sarah picked up her head and looked around the coffee shop as if one of its patrons could explain. "Seriously?"

"We talked yesterday. She agreed with what you were saying, that she's not caring about what happens to people. You were just really brutal about it."

"I know. I really need to calm myself down." She took another sip. "The coffee's probably not helping."

"Might help to see a therapist."

"Am I that messed up?"

"I go to one."

"Really?" She couldn't imagine him trusting a therapist enough to open up.

"Yeah. Started a month ago. I'll send you his email."

"Wow. Appreciate that, man. Don't think it'll work, but I'll try."

"Exactly. Try things. You're in a different coffee shop?"

"Yeah. Starbucks. Pretty big one."

"Is that helping? Is it better than what you usually do?"

She looked around at the customers – almost all of them coyotes – sitting and chatting around her. She didn't feel safe or welcome, but the decor wasn't too off-putting. Uncomfortable, maybe.

"Not really. Coffee's fine, at least. Just not my place."

191

"Okay. So, you tried something and it didn't work. That's okay. I know you, you've got tons of routines. Just change one of them, see how you feel."

"I guess." She thought through all the routines she had. "You think I should leave the movie group for a while?"

"No, no," Sean insisted. "I mean... okay. If you need to, then yeah, take some time off. If that's what you need. But, we'd all miss you."

"Alright. I'll think about it. Thanks for letting me vent."

"No problem. Let me know if you'll be there Sunday."

She paused. "Think I'll skip this time."

Her coffee was getting cold. The conversation helped her stall and avoid thinking about what to say to Alex, but that time was over.

She couldn't believe Sean was willing to forgive. Sean, who seemed to trust nobody, not even himself. Who still brought up embarrassing moments to tease her with from when they first met. They had a good friendship, but nothing as deep as she had with Alex. If he were willing to let live, maybe Alex would too. Maybe things would be okay.

She committed to putting two words down: *I'm sorry.* She hoped that it would work like drawing. Once the page was no longer blank, things would start flowing. Her drawings were abstract, so it didn't matter where things went. Here, it mattered.

Progress was slow, but eventually, she had something.

Alex,

I'm sorry. I'm sorry for yelling, I'm sorry for pushing you so hard. I just hate to see you struggling. I want to help. I still really care about you. You deserve better than what you're dealing with, I just wanted to try and get you there. But that's not something I can do for you.

I want to talk in person at some point, apologize in person and all that. When you're comfortable with it. I won't come to the exhibit on Wednesday unless you ask me to. I'd totally understand if you need space. Just let me know.

192

Sorry.
Sarah

With each sentence, she read and re-read. She obsessed over her words and her tone. It didn't feel ready. Maybe it was too tense? Too brief?

She pushed her laptop to the side and grabbed her notebook from her purse. It still had notes from Sinclair Manor in it. She ripped out a fresh page and started drawing what she saw out the window. It didn't matter what it was or how well she drew, as long as it helped her avoid sending the email.

Her laptop reclaimed her attention when its screen went black. Her coffee was cold and undrinkable. The drawing was barely started and barely showed promise.

"Fuck it." She turned the computer back on, sent the email, and closed the lid. She collapsed back into her chair as if a demon had been exorcised from her body.

CHAPTER THIRTY-EIGHT

Sarah stared at the white stucco ceiling, paying attention to every crack in the surface and every shadow that her TV cast against its bumps. The couch was almost too short for her to lay on comfortably, but it hardly phased her.

Jesus. I'm acting like I'm in a John Hughes film or something. This is pathetic.

She feigned illness to claim the Monday for herself. Her gut told her she should be at work. For that matter, she should be looking for a new job, or for a new apartment. She should be doing something, anything other than staring above, divining her future from the bumps on the ceiling.

Probably should look for a new circle of friends while I'm at it. Kate apparently forgave me, but hell if I know if that's true. It probably isn't. Sean's gonna just kick me out of the Facebook group and that'll be that. Can't say I'd blame him if he did. He can't possibly trust me. Doubt he ever did, with all the secrets he's been keeping.

Her mind wandered back home, to the Midwest. She wouldn't move in with her parents – she didn't need to – but at least things were safe and familiar there. There wasn't a mess there. It was quiet, boring even, but she had enough excitement. Most of it was her own fault.

Sarah hadn't talked with her parents in months. She never felt bad about it since the conversations rarely had anything interesting to them, but even so, she considered giving them a call. It would be a different point of view, but she knew what they would say. "You're a big girl, Sarah, you can work it out."

The room darkened. *2001: A Space Odyssey* played on the TV, the main source of light during the overcast morning. Sarah wasn't watching it, much less listening, but it offered company. She saw it a dozen times before. It was an old friend of hers, one she had no way of angering.

She closed her eyes and imagined herself on Discovery One, floating alone through space towards nothing in particular. Stars and planets passed in the distance, ones she could never interact with. She imagined herself lost out there, away from Earth, lost to everyone she cared about.

Her eyes opened. She took a deep breath. "Alright," she said out loud to nobody, "let's just get one job lead and one apartment. That's all. Then I'll feel okay."

Another scene of the movie passed before she got up and grabbed her computer from her desk. She sat back down on the couch, laptop on her legs, and stared blankly at the screen. The bright interior of a spaceship glowed at her from the TV.

Wonder if Alex ever replied. The idea got her arms moving. Her email had nothing new in it beyond the usual newsletters. She checked the spam folder to be safe. She checked her work email on the impossible chance that he responded to that address instead. Nothing.

She found herself watching familiar scenes with a fresh intensity. She knew she was wasting time, but nothing was appealing enough to snap her out of it. Certainly not the idea of reading through job descriptions or apartment ads. Doing nothing felt like a good way to spend the morning.

Or was it afternoon now? She lost track of time.

Hunger worked as a better alarm clock. She wasn't interested in cooking anything, but none of the myriad options near her apartment were

196

interesting either. The movie kept distracting her from considering her options. It gave her a chance to avoid thinking, so it had her attention.

The credits rolled. *Alright. Alright. I'll just get something delivered. Whatever's fastest.* She grabbed her phone and pulled up a list of options. There were plenty of them there; Portland was growing on the backs of people who claimed to have too little time for pesky little things like getting their own food. More and more people were racing around, catering to their needs and wants.

She thought about the last delivery guy that came to her, months back, the last time the gang got together early and ordered pizza. She remembered noticing how tired the hedgehog looked. He clearly spent his entire day biking around the city non-stop, rain or shine. Sure, he was in good shape, but the delivery fees meant he was hardly made much money.

It started raining outside. She watched it fall quietly. *Can't make someone deal with that.*

She got up and put on her coat. With no direction in mind, she found herself instinctively walking to the Deadline Cafe.

CHAPTER THIRTY-NINE

For as often as she came to the cafe, she never ate there. Her routine put her there in the afternoon, after lunch, so she simply grabbed her latte and carried on without a thought. She wasn't positive the cafe would even have food.

It did have food, but it lacked a crowd. The tables were mostly empty save for a handful of retirees reading newspapers. Even with the cloudy sky, the inside felt bright and warm.

"Hey Sarah," the barista said. He was the same red fox that she saw every Sunday. "Didn't know you came in on Mondays."

"I don't." She had no enthusiasm for conversation.

"This is Monday, then, right?" He gave a playful laugh. "I'm not stuck in Groundhog Day?"

"You don't look like a groundhog."

"Well, thank you."

It seemed an odd thing to be thankful for. "But yeah, I'm usually at work. Just had to take a day."

"Can understand that. Most of the regulars are like that, only around on weekends or nights, then they show up middle of a Wednesday and you're like 'what the hell's going on?'"

"If I knew what was going on I'd tell you."

"Sounds good. The usual?"

She looked around at the menu. "Eh. You know what. Let's do a mocha instead. And whatever vegetarian sandwich you have, doesn't matter."

"I hear ya. Changing it up, are we?"

"Everything else is changing. Might as well."

He got to work on the espresso machine. Sarah stood and waited. She was uncomfortable, glancing around idly. As awkward as it was, having someone talk to her was probably better than standing in silence.

"I know what you mean, though," he said. "It's alright, keeps things interesting."

"Good interesting or bad interesting?"

"It's always a bit of both, isn't it? Well, no, you can have stuff that's just good."

"I don't know. Don't think I have any good interesting going on right now. It's all just crap."

"Sorry to hear that. I'd offer to help, but I'm not particularly good with advice."

"That's fine. I just needed to vent. Don't know what I'd do with advice anyway."

"Think you're supposed to take it," he said with a smile.

Sarah wasn't impressed with his pleasant attitude. "I guess." She grabbed her coffee. "I'll be in the back."

She carried her cup, keeping her usual seat in view. When she got near, she stopped. Virtually every other seat was available. There was no reason not to change it.

Around the corner was a beat-up loveseat situated next to a coffee table. A mismatched set of armchairs surrounded it, making the corner feel like a living room. It seemed like a natural layout, almost accidental, yet the room required that it be there. To do otherwise would sell it short.

The act of moving around reinvigorated her spirits. She opened her laptop and recited her mission in her head. *One job, one apartment. One job, one apartment.* The apartment would come first. She already knew how to look for that. But both had to get done, so she reminded herself. *One job, one apartment.*

Sarah could see the barista wandering, lost. It brought a small smile to her face. Even though the cafe was virtually empty, he had a hard time finding her.

200

"Sheesh, there you are!" he said. "Thought you left or something."

"I did say I was changing things."

"There you go. Let me know if you need anything."

She set the sandwich to the side and took a sip of her mocha. It was a small change that she could feel in control of. It was too small to matter, but she focused on the scent regardless. A small victory was still a victory.

Her body sank into the fabric. She spent over an hour in the loveseat, comfortable and focused, flipping through apartment listing after listing. It didn't matter how practical any of them were anymore. A townhouse far from city limits, a penthouse in the Pearl, anything was worth a glance. She dreamed of the lives she would have if she lived in them. Some were unappealing lives of austerity or desperation. Some were implausible lives of ease and elegance. Some were as dull as the one she had already.

She looked at the job hunt the same way. Only one or two places advertised that they needed a marketing manager, but there were plenty of other options available. Even if she ignored the intensely technical and stayed with jobs that sounded like a loose fit, she had opportunities. They weren't companies she knew, and she wasn't sure some of the job titles were real. They were bookmarked anyway. She could be a sensible rabbit later.

Her lunch sat hardly touched. She enjoyed the daydreaming. It was genuine progress, more than what she usually pondered over. No matter what apartment or job she chose, it would change her. The least she could do was make the change on her own terms.

CHAPTER FORTY

Sarah could feel the difference in her mood. The rain stopped falling while she was inside, the clouds started thinning out. It was still grey and overcast, but it was October. She didn't expect anything better.

She walked with a light step, handling the slippery leaves with ease. It was a sign of a local to walk gracefully in the autumn muck. After four years she wasn't quite a master, but she was good enough to feel content.

Stepping into the apartment building's doorway, she shook her head to knock a few errant drips off her ears. Andrew was inside, stepping out of the building's management office with a small stack of papers in his paw. She caught an exhausted expression on his face that disappeared as he noticed her open the door. Sarah smiled, causing him to smile back.

"Well, hey there! Sarah, was it? 309?" His voice had a professional tone that Sarah knew from meeting after meeting of pleasantries. He wasn't particularly happy to see her.

"Yep! Funny running into you here."

He offered a polite laugh. "I do work here, after all. Though I guess this is good timing, I was about to go put these on everyone's doors. You'll need to sign the new lease by the end of the month if you're going to stick around."

"Not doing it."

She quietly cheered to herself. Sure, he was forcing her to move out on Waterknell's terms, but even a small chance to do something on her terms was worth being happy about.

Andrew's ears sagging slightly. "Well, I'm sorry to see you go. We'll just need a formal notice of your intent to vacate, and if you're out before Halloween, we'll prorate and refund the last of your rent. Assuming the key return and damage assessment and all that stuff works out fine."

His tone was all business, the lines recited with a tired familiarity. He had clearly done this plenty of times before.

"No problem. Should it just say, like, 'peace out' or something? 'Sayonara suckers?' Anything in particular?" She laughed to herself.

Andrew laughed nervously in response. "I don't think 'sayonara suckers' will go over well with my bosses, but yeah, it doesn't really matter. Long as you say which unit and sign it, I don't care."

"Alright, I'll go with the 'peace out' one then."

"Sounds good." He shuffled his feet. "Where are you off to?"

"Oh, I have no fucking clue." She noticed her confident voice. She couldn't remember sounding like that in a long time. "But I'm not staying here. Not paying that kinda rent."

"Well, best of luck to you." He looked unfazed by the news. "It's pretty crazy out there. The sooner you can find a spot, the better."

"Oh, I know. I've been looking. Hopefully, I'll be out before Halloween. Figure everyone's gonna be trying to move out that day."

Andrew sighed. "There are a couple, yeah. But I mean, I'm not in charge of setting the rents, that's higher up. I'm just here to help you folks out, whichever way you're going."

"Well, I'm going... up to my apartment, I guess."

She walked away, pleased with herself yet confused.

Man. He did not care that I'm leaving. You'd think he wanted us to stick around. Now they're gonna have to clean the place up, probably lose a month or two of rent. And that's if they rent it out right away. Which they're not going to, not at that price. Completely not aligned with the market, there are some pretty fancy places for that price.

It'd be kinda weird living in one of those. Like, I could have a doorman. The hell kinda person would I be with a doorman. That's rich people shit. I'm not that rich. I can open my own doors.

As if to prove her thoughts correct, she opened her apartment door, letting it swing wide before dropping herself on the couch.

Kinda wish he reacted more, honestly. Wish he was all "no, don't leave!" so I could be "I'm leaving, deal with it." Like, I'd be in control of things. Could tell him off a little bit. Could've – I wanted to yell at him, didn't I? Dammit. I'm yelling at too many people as it is.

He sorta deserves it, though. Making such a mess of everything here. Well, unless he really is just being told what to do. Then it's more like, why aren't you fighting it? But man, I probably did some shitty stuff with work and didn't really question it. Ad campaigns can get pretty sketchy. I don't think I'm gonna do that stuff anymore. If I can.

She split her attention between writing her notice and pondering her next job. As she did, Andrew approached down the hall. She saw him stop at Carl's former apartment and begin to tape a piece of paper to the door. He stopped suddenly, put the paper back in his pile, and turned around. His ears drooped.

CHAPTER FORTY-ONE

Sarah woke up with a mission on her mind. Whether from the day of rest or the sense of direction, she had a newfound level of energy. Her body was optimistic.

She also had a plan. Her first meeting was early, making it a good time to gather contact info for a bunch of apartment buildings. Then a long gap between meetings when she could call each one and ask if they had any openings. She didn't care if they actually advertised any. If she was going to find an apartment, she was going to be in control of every part of the hunt.

"You feeling better today, Sarah?" Michelle asked in a concerned, motherly tone.

"Much," she said, grabbing her computer from her desk and hurrying off to an office.

Michelle huffed. "Well, since when were you so busy?"

Sarah shrugged and walked off. *Not like I'm doing work.*

The length of a single conference call gave her two dozen leads to work with. She regularly did research for her clients, digging up competitors and loosely-related marketing campaigns. She never put this much energy into it before. That made sense to her; she never cared before.

After the call, she loitered in the office, making her own calls. Each one, she inquired innocently about their offerings. Each one, she was shot down. There didn't seem to be any hidden underbelly of available apartments for her to uncover; they simply didn't exist. Her kinetic enthusiasm waned with each call.

Man. This is like the worst training montage ever. She laughed, imagining the visual. The theme to *Rocky* played in her head, cracking her up again.

A faint reflection appeared in the office window, showing her disheveled face, the stress of a hyperactive morning wearing on her. She looked defeated and beaten, but with a wide smile on her face.

It made her laugh harder. *Okay. That's enough, Sarah. You've clearly gone insane. Go get food.*

Roger was walking the main aisle when she made her way out. He gave a small nod to get her attention. "Hey, Sarah, can I grab you for a-"
"Can't, too busy," Sarah said, walking past without hesitation.
"With what?"
"Everything!"

It came out of her faster than she could think. She had no idea what it meant, but she hurried out the door before Roger could challenge it.

She felt like she could walk miles out of pure momentum. Each stop light was a nuisance that left her bouncing impatiently on her feet. After the fourth, she stopped at the first restaurant she could find, an unremarkable Chinese place. It didn't matter where she found herself. She wasn't going to eat much anyway. She was just going to think.

The chow mien sat untouched, steaming in her face. *Alright. Idea. Henry said that they go through two bedrooms pretty slowly with that whole co-op thing. So, let's get a list, call every place that's part of the co-op. Tell them Henry said they had a two bedroom available but say you could have the building wrong. Plausible deniability. See if you luck out with any of those.*

She wanted to try her plan then and there, but she never liked making calls in a restaurant. It annoyed her when others did it, so doing it herself had to annoy others. Instead, she saved it for the office.

The first attempts came up dry. The third was interrupted by Roger peering through the window, gesturing to get her attention. She waved him off; he responded with a curious stare before wandering off. It distracted her enough to break her focus and make the lie unconvincing.

Her fourth attempt put her on the east side of the river. She preferred the west side and wanted to stay there if possible, but she was positive it wasn't going to be. Everyone else preferred to be on the west side as well.

With a sigh, she called the number. "Alright," she said as the phone rang, "let's see what happens."

"Arbor Manor, Danielle speaking." Her voice was soft and small, but clouded by background noise.

Construction, I guess. "Hi Danielle. I was hoping to talk to you about a two bedroom?"

"Um... give me a moment." The gamble was already working better than Sarah expected. "Who mentioned that we had a two bedroom?"

"Henry, at Sinclair? I think he said it was at your place, I might be mistaken."

"No, no, we do have one, just opened up yesterday. We haven't even put it on Craigslist yet."

"Well, perfect. Would it be okay if I came by tonight to take a look?"

Danielle hesitated. The construction noise grew clearer. "Sure, sure. We can do that. What's your name?"

"Sarah. Can we do 5:30?"

"Sure, Sarah. See you then."

She hung up in time to see an email arrive from Roger.

Just paperwork stuff? Really, that's what he was trying to get to me about? Could've just emailed me in the first place, no need to break my focus.

She shrugged it off and called Sean, pacing across the office while the phone rang.

"Sarah?"

"Sean, hey. I- am I interrupting something?"

"Not really."

"You sure? You sound a bit distracted."

"Just had to get away from my desk."

Sarah looked at the clock. It was the middle of the afternoon; she was definitely interrupting something.

"Sorry. Didn't even think what time it was."

"It's fine. What's up?"

She couldn't contain her excitement. "I think I got a place. Two bedroom, Hosford. Think you can come check it out with me tonight?"

"I guess, sure. Do you really want to share a place?"

"Sean, I would live with a total fucking stranger if it gets this sorted out. I don't care. But I'd rather live with you, so please come with me and give it a try."

He sighed loudly. "Alright. Just tell me where and when."

"Thanks. I'll pick you up at the office. I owe you one."

CHAPTER FORTY-TWO

Sarah drove away from the sunset, heading into the southeast part of the city. The skyline glowed red behind the trees. This far out, there weren't many towers or tall apartment buildings to create an artificial skyline.

She drove fast. That is, until she hit the first speed bump that gated the residential neighborhood. The thud jolted her eyes open and made her slow down.

"Seem a bit excited today," Sean said flatly.
Sarah exhaled. "Just wound up."
"Breathe. You're fine."

The Arbor Manor was surrounded by small, old bungalows, all decorated with hippie eccentricity. It formed a plain horseshoe on the corner with a gate protecting its gap. An old school under renovation sat across from it, claiming an entire block's worth of parking. Even with the obstruction, Sarah had plenty of options, more than she ever had at her old place.

A raccoon stepped out of the front door as Sarah got out. She looked younger than Sarah, dressed in the full Bohemian look. She fit the neighborhood perfectly. "Sarah?"

"Yep! You must be Danielle," she answered. She gestured behind her as Danielle opened the gate. "This is Sean."

"Well, hello you two," she said, eyes on Sean.

"Nice to meet you," he said. "You're in charge of the place?"

"Yes and no." Danielle was still watching Sean. She reached to open the front door and fumbled around for the doorknob. "Sorry!"

211

Sarah bounced lightly. "No worries."

"Yeah, so, I do most of the office stuff nowadays. My brother actually runs the place, though."

Sarah nodded. "Family business."

"Yep! The building's been handed down over the years. My great grandpa built it. Or, he had it built, I guess. I don't know, I just know he had a lot of land around here, back when it was mostly just farms."

Sarah looked out the front door, back at the west side skyline. She could barely see Sean's building, a thin vertical line far off to the side. Her office building was nowhere to be seen.

Sean carried the conversation as they walked to the elevator. "Man, can't imagine this place being just farmland."

"I know. Can barely remember how the neighborhood looked ten years ago. I mean, the houses were the same and all, but a lot of it got cleaned up."

"Good to hear," Sarah said.

"Definitely cleaner than downtown," Sean said.

"You live downtown?"

"Well, Pearl. But we both work down there."

Danielle sighed in admiration. "Nice. I kinda like those buildings, honestly. Must be cool living in one."

"It's okay."

They got off the elevator on the fourth floor. Danielle moved her focus to Sarah, snapping into sales mode.

"Anyway! This is a pretty good neighborhood too, much quieter, low-key. Lot of local shops are popping up nearby, places getting cleaned up."

"Must be getting more expensive, too," Sarah said.

"It has, yeah. But the neighborhood association's been really good about keeping an eye on that. I mean, you can't stop it, but they do kinda make a fuss if it's getting out of hand. Plus, the whole co-op thing, we're all about keeping these places affordable."

Sarah looked around the hallway. The carpet and walls looked worn yet clean. The lighting fixtures were vintage, ornate enough to stand out against modern designs.

"How old is this place?"

"Ninety-some years," Danielle said. "Ninety-six, I think."

"Feels like it. My current place is at least a hundred."

"Yeah, this is one of the older neighborhoods. And we've tried to keep the place in good shape."

Danielle opened the apartment door, flashing a confident smile. The apartment was visibly lived-in despite being unfurnished. The hardwood floor was scuffed and darkened in patterns that implied how the furniture used to be laid out.

"Sorry about the mess," Danielle said. "The last resident just moved out Sunday. We were able to sweep up, but we haven't gotten the full cleaning crew in. That will definitely happen this week, though."

Sarah nodded and pulled out her notebook. She wandered the space, inspecting, noting anything of interest.

"Any idea why they moved out?" Sean asked. He seemed more interested in Danielle than the apartment.

"Yeah, they moved out of town. Off to Denver, apparently."

Sarah's ears perked. *It is Thomas's place. Rabbit's luck, huh.*

"Wow," Sean said, idly looking around. "I couldn't manage living there. Gets too cold here as it is."

"I know!" Danielle said with a fake shiver. "I've never really gotten used to it. But I love when it snows here, this last winter was awesome."

"Was crazy. Couldn't do anything."

"Not on a bike," Sarah said. "People were skiing in the street, though. I managed to drive a bit, but it gets way worse in Illinois, so that was like-"

"I know," Danielle said dryly, "must've been nothing."

"Not nothing, but, yeah. Not that bad."

Danielle nodded. Her attention was still centered on Sean. She had a small smile on her face, her tail swaying and pushing her skirt behind her, a lighter breath to her voice when she talked to him.

"So..." Sarah said.

"So!" Danielle jumped to attention. "Any questions so far?"

"That construction across the street."

"Right. It's been a little noisy, mostly during the day. They get in a lot of trouble if they make noise at night, though, since it's residential. Not a huge issue, usually."

"What's going in there?" Sean asked.

"Bunch of offices. The auditorium is gonna be a concert venue."

Sarah's head tilted in thought. *Could get kinda loud. Or at least, people leaving late, might get annoying.*

"Anything else?" Danielle asked, matching Sarah's tilt.

"Oh. No, I think I've answered my own questions. Done this a lot lately."

"Bike parking?" Sean asked. "Security?"

"Well, there's the gate, of course. That's resident-only. Bike parking is in the basement, first come first serve."

"Right. But, like, any nearby concerns? Any incidents?"

"I don't think so." She gave Sarah a quizzical look.

"Boy's got computers."

"And I just try to be mindful of the stuff, that's all."

We're bickering like a couple. Sarah smiled.

"You'll be fine," Danielle said. "This high up, nobody's gonna come through the window or anything!" The enthusiasm in her voice dipped, but she still had a cheerful air.

Sarah gave Sean a curious glance. The two knew each other long enough to communicate silently. Sean's cheeks gave away his hesitation, but Sarah was eager to move and he wasn't going to stop her.

"Right," Sarah said. "Danielle. How should I go about claiming the place?"

She bounced as if renting the apartment would somehow be difficult. "Awesome! I have all the forms you'd need down in the office. Just take those, fill them out, get them to me as soon as you can. Are you both moving in?"

Sarah looked to Sean for confirmation. "Not sure," she said. "I'm definitely in, he might be."

"Yeah, not positive yet," Sean added.

"I'll figure something out, though."

"Alright." A hint of disappointment emerged. "Well, we can do it for just you, Sarah. And Sean, if you decide to tag along we can definitely take care of it. We'd love to have you!"

The two gathered the paperwork and went back to the car. The occasional hatchback passed by, interrupting the quiet. Sarah opened her car door and dropped herself on the driver's seat with a sigh.

"That's your place, huh?" Sean asked.

"That's my place."

"Congrats. Wanna grab food?"

"Yeah, probably should." She looked around; a taqueria and a Thai restaurant both sat near enough that she wouldn't need to move the car. "Feel like pizza? I know this place more in the central east side."

"That works."

CHAPTER FORTY-THREE

A part of her was afraid that she'd run into Alex when they got there. She was encroaching on his turf and bringing an outsider like Sean to boot. Yet, it seemed unlikely, and the place had been calling to her all night. She wasn't sure why. The familiarity, perhaps, or the romanticism it carried for her. Some emotional connection.

It certainly wasn't the pizza. There were plenty of better places.

"How'd you ever find this place?" Sean asked.

"Used to come here with Alex all the time. He loves it. Plus, for me, it's something different."

"Definitely different than the stuff near my place. This is more..."

"Old Town?" Sarah offered.

"I was gonna say New York. But, I guess I can see that."

They shared a table near the front, the same that she and Alex shared most of the time. She always sat facing the door, watching the customers come in and out. She never knew who they were, but she still found them interesting. Even the unnerving ones. Some would know Alex, recognizing him instantly, initiating a conversation that she had to sit sideline to.

"Okay, so," Sarah said, "I have a question."

"Alright. I've got one too."

"Actually, I have two questions."

Sean chuckled. "Because I have a question?"

"No, probably not."

"Sure, sure."

She rolled her eyes. "Okay. One. Did you not realize Danielle was flirting with you?"

Sean stared. "She was?"

Sarah laughed. "She was so obvious! Making eyes at you, talking with that, sort of, manic pixie dream girl kinda thing. I wasn't sure if you were stringing her along or what."

"I wasn't even thinking about it. Seriously!" He started to laugh along with her. "I just figured, you know, you're the one actually looking at the place, I'll just make small talk. Not like you want to deal with people."

"Okay, that's fair. Still, how do you not notice?"

"Is that question two?" He smirked.

"That's- I have as many questions as I need, okay?"

"Three."

Sarah narrowed her eyes. "Sean."

"I wasn't thinking about it! Like, we were there to look at the apartment, not flirt. Right?" He paused to take a sip from his soda. "Besides, I don't think she'd be my type."

"What is your type?"

"Four."

She softly kicked his leg beneath the table. "Dammit, stop counting how many questions I ask!"

"Hey! No violence."

Sarah looked over at the counter to make sure Tommy wasn't around. She knew he would have too much fun giving them a hard time, and she hadn't prepared Sean for the possibility.

"Then c'mon, tell me."

"Alright, alright." He looked down at the table and squirmed in his chair. "I... I don't really know. Like, I know I don't want someone like Angela. She was just a spoiled brat. But it's not like 'oh, she's gotta be this tall or this species' or anything like that."

Sarah could tell the question made him uncomfortable. "Alright, that's fair."

"What about you?"

His softened voice made her assume he was asking honestly, but it still made her nervous. She looked up at the ceiling in thought. *I could probably describe him to a T and he wouldn't realize what I was doing.*

"I guess... more interesting than me. Think that's why I liked Alex. But we just didn't match, so like, I don't know. Probably more important that we just get along."

He nodded. "So you have no idea either."

"Guess not." She hesitated. "Now I kinda don't want to ask my other question."

"It's alright," he said. "Shoot."

"Okay." She exhaled. "Do you want to move in with me?"

Sean avoided eye contact. "Well... okay. Here's my question. Why do you want me to move in with you in the first place?"

She looked for an excuse. If he didn't catch on to Danielle's overt flirting, he definitely didn't catch on to her more subtle approach. But she didn't want to dump the idea on him right now.

"Because you're my best friend. We spend all this time together anyway, we know we can stand each other. And, like, I think I can trust you to be a good roommate."

"You think so?"

"Well, I mean, I don't know. You don't know how good a roommate I would be, either. But I assume you would, at least, do the dishes, not be super annoying. Not, like, steal the internet and get us arrested."

Sean laughed. "You have no idea how the internet works."

"I do not." She laughed to herself.

"Besides, I kinda figured you wouldn't want to live with anybody else anyway."

"Really? I'm looking at two bedroom places. I have to live with someone."

"I know." He looked down. "I don't know why I thought that."

"Sean." They regained eye contact. "You can say no. You don't have to move in with me if you don't want to. It's fine."

He sighed. "I don't know if I want to, that's the thing. Honestly, I'm so used to where I am now. It works for me."

"Then stick with what works."

"Yeah, but it's nice to change things every now and then. I could stand to do it more often. Like, hell, I never would've come here. Would've gone to Schmizza."

The pizza place definitely wasn't Sean's style. It was too low-key, too run down. The sort of place that was becoming too rare. He stuck to the more reasonable restaurants. These days, even those seemed to vanish week after week, replaced by conceptual and experimental places. She couldn't imagine him in those, either, though he could go if he wanted. He could afford to. They were too expensive for Sarah to try.

"And, you're kinda right," Sarah said. "I probably wouldn't want to live with anyone else. But, I mean, I have to change anyway. Might as well change a whole lot of stuff, get it over with."

Sean stared, nibbling at his pizza. "Who are you and what have you done with Sarah Madsen."

Sarah choked with laughter. "Come on, man!"

"You won't watch a comedy."

"Bullshit I won't watch a comedy!"

"You barely sat through *Young Frankenstein!*"

"It's not my style, okay?"

"Fine. Saturday, I'm coming to your place, we're marathoning Mel Brooks movies. We are going to find one you like."

"Fine," Sarah said with a huff. "It's a date."

Sean nodded sternly. Sure enough, he didn't seem to catch on.

CHAPTER FORTY-FOUR

Sarah felt compressed in the queue. It was more disorganized than tight; the layout of tables interrupted what would otherwise be a perfectly orderly line. Instead, it snaked into tight aisles, shuffling around as people tried to come and go. It made for an unpleasant dance.

She knew the Deadline was busy on Saturdays. She had seen the crowds once, years ago, and declared Never Again. Yet, there was an impulse to show up, to send the place off once and for all. Sure, she would be around for a couple more weeks, but packing would be increasingly important. By the time she was done, she would live miles away, too far to return frequently.

Only one table remained available, situated beneath the rafter that used to hold the wire sculpture she always noticed. It was gone, along with the photos that hung from the post nearby. Most of the cafe's artworks were shuffled around; moderately-sized paintings replaced by arrays of framed photos, minimal drawings replaced by kitsch pieces of mixed media. The shop always cycled through artwork here and there, but this amount felt more drastic.

She held her ears down. There was too much noise for her to do any heavy, focused thinking. The fact was somehow comforting. She had been overthinking the process; the work became too analytical for her own taste. A bit of stray, mindless thought would help her break the pattern.

A laptop or tablet sat at nearly every table. She couldn't avoid spotting some of the screens as she walked. Some had Photoshop open, creating digital art underneath analog examples. Others looked like they were writing code or essays. The cafe always felt like a place to make things, and from what Sarah observed, that energy was hard at work.

She put in headphones and closed her eyes to shut out the distractions. *Alright. Let's just take a stab at it. What am I looking for? What do I want to spend my time doing? No job titles.*

Her apartment hunt notebook still had empty pages. She tore one out. *Let's see. Definitely want to keep working with people. No staring at screens all day. I'm not really good at design. I mean I know it, I just can't make the actual graphics. Could learn it. That'd be nice. So, okay, there's one. "Willing to learn."*

She wrote each idea down, along with scattered thoughts on what she liked and disliked about her current job. With her mocha half-finished, she decided she had enough to work with. She pulled out her laptop and started swapping her attention between writing notes and browsing jobs.

"Job hunting?"

Sarah jumped in her seat. Even though the soft-spoken voice barely rose above the noise, it was more sudden than she expected.

It came from a brown coyote, sitting at the table behind her. He had a familiar look to him, average yet somehow attractive. Easy on the eyes, perhaps. From his posture, Sarah figured he had been looking over her shoulder for a while.

"Sorry," he said.
"It's okay."

She laughed nervously. It could help defuse the situation, but she was genuinely nervous. He was a coyote, after all. Her instincts said to run.

"Pretty shitty market out there, huh." He sounded depressed.
"Yeah. I mean, there's a few around, but, yeah. It's been tough."
"How long you been out of work?"
She hesitated. "I'm not, really. I guess."

"Oh." He looked down at his screen.

Her eyes widened as her mind put together the pieces. She had seen him before. He didn't come every Sunday, but over the last few months, she saw him half a dozen times. Maybe more.

Y'know what. It's worth a try. Probably never see him again anyway.

"What about you?"

He looked back up. "Um, four months now. Was doing microprocessor design."

Sarah blinked. "Wow. You can't get a job doing that? Sounds crazy hard."

He shrugged. "It's pretty much just Intel anymore, and that's not happening."

"Sorry, man."

"No worries. What about you?"

"Marketing manager. I-"

She was ready to go into her usual story, the one she designed to get recruiters off her back. The one that was meant to push people away.

"I took a layoff. Keep my team from having to deal with it."

"Ballsy move."

"I do dumb stuff sometimes." She extended a paw. "Sarah."

"Daniel." He paused. "Well, um, good luck with it."

"You too. If it helps, don't worry about titles or anything. Just think about what you want to do and what you're good at. It's a little harder, but it makes you feel more optimistic about your chances."

"That work for you?"

She shrugged. "We'll see."

There we go. I helped someone. Good deed done for the day. She smiled to herself.

A backpack dropped on the seat across the table, startling her again. Daniel stood next to it.

"Might as well keep each other company, right?"

Sarah hesitated. "You know. It's worth a try."

They commiserated over the job ads, sharing anything that the other might find interesting. Daniel was more fond of the ones that were laughably bad. Even those, embarrassing as they were, occasionally gave Sarah ideas.

She was surprised how well they got along. As well as she could remember, she never had a coyote friend. Then again, she couldn't remember trying to make one. She hadn't tried to make friends since she found the movie group.

Maybe I'll invite him along. Couldn't hurt.

An hour had passed before Daniel started packing up. "Thanks for keeping me company."

"No problem." *Yeah, what the hell.* "If you need company tomorrow, I'm going to Laurelhurst Theater with some friends. Probably see some weird indie movie or something. You're free to tag along."

He considered it for a moment. "You mean, a date?"

"Just friends. I mean, we only just met."

"I was gonna say, you didn't seem like that kinda rabbit." He put on his backpack. "But, sure, why not."

Sarah headed home to pack. There was still plenty to do there. The rote work let her mind wander.

I made a friend. I went and actively made a friend for once. Good work, Sarah. I think he'll get along with the gang, too. And... if I didn't have Sean I totally would ask him out.

CHAPTER FORTY-FIVE

Sean's bike always had two satchels attached to it, one on each side. Normally they were evenly-shaped red rectangles, but as he wheeled his bike into Sarah's apartment building, she noticed they were bulging.

"You appear to have stuff," she said.

"Well, you're moving out. Figured you could use more things to pack up."

"How considerate."

He detached the bags from the bike and stood it up in the elevator. "So, I said we were going to marathon some Mel Brooks movies."

"So you brought DVDs? We stream movies nowadays. Maybe you remember two weeks ago when we streamed movies?"

Sean gave her a playful bat on the head. "I brought popcorn. If we're gonna put up with each other the rest of the day, we might as well make it enjoyable."

As the elevator stopped, he pulled out a bag of popcorn and handed it to Sarah. The entire satchel crinkled; it was full of bags, each a different variety. They came from a shop a few blocks from the apartment, a bright pastel place that exclusively dealt in gourmet popcorn. Sarah passed by several times, but never went inside. The idea was a bit too ridiculous for her. Too twee.

"You actually went to that place."

"Sure. Why not?"

"I have a popcorn maker. I have a ton of popcorn. I'm set."

He closed the satchel and wheeled his bike down the hall. "I figured you would've boxed it up by now, what with the whole moving out thing."

She opened her apartment door. The bookshelves were still full, her desk still adorned with photos of family and friends. There were a handful of boxes sitting in corners, but the living room otherwise looked untouched.

Sean looked around. "Okay, I was wrong."

"I know, I'm way behind."

"You've still got a couple weeks."

"I guess. And I've already got the kitchen more or less done."

"That's not so bad. Though, you probably don't wanna go too fast. It'd start to feel weird. Everything empty, bunch of boxes sitting around."

"The whole thing feels weird." She tossed the bag of popcorn onto the couch. "I don't really want to say goodbye to the place."

"I know. Did you hear back from the new place yet?"

"Still waiting for the credit check to pass. Once that's done, though, I'm good."

"Not worried about it going through?"

"Nope." She smiled, pleased with herself for not worrying about something for once.

Sean exhaled nervously. "Did you just put yourself on the lease?"

"Yeah. Wasn't sure if you were up for it."

Sean nodded. "Right."

They shared an awkward silence. "You don't want to move in with me, do you?"

He stammered, shuffling his feet. "I don't..."

"It's okay, man. You don't have to. It's just an offer."

"I know. I just don't wanna be mean."

"How are you being mean? Yeah, I would like it if we lived together, but that's asking a lot of you. And I can't make you do it. I can't tell you what to do. Alex snapped at me for doing that."

"You sure you're gonna be okay?"

"No, I'm not," she said after a pause. "But I guess I should be."

Sean offered a pat on the shoulder, his ears splayed sympathetically. Sarah accepted.

"Like, I don't know. Maybe I will get a bit grumpy at you about it. I don't want to, I don't wanna be telling everyone what to do, but I mean..."

"You do have that habit."

"I know. To be fair, you lead the whole group. You kinda tell us what to do."

"Everyone goes along with it, though. And I'm always worried someone's gonna get pissed off and hate me."

"Pshaw. Nobody's gonna hate you, you're too fun."

Sean laughed. "Really?"

"Yeah."

"Huh. I honestly thought everyone thought I was annoying."

"You're, like, the least annoying one."

"I guess." He leaned against a bookshelf. "But I mean, you're all putting up with whatever I suggest, so if it sucks, then..." He trailed off. "I really expect Lee to just stage a coup at some point."

"Lee?" She chuckled as she sat on the couch. "I wouldn't worry about it, man. As long as you don't go full dictator, you'll be fine."

"Alright then." He grabbed the remote from an end table and tossed it to Sarah. "I hereby cede my power. You may pick the first movie."

She stifled a laugh. "You're going to give control over to the woman who just said she has problems taking and giving up control."

Sean smirked, sitting down next to her. "I make bad decisions sometimes."

"So you are moving in with me."

"No, no," he said in a sympathetic yet insistent voice. "I couldn't do it. I'll visit, though."

"Damn straight you will."

She was hurt, but it didn't feel right to show it. She hoped he would agree, even after his initial hesitations, but there were a dozen different ways it could've gone. Maybe he'd come around for some reason, or the nagging would damage their friendship the way it damaged the one with Alex. A kind rejection seemed like one of the better options, even if it was disappointing.

Y'know, if this is how he turns people down... I gotta try.

"Also. Since I've been declared queen of the movies-"

Sean burst out laughing.

"Since you put me in charge, I have one more demand. Give me your tail."

His laughter turned incredulous. "Wait, what?"

"You heard me. Tail. Lap. Let's go."

"You're drunk with power. Give me the remote."

She laughed and held the remote as far from Sean as she could manage. He played along, reaching as far as he could without climbing onto her.

"You're just mad you can't tell me to do that. Not without me sitting in your lap."

"And it's not that kinda friendship."

"Could be," she said with a smile. It seemed to pass Sean's notice. "Seriously, though, I'm jealous. You have a real tail."

"I see how it is. You just want to cuddle it. Not interested in the guy it's attached to."

"Would you rather I cuddle you? C'mon, put on some bad horror movies, I'll grab the beer. We know how that works."

Sean put a paw up to catch a laugh. "Oh, jeez, don't remind me of that. I was so grabby. Surprised we didn't make out."

Sarah bit her tongue. At this point, Sean might be flirting back, but it was hard for her to tell. Their usual playful sarcasm resembled flirting more often than she wanted to admit.

They took turns picking movies. Sarah considered picking a dramatic movie each time her turn came. She was always up for something more to her taste, but it didn't fit the evening. It only felt right to be lighthearted.

The popcorn bags emptied quickly, along with more beers than they should've had. By the time midnight rolled around, the two were laying on the couch, holding each other, fading in and out of sleep.

Sarah woke up somewhere in the dark of the night, hung over. She realized the position they were in and worried how Sean might react if he woke up too. With a grunt she stumbled off the couch, trying not to wake him, and dragged herself to the bathroom for some aspirin. She left some on the end table for Sean along with a glass of water and climbed into her bed.

Her hangover was still there in the morning, but Sean wasn't.

CHAPTER FORTY-SIX

By Monday, Sarah was well over the hangover. The long night had interfered with her packing, but she told herself it was okay. She had two more weeks.

She also had bags of popcorn. So she dropped one on the end of her desk. It grabbed Michelle's attention.

"Chipotle lime," Sarah said. "You're free to have some."

"Thanks," Michelle said, reaching for the bag. "But, y'know, Roger will bring the treats for your last day. You don't have to get stuff."

"Oh, I didn't. Sean and I had a movie marathon over the weekend."

"Nice!" She munched on some popcorn. "See anything interesting?"

"Bunch of comedies, mostly. Sean's really into them, he's been trying to get me to watch a bunch. Mostly Mel Brooks. Finally just kinda gave in."

"Well, that's good. I haven't been able to see anything but Disney movies since I had the boys. Just, no energy to go on my own." She took another paw's worth of popcorn. "Good thing he's just your boyfriend, huh?"

Sarah bit her lip. She wanted to say "yes," expecting that Michelle would never meet Sean to contradict the claim. Or, if she did, it would be after Sarah asked him out. She had been thinking about it since her head cleared the day before. When she would do it, how she'd phrase it, what to do in case it went wrong.

"We're not dating," Sarah said. "Not officially. I mean, sure, we hang out all the time, we do all these things with each other, but... I don't know. Either he's not interested or he's waiting for me to make the first move."

"If those are the options, he's probably not interested." She tossed more popcorn into her mouth. "I'm sorry, I'm taking the whole bag on you."

"It's fine. I've got two more at home. He brought a ton."

"Oh, well now. If he's bringing you gifts, maybe he is interested."

Sarah rolled her eyes. "I don't think popcorn counts as a gift."

"It could."

Sarah chuckled. "Either way, I guess I should probably ask him out."

"Definitely! Won't know until you try."

She wasn't sure if she wanted to know. The certainty would be nice, but if he turned her down it would remove any lingering hope of a relationship. She liked to imagine what their relationship would be like. Probably the same as what they already had, but more intimate. Such a small change that it'd be easy to handle.

Sarah made her way into an office where Jessica was already sitting. As far as she could tell, she was already finished moving her work around. The meetings where she felt unnecessary before now had Chris or Jessica taking on what little work she did. So she drew swirls on her notepad and let the badger take control of the meeting. Her presence was only for moral support.

The phone beeped. "Ron, is that you?"

"Hey, Sarah," an old, male voice said through the conference call.

"And Jess," she added, introducing herself.

"Jess is going to take over this account," Sarah said. "I already let Dan and Allison know, but Dan suggested I reach out, make sure we talked one level up as well."

"That's good to know, then. They haven't joined the call yet, have they?"

"Nope, still waiting," Jessica said.

Sarah already checked out of the conversation. The meeting was a formality that required just enough input for her to be present. But, Jessica was present. Sarah considered ducking out entirely, confident that she wouldn't be missed.

"So, Sarah," Ron said, "what's the story with the transfer? You moving on?"

"Afraid so," she said. "There's been a, uh... a bit of stuff going on. I'm sure you heard, I know you and Gary talk every so often."

"Of course, of course. But, Wallace Sport is glad to remain a client, so I'm sure that puts him at ease."

"I'm sure it does."

"And you're not quite as loyal to Roger as Sarah is, are you Jess?" Ron asked with a chuckle.

She and Sarah exchanged confused looks. "Come again?"

"Well, hmm. What's the situation been over there, then?"

"We heard that there was some embezzlement scheme with a few sales guys. That chopped a ton off the budget, so people had to be let go."

"Yes, yes. And I thought Roger had been let go."

"No, he wasn't," Sarah said slowly. "He asked us to take severance."

"Is that so?" Ron let out the curious grunts of a professor. "Bit surprising. Gary mentioned he was ready to let Roger go. Didn't know he changed his mind."

The phone beeped with another connection. Ron immediately changed the subject back to business. Sarah grabbed her notepad and wrote on it. "Gary didn't change his mind." She slid it in front of Jessica, who looked at it with a nod.

As Jessica took control of the meeting, Sarah quietly let her anger at Roger sit. It was becoming a familiar emotion and she was embarrassed to have it. She thumped her foot and thought about Sean instead, hoping to calm her mind. Jessica heard the thumps and nodded, but kept the tone of the call professional.

When the call finished, Jessica let out a loud hiss.

"The meeting wasn't that bad," Sarah said.

"No, fucking Roger! I knew that whole thing was sketchy!"

"Same," Sarah said, indifferent.

"I mean, sales rips us off and we have to take the flak? Bullshit."

"Let's be honest, wouldn't be the first time we had to clean up their mess."

Jessica was too consumed with her anger to listen. "You wanna go chew him out? I'm ready to go chew him out."

Sarah shook her head. "Naw. Don't go chew him out. You have to stick around, and you'd be on his bad side. I'll save it for my last day."

Jessica's eyes widened. "Oh, I get it. Little last minute 'fuck you' for him, huh?" She gestured a small stab.

"Well, he gave me one."

Jessica smiled at the idea of exacting revenge. Sarah was more measured; she was learning how mean she could be, and despite Roger's behavior she didn't want to let it out again.

"Can I ask you a favor, though?" Sarah added. "Try and keep him away from me until then."

"Someone's gonna need to keep me away from him, too."

"We'll make Michelle do it, then. She either doesn't know what's going on or she doesn't care."

"Well, Roger hasn't fucked her over."

"Not yet, anyway."

"Yeah. Give it time," Jessica said. She quieted down as she got to the door. "I swear, this whole place is fucked."

CHAPTER FORTY-SEVEN

Alright, Sarah. Get to Laurelhurst early, hope Sean's the first to show up. Ask him out.
You can do it.

Sarah parked outside the theater. Sean was standing outside, as attentive as ever. His bike looked to be in better shape as well. The handle wraps were refreshed, the tires smoothed out. Her leg bounced with nerves until she stepped out of the car.

"You're here early," Sean said.
"Well, you know. Needed to get away from packing."
"Can't blame you."

The small talk died off quickly. They hadn't seen each other since the movie marathon the weekend prior, and Sarah wasn't sure how he felt about that evening. For that matter, she wasn't sure what he remembered.

Just a quick, y'know, "I liked doing the marathon with you, it felt kinda romantic..."
Ease into it.

"For the record," Sarah mumbled, "the marathon was fun."
"Hmm?"
"Said the marathon was nice."
"Yeah," Sean said, upbeat. "You like Mel Brooks now?"
"A little bit. *Dr. Strangelove* was more fun."
"I figured. It's Kubrick."

She had just gathered the air necessary to move the conversation further when Kate emerged from the theater. She swallowed her breath in surprise, making her cough.

For all her worrying about their argument, Sarah didn't have a plan for what to do or say when she saw Kate next. She hastily tried to throw one together, but Kate approached too quickly for anything to come to mind.

"Hey, Sarah made it!" she said. She was as upbeat as always. It made Sarah suspicious. "How's the move going?"

"It's going," Sarah said. "Just about done, been taking it kinda slow."

"Well, good! Looked like you could use a bit of slowing down, you've been on edge for a while."

Sarah sighed. It felt like a good opportunity. "I know. And, I kinda wanted to apologize for blowing up at you. Been really worried about Alex, and I didn't handle the whole 'shit's going crazy' thing very well."

"It's fine." She sounded sincere. "You were just defending Alex, that's totally fair. I should've been more thoughtful and all that."

"So, we're cool? I wasn't sure if Sean was just messing with me, he said you were over it pretty quick."

Kate smiled. "Well, I mean, I'd rather you not do that again, but sure."

"I'd rather not do that again, too."

"I'd rather you didn't do it again, too," Sean said. "I mean, just to round it out. We're all in favor of no yelling."

Sarah laughed. Sure, she had missed the chance to ask Sean out, but her spirits lifted nonetheless. A bit of guilt over creating tension still lingered, but if Kate wouldn't hold a grudge, then she could let it slowly fade. Things would be okay.

Lee arrived with Ian in tow. He was a fellow ferret, taller, with an athlete's demeanor about him. It was the first time Sarah met him; he had only joined the group two weeks prior. Lee never said how they met. Sean and Sarah both assumed they were a couple, but decided not to say anything.

"Evening gang," Ian said. "You must be Sarah. Lee warned me about you," he added with a laugh.

"Did he now? Wasn't aware I was dangerous."

"Oh, she's totally dangerous," Sean said. "She's a total rabbit, flirts with everyone. She flirts with me all the time."

She gave him a playful shove. "Asshole."

He laughed. "Well, hey, I'm gonna make it harder for you then. It's your turn to pick."

Sarah wasn't sure she heard correctly. "Wait, what?"

"You always pick, Sean," Kate said. "That's the rule."

"I can let other people pick sometimes," he said. "It's not a crime."

"Can I pick next time?" Lee asked.

"Sure. I'm just putting Sarah on the spot 'cause she called me an asshole."

"You accused me of flirting with everyone. Jerk."

Ian chuckled. "Man, Lee, you didn't tell me they were a couple."

Sarah gagged, embarrassed. She considered disagreeing, even though she hadn't asked Sean yet.

He burst out laughing and interrupted her thought. "Alright, can we just go?"

Kate was unamused. Sarah could feel her staring her down. She had accepted the apology, but now it felt insincere. There was some ulterior motive present that Sarah couldn't nail down. It was probably romantic. The fact that everyone seemed to believe that Sarah and Sean were now officially a couple definitely played a part. But the look was more aggressive, more bitter, more like a predator's eyes.

Sarah tried to shrug it off. Rather than dwell on it, she focused on which movie to pick. The theater was small, so there were few options, none of which were precisely the sort of film she'd go for. It probably wouldn't matter if she picked or if Sean did. Still, the power felt good.

Yet it also felt like a test. One option was close to what she would go for herself, but picking it would mean subjecting the group to her tastes. She wasn't sure if she should do that. The other option was a lighter film that Kate and Sean were more likely to enjoy.

She started to understand why Sean had such anxiety over leading the group.

He didn't seem to have any anxiety now. He watched, patiently smiling, as she dithered and hesitated. Eventually, she picked the movie she preferred to see. Sean nodded, looking pleased. If it was a test, she seemed to pass it.

She kept a nervous eye on the group when they took their seats, looking for any hint that they were dissatisfied with the choice. They were all too polite to show it to her face, but if they thought she wasn't looking, perhaps they'd let their guard down. She had to know what they thought.

Sean gave her a light jab in the side. "You alright?"
She looked at him, then back at the rest of the group.
"You're fine," he whispered, picking up her concern. "It's hard to fuck up with this crowd."
"You worry about it all the time."
"I pick all the time. You're not gonna annoy everyone right away."
"Yeah, you have practice." She smiled.

After the movie, the group left the theater with cheerful steps. Sarah's pick had been successful, as much as any of Sean's choices had been.

"So, Cardinal Club?" Kate asked.
"Sure," Ian said, "assuming they're as good with Old Fashioneds as you said."
"Might as well," Sean said. "Sarah?"
"Naw, I've been drinking too much lately. Plus, I still need to pack."
Sean nodded. "Fair enough."

They were excuses. Valid ones, but Sarah mostly wanted to end the night on a good note. More time around Kate only threatened that.

CHAPTER FORTY-EIGHT

The office was decorated for Halloween. The office administrator had a particular fondness for the holiday, even over Christmas, and the number of paper pumpkins and orange-and-black streamers along the walls made the fact obvious. They clashed with the company decor. The designers Sarah worked with could tell her why, but to her, they were just tacky.

This year, she felt a certain appreciation for them. Halloween meant change; it would be her last day of work. She knew what her weekend would entail, but after that, her calendar was empty for the first time in years.

She had never been truly unemployed before. There were months, during college, where she didn't have anything part-time. But she wasn't dependent on those part-time jobs to keep her going. Now, grown up, she did depend on her job, and the severance would only last her so long. It made her nervous, the fear pushing bluntly into her stomach.

Michelle seemed excited. She was already at her desk, tail slowly wagging, when Sarah sat down.

"Just one more day for you, huh?" she said with a smile.
"Guess so," Sarah said. "Went by kinda quick."
"I know. Been a hell of a month, and I wasn't even that busy!"
Sarah leaned back. "Surprised I got everything squared away. Keep worrying there's something I missed."
"Oh, I wouldn't worry about it. You've been rushing around like a mad woman, from the looks of it. Besides, you've got plenty of time!"
"Eh. It's only one day."

"Lot can get done in one day, right?"

"Yeah, guess so." She sighed. "I don't know. At this point, I probably shouldn't even care anymore. It's out of my hands."

Michelle gave her a knowing look. "You've been checked out for a while, haven't you?"

"Oh hell yeah," she said with a laugh.

"Well, good for you! Sounds like taking the walk was a good idea."

Sarah nodded. *Guess it was. I mean, I'm fucked if I don't find anything soon, but...*

"Having any luck with something new?" Michelle asked.

Sarah chuckled. "Why, are you looking for a way out too?"

Michelle laughed. "Oh, I'm gonna miss dealing with you."

A pause. "Yeah. Same here."

Sarah made herself look busy. Few emails arrived, far fewer than a typical Thursday. She relaxed, knowing that her projects were handed off successfully and were now someone else's problem.

An email arrived from Vinish, inviting her to lunch. Halloween would be his last day as well. A few people from sales and design were included on it.

Team lunch. Might as well, gives me something to do.

The three – Ash, from sales, joined Vinish and Sarah – walked as a group to a Mexican spot several blocks from the office. Sarah huddled in her jacket the whole way, hoping in the back of her mind that her new apartment would have good heating. Winter was never as brutal as it was back home, but it would certainly be unkind soon.

The restaurant was warm in temperature and in decor. It was a crisp, new place, stylish but not overly so. There were several restaurants downtown like this, filling a dozen different culinary genres, and Sarah had never gone to any of them. She would have if she ate out more frequently, but that cost money. She always worried about money.

"It's an interesting place," Vinish said, leading the group inside and to a table. "A sort of Tex-Mex approach. But they throw in some fairly clever French cues as well. I was surprised how well it works, honestly."

"Long as there's vegetarian, I'm cool," Sarah said.

"Since when were you a foodie?" Ash asked.

"Always," Vinish said with a nod. "Dropped out of culinary school. Couldn't stand those people, so aggressive. Still like the food, though."

"Should've brought Sean along," Sarah said. "He could use his horizons broadened."

"He's your boyfriend, right?"

Sarah grumbled to herself as she sat, annoyed that she even brought him up. She was getting sick of the question; or at least, sick of the answer.

"No, no, he's just a friend."

"He's not your boyfriend? The otter?"

"Oh." She huffed out embarrassment at the mixup. "No, that's Alex. We broke up a while ago."

"Yes, sorry, I remember that. Couldn't remember the name."

"How's he been?" Ash asked. "Thought you two kept in touch."

Sarah laughed. "Was there this whole gossip channel I wasn't aware of?"

Ash stared. "Apparently."

"Oh. Okay." She paused. "He's... been better. The art market is pretty tough, hasn't been having much luck. Last I heard, at least."

"What does he do?" Vinish asked. "He's a painter?"

"Yeah. Traditional stuff, occasional mixed media. Pretty dark, honestly."

"What's his niche? Just being dark?"

"Pretty much. He just hates the whole marketing side of it."

"It's unfortunate," Vinish said with a slight shake of his head. "He's a business, he needs to do marketing. Otherwise, he's out of luck."

A waiter interrupted the group to take orders. Sarah kept hers simple. She would be unemployed soon, after all, so being lavish with her meal felt unwise.

"Anyway," she said as the waiter left, "I've been telling him all that. That he needs to market himself and such. But he gets really angry about it."

"How does he expect to succeed if he's not concerned with positioning himself in the market?"

"Exactly! And I know he knows the market. He's got so much opportunity to make himself stand out, that's not hard for him. He just has to channel that into something useful."

Ash chuckled. "You two don't turn it off, do you?"

"Turn what off?" Vinish asked.

"The whole marketer thing. I half expect you to start talking about Warhol's KPIs or something."

"Well," Sarah said, "he's right. Alex runs a business. He needs to do this kinda stuff. He needs to do sales, too, for that matter."

"And he won't?"

Sarah started gesturing. "He gets so pissed about it! He yelled at me the other day because I was trying to get him to just think about it."

"Seriously? Ash asked. "Were you getting mean with it or something?"

Sarah sighed and looked at the table. "I... yeah. I guess I was a bit too persistent."

"Not a huge surprise. I have some kinda mean emails from you during the Wallace project."

"Really?"

Ash nodded.

"Shit. I'm sorry."

"It's part of the job," Vinish said. "If you have to be a bit forward to get things done, that's fine."

"No, no. I really need to stop."

Vinish shrugged. "It's just work."

Sarah exhaled, restraining herself. She felt herself tensing up, but there was nothing to be tense about.

"I can never leave my work at work, though. That's the problem. Like, I'll get annoyed with a client and then I'm grumpy the whole rest of the night." She sunk in her chair. "I probably put that on Alex a ton of times and never noticed."

"It's probably fine," Ash said.

"Well, he won't talk to me anymore, so."

Ash stared, confused with a hint of disgust. "What did you say to him?"

Ashamed, Sarah sighed and closed her eyes. "I just said he was gonna have to do the whole marketing thing. He won't, and like, that's why he isn't having any luck. He's not putting in the effort, so he's not going to succeed. And I told him that, and I just... he really needs it drilled into him. And I apologized, like, right away. Once I realized I went too far. But, nothing. Haven't heard a word from him."

"Call him?" Vinish asked.

"Voicemail. Hasn't answered emails either."

"Were they actionable?"

Ash gave Sarah, who finally realized what the earlier remark meant, an incredulous look. Vinish probably did see the world in marketing terms. Sarah could see Alex's work that way without feeling strange, but not their whole relationship.

"I guess not, honestly."

"Well," Vinish said, "give him something to do. See if he'll do it. Even if he doesn't respond, maybe he's still listening."

"Sounds like it'd make things worse, though," Ash said. "Probably better to just leave it alone and move on."

"No. I gotta." Sarah paused. "I mean, it's worth a try, anyway."

Their lunches appeared. The conversation moved to idle chatter; Vinish and Sarah discussed the job market and debated what they might do next. All three commiserated over aggravating clients and annoying coworkers.

It felt like any other lunch with friends. As they left, Sarah wished they had done these sorts of lunches before, when they were all safely employed. It would've messed with her routines, but they got along well. And Vinish had advice to offer. It might not be good advice, but it was worth trying.

Besides, she didn't have anything else to do.

CHAPTER FORTY-NINE

Sarah grabbed her laptop from her desk and wandered to a nearby Starbucks. She hadn't been in it before, yet it felt almost the same as the others she had been in. The uniformity used to bother her, but she couldn't get upset about it anymore. It wasn't the Deadline, but it wasn't trying to be.

Foot traffic was light but enough to keep her interested. She watched them pass by, people who spent large portions of their lives in offices downtown, building and selling hundreds of different things. Always in a rush, always distracted. For the last four years, Sarah had been no different. Now, looking out from the window at the cloudy and cold afternoon, it all seemed so foolish.

Maybe she could avoid it next time. There were companies, most of them small, popping up offices in nooks and crannies across the city. There could be someone in her current neighborhood, or in her new one, that needed her exact set of skills. She doubted that she would ever notice, but she was drawn to the idea. It would still be a job, but it would be a change. Change was starting to feel good.

She looked around idly at the empty cafe. Her prospects were starting to look up. Every time she sat down to hunt for a job, there seemed to be more openings listed. Companies had to hire to justify their budgets. Even though they weren't looking for Sarah's exact job title, she still felt optimistic. Maybe it was time to change that, too. There were opportunities to do it.

A fellow rabbit, reminding her of Ash, passed through the cafe. Sarah sipped at her mocha and watched her, thinking about her coworkers. They always seemed comfortable in an office. Michelle thrived in it, even if she always talked about wanting to be around her kids. After four years of working together, that was all Sarah really knew about her. There were plenty of opportunities to learn more about her as a person – Sarah was positive of that, even if she couldn't think of any examples – but she never put the effort in.

Maybe that was the reason she didn't enjoy the office. She knew that she didn't deeply care about her job. She cared enough to make sure she didn't get fired or in trouble, but past that point, she doodled or zoned out. If she didn't like the work, there was no way she would like the place it happened in.

Vinish seemed to enjoy the work. She was surprised to hear that he took the layoff; he always seemed attentive and concerned. Sarah always assumed he was much better at the job than she was simply by his demeanor. He always had a calmness about him that Sarah envied. If he were that good at his job, he could definitely do better for himself elsewhere. Maybe he knew that; maybe that was why he took the layoff.

He had advice, too. She wasn't sure if it was well-considered or, as with the advice she often gave, made up on the spot. But the thought of giving Alex something actionable made sense, even if the phrasing made her uncomfortable. It would provide certainty. If she asked him to do something and he didn't, then, that was that. He might not respond to it well – she would effectively be telling him what to do – but it couldn't possibly make things any worse.

She pulled out her laptop. A dozen emails sat in her inbox, waiting to distract her. Many were congratulations or condolences for a job soon to vanish. They all felt bland and anonymous, as though nobody had gotten to know her over those four years either. Still, at least people were willing to act as though they cared.

She allowed herself a moment of distraction. When it started to turn into a moment of stalling, she closed her work email and opened her personal one. She went to the end of the email chain she sent to Alex over the past weeks and started a new draft.

Alex, I know I've been sending a lot of these. Probably too many. I don't blame you if you're just marking these as spam. But I really do want to talk. I want to apologize, and I want to do it in person. I think we both need to see it in person.

So here's the story. I'm gonna be at the pizza place on Saturday. 2 pm. Same seat as always. If you want to talk, come. If you don't, don't. Either way, I won't bother you again.

Her stomach twisted with anxiety. She hesitated on sending the email, as she did with every other one she sent him. Maybe the language wasn't right. Maybe she shouldn't send it at all. But she knew what would happen if she didn't give any direction. She had been giving no direction for weeks.

It was time to trust Vinish.

She sent the email and sipped her coffee, taking in the aroma. She was calmer than she expected. Meeting Alex again would give her something to stress over, but for now that meeting only existed in the abstract.

Work stopped stressing her out as well. She had assumed there would be a million small things to take care of, loose ends to tie up. Instead, she could wander out of the office mid-afternoon and into a coffee shop without anyone raising an alarm. Either the storm was waiting for her final day, or it would never come at all.

The evening matched her calm. The air was still cold, but there was no wind to make it worse. Traffic was present all along her drive home, but it existed more as a matter of fact than a source of aggravation. Her neighborhood was quiet, the roads as empty as at midnight.

She made a quick dinner and packed more boxes. The work was almost done. Every box of progress gave her another small shot of success.

Before going to bed, she checked her email one last time, using a stack of boxes as a makeshift laptop stand. Alex still hadn't responded. She wasn't happy with the fact, but she accepted it. She had her final day of work to think about first.

CHAPTER FIFTY

A mass of office workers, dressed as movie characters and figures of legend, shuffled impatiently in the break room.

There was no cake.

It was Halloween, but it was also Sarah and Vinish's last day there. The confusion between the holiday party and the going-away party meant that neither was stocked as well as anyone preferred.

Michelle was absent from the crowd, having gone to fix the situation by getting cupcakes. Roger stood in the corner of the room, guilty.

Sarah stayed at her desk, lacking a costume. Her desk was already cleaned off and packed up. She kept her papers and belongings organized the entire time she had the desk, so when it came time to pack up, the required effort was minimal. Certainly, far easier than packing up the apartment.

The occasional straggler passed by her desk, offering goodbyes before heading to the delayed party. Sarah didn't know all of them, but she did her best to accept the kindness. No sense leaving on a bad note.

She idly checked her email. Alex still hadn't responded, but only a day had passed. She didn't expect any response, but she still hoped for one.

"Alright, party's back on!" Michelle backed into the office, dressed as a superhero, carrying boxes of cupcakes. Those near the door reacted as though her outfit wasn't a costume at all.

Sarah followed far behind. She wasn't interested in the party. She certainly wasn't interested in Roger's inevitable speech and jokes. But the party was, at least in part, for her. So she felt obligated. It would be poor form to miss your own celebration.

Roger made a weak effort to help Michelle lay out the boxes of cupcakes, then gestured for the crowd's attention. "Alright folks, really sorry about that whole mix-up. We can't have people leaving on a holiday, huh?"

"Well, we'd be glad to stick around," Vinish said with a crocodile smile.

Roger laughed nervously. "Yeah, it kinda sucks, doesn't it? Like, we could totally handle just one of you leaving, but both at once, I tell ya. Really put us in a tough spot."

"Wasn't our idea," Sarah mumbled.

"But anyway, you know, these things kinda happen, and I'm sure we'll be alright. Vinish, you've done a lot for all of us, been really loyal. That's great."

"Thank you."

"And Sarah, man. Four years? You had a pretty good run, grew into the role a ton. I know a lot of clients liked working with you, I heard a lot of 'oh, y'know, it's great to work with a rabbit,' stuff like that."

Wait, what? The hell does he even mean by that?

"So, yeah. I know we'll all be a ton busier now, but I guess you don't have to worry about it."

"Wasn't about to," Sarah said.

"Um... okay." Roger's jokes usually went without comment. Even Thomas had played polite. Sarah clearly knocked him off his pace.

Sarah mingled with the designers and salespeople. Vinish did the same in the opposite direction. She sought to get his attention and silently agree to trap Roger for a confrontation. She succeeded in the first but failed in the second.

Undaunted, she worked her way to the corner where Roger was cheerfully talking to the Rachel, the VP of sales. She stood, stern and quiet, waiting for them to notice her presence.

"Oh, hey Sarah," Rachel said, extending a fox paw. "I don't think we ever actually met."

"Well, we are in different departments. Wouldn't be necessary."

"You're right," she said cheerfully. "Sorry to see you go, though. I know Ash appreciated working with you."

"Thanks," she said before turning. "Roger, you mind if we grab an office real quick? I'm gonna need to talk for a bit."

She walked swiftly to the nearest office and stood behind the desk. Roger sat, fidgeting heavily.

"Suppose I should congratulate you, then," Sarah said. "You did a good job saving your own tail."

"What do you mean?" he asked with a smile.

"I've heard a few details the last couple days. And, y'know, without anything left to do it's pretty easy to dig into the politics for a bit."

"I thought you hated the politics."

"I thought you did too." She sat down and leaned onto the desk with a cold glare. "But, I think making a deal to throw people out and save your own ass qualifies."

He fidgeted. "Well, I mean, things have been rough. Gary was getting ready to pick for me, and-"

"He was gonna pick you."

"I... I mean, it would've been way more disruptive to find a new department head."

"As opposed to losing half the team?" she said, insulted.

"It sucks, I know, but like, I had to do something about it."

Sarah leaned back in her seat, glaring. She knew, in the back of her mind, that she had no idea how she would handle the situation if she were in his position. She would probably be honest about it, at least.

"Look. I know you did a pretty shitty thing here. You know it. And I could sit here and growl about how much of an asshole you are, but I'm not going to. I'm not forgiving it, I'm not excusing it, but it doesn't seem like you did it out of malice."

Roger smiled, immediately throwing her claim into question.

"The point is, this happened, it's over, and I'm gonna be okay despite what you did."

"That's... really nice of you."

"You don't deserve it." She stood up. "I'm still angry with you, for the record."

"Well, have a cupcake, should make you happier. Right?"

Sarah rolled her eyes and walked to the break room. She was looking for Vinish. He was at his desk, quietly packing up the last of his belongings.

"I don't think the people in the party even notice that we're not there," he said without looking up.

"Don't think we really mattered. It's just a Halloween party, far as anyone's concerned."

"I wouldn't say we didn't matter."

Sarah shrugged and sat at the empty desk across from him. "Don't think we mattered to Roger. Just talked to him. He pushed us out to save his own ass."

Vinish nodded. "I'm more surprised you confronted him about it. I certainly wouldn't."

"Yeah, it was awkward. He didn't even really apologize. I don't think he's sorry about it."

"Of course he isn't." Vinish looked up; he seemed distressed, his eyes weary. "A squirrel doesn't get that far ahead without being a bit cruel."

Sarah was offended by his candor. Rabbits weren't expected to get that far ahead either.

"Well, I mean, I'm not saying he's a villain. Maybe I would've done the same thing."

"You did show you can be mean to people."

"Yeah." She sighed. "No word from Alex yet, by the way."

"Was it actionable?"

"Yep. Told him I'll be at this pizza place, on this day, at this time. Said, if he wants to talk, come."

"There you go." He started walking to the break room. "Hope things work out for you."

"Same."

CHAPTER FIFTY-ONE

It was time to pick up the keys. Sarah officially had a new neighborhood to call home, with new landmarks to become familiar with. There were new routines to establish.

She left her new building and drove straight down the street, away from the river. She made mental notes of everything she passed. It was mostly homes with the occasional small store mixed in. She would have to pick a different street to use as her main drag. Belmont was close enough.

On one corner, away from any shops, was an A-frame sign. According to it, there was a farmer's market at the school a few blocks away.

Why not.

Tents lined the elementary school's yard, curving around the playground equipment. It was a large and organized affair; racks stocked dense with grains, tables overflowing with produce, plants and flowers hanging from awnings. There was even an information booth, staffed by a rabbit in a heavy jacket. The air wasn't unusually frigid, but if he had been sitting there all day, she could understand the need.

She wandered slowly from stand to stand, running through her mental shopping list. It all felt more expensive than just going to a grocery store, and shopping outside was certainly colder, but she enjoyed the idea. Maybe she wouldn't come every week, but once in a while. Something to change up the routine.

Scattered among the farmers were craft booths and artists offering modest creations for sale. She stopped at one booth where an older meerkat sold burned wood scenes. She was a life-long artist, she'd say casually to nobody in particular, but now she teaches too.

One of her pieces caught Sarah's eye. It was a simple scene, looking down Broadway, but it had to be from years ago. She recognized some of the buildings, but their signs were different.

"Looking for anything in particular?" the meerkat asked, now directing herself at Sarah.

"Not really. Just need to spruce up the new place. How much are these going for?"

"Sixty-five."

Sarah nodded. "Alright. Deal." She paid and stuffed the artwork in a bag she received from the info booth.

In a corner far from the parking lot was a booth decorated with wire sculptures. Most were sharp, geometric, abstract pieces. Sheets of metal, folded in origami, filled out the display. The metal shined subtly; the overcast sky meant only the lamp in the booth offered any real illumination. Carl sat in the corner, bending wire.

"Funny meeting you here," Sarah said, grabbing his attention.

"Well, hello Sarah, didn't expect to see you either." He put his work down and offered a friendly hug.

Sarah obliged. "I take it you're living in this area now."

"Not quite. Paula's place is a ways south, she had to give me a ride. Won't let me drive! I mean, my leg's beat, but it's not that beat. Now, what are you doing around these parts?"

"Found a place."

Carl smiled. "Well, there you go. There you go. Got your tail away from those suits for good, huh?"

"Yep. Does mean I have to find a roommate, though. Only reasonable thing I could find was a two bedroom, and that only makes sense if I split it with someone."

"Then I'd say it doesn't make any sense. But, I guess it's about all you could do at that point."

"Yeah, our paws were tied. Wasn't about to risk it and put it off much longer."

"Then it makes a bit more sense. Is the raccoon moving in with you?"

Sarah bounced on the balls of her feet. "Hopefully."

"Well now, don't get excited 'till you get a yes out of him."

"I know, I know. Been trying. Hell, I tried to ask him out, he hardly even noticed."

"Then you gotta try harder."

"I will!"

She let out a small laugh. Even with things changing around them, they still had the same relationship as always.

"So anyway," Sarah said, "how's business?"

"It's alright. Quiet. Gives me a little space to work, though."

"That's good."

She looked around the space he had. Some wire sculptures were hanging from the wall, identical to the one that used to decorate Carl's apartment door. She couldn't imagine anyone else's door with one on it, but now it didn't seem impossible.

Another piece hung from the back corner, all on its own. It was identical to what Sarah kept noticing in the Deadline Cafe. She had always suspected it was Carl's work but never bothered to check.

She gently brought it off the wall. "This is yours?"

"Of course it is," he said with a smile. "It's in my booth, isn't it?"

"Well, yeah. But I used to see this hanging in a cafe all the time. Didn't know you sold things that way."

Carl chuckled. "Oh, no, I don't. Probably some kid."

"What, someone bought your thing and sold it?"

"I doubt it." He pointed at the wires in Sarah's paws. "I've been making stuff like that for, say, fifteen years now. First bit of wire work I ever did.

Had a book with a bunch of patterns, that was in there. I just copied it a bunch of times, nothing fancy. It's why I don't sell it for too much."

Sarah checked the price tag tied to it. Twenty dollars. Not quite as much as the other one. "Huh. Well, now I know."

"Yep. You can have it if you'd like."

She paused for a second. "Sure, alright." She reached into her purse and grabbed her wallet.

"No, no, don't worry about that," Carl said. "Call it a gift."

She grabbed two tens. "Like hell I'm gonna steal from you."

"Fine, be stubborn." He smiled.

"I kinda am."

"Coulda told you that. Now, you better be back sometime. And you better bring that raccoon with you."

"Don't worry, I will." She smiled and went back to her car with a slight bounce to her step.

Only then did she tally up the groceries and craftwork she purchased. *Well, that kinda fucked up the budget a little. Didn't realize I bought that much. Ah well. It was worth it.*

She started the car and noticed the time. 1:45.

Oh, shit.

Sarah had to be at the pizza place at 2 pm. She pulled out of the parking lot quickly, jostling herself on the speed bump. She hated being late for any meeting, especially this one. This one mattered to her.

CHAPTER FIFTY-TWO

It was 1:56. Sarah fidgeted.

She sat in her usual seat at the pizza place. Near the window, facing the door. She would know if Alex was arriving. She could avoid the surprise.

But she didn't know if he would arrive at all. He didn't respond to the email, so she had no way of knowing what he was thinking. Maybe he didn't even read it.

She tried to steel herself against the possibilities. What if he didn't show up? Would she try to reschedule, or were they so thoroughly done as a couple that he wouldn't offer a chance for closure? If he did show up, what would she have to say? She had no apology rehearsed, and besides, he could tell if she was giving some scripted line. It would depend on how he was acting. Maybe he was okay.

She glanced at the walls. They were lined with memorabilia from decades past: yellowing newspaper clippings and banners with retired team logos. The occasional framed photograph filled in gaps. Probably local celebrities from before she moved to town. She never really paid attention to the decor, to the worn-down paint or the charred ovens. She paid attention to Alex.

1:58. 1:59. She checked her phone obsessively, her stomach turning with each minute. If Alex were going to show up, it would be soon. He was rarely early, but hardly very late.

She tensed up. An otter approached down the sidewalk. He wore a black skirt and matching suit jacket, a tuft of orange sticking out under a newsboy cap.

Alex sat down across from Sarah, tucking his skirt and dropping his tail to the side. He stared, silently, waiting for her to make the first move. She could feel tears coming already.

"I didn't think you'd come," she said.

"Wasn't sure I would. Darien told me not to. Said it'd be a bad idea."

"Well, thanks." She avoided looking him in the eye. "I just needed to apologize."

"For what?" Alex asked, dryly.

"I shouldn't have yelled at you."

"Right."

Alex never felt so intimidating. Otters weren't supposed to be intimidating.

"I guess... I'm just frustrated. For you. Like, I know things are really hard for you, and I just want to help. I still really care about you."

"You want to do something about it."

"It's not even that. I want you to be... better. In a better place. And I know you can be, it's just..." She stumbled on her words.

"Sarah."

"Yeah?" Her voice started to break.

"I appreciate the concern. I appreciate that you care. I don't have a lot of people that do anymore. But you have been such a pushy bitch about it."

"I know." She hung her head, trying to hide her tears.

"Trying to hook me up with that designer startup jackass guy... whatever. That was stupid, but fine. But you pushed me about that, you pushed me about your marketing shit. I don't want to do it, I'm not going to do it. And then you unload on me? In public? At the art walk? The fuck is wrong with you?"

"I don't know," she said, fighting for her composure. "I don't know. I just wanted to help."

"You wanted a project."

"What?"

"That's what you do, isn't it? At work, it's always one project, done, then the next-"

"Well fuck, that's what you do too, isn't it? One painting, one sculpture, then the next."

"But I didn't treat our relationship like a project."

Sarah felt queasy. She was embarrassed and guilty, but now she was angry. It was a bitter cocktail and hard to keep down.

"How did I ever treat our relationship like a project?"

"You were doing this same shit the whole time. Dragging me to those workshops and whatever."

"I thought you would appreciate it. You're always talking about how hard it is to be an artist, so I thought 'hey, maybe this would help him.' And I stopped! It was obvious it wasn't helping."

"Of course it wasn't going to help. It's all rich people business bullshit. It's your thing, not mine."

"Well, I guess it felt like your thing wasn't helping you enough." She slumped in her seat. "I just wanted you to try something new, maybe it would help you. And yeah, I wanted you to do it, but for your own sake."

Alex rolled his eyes. "You could've just asked."

"And you would've said no."

"Because it wasn't going to help!"

"You don't let-" Sarah grumbled. "Are you going to get this pissy at me just because I care?"

"It's because you always wanted to be in charge. You always had to be in control."

Sarah wiped her nose with a napkin, taking a moment to gather herself. "I don't like seeing you struggle. I don't like hearing you complain all the time. And yeah, it's valid stuff, but it's like..."

"I'm just trying to vent, Sarah. That's all I need. But you never let me do that. You'd immediately try to take over and start solving my problems for me. You can't do that."

"Alex... I just want things to change for you. They can change for the better, I know they can."

"You need to change too."

She sat in silent agreement. She finally gathered the courage to look him in the eye. He was tearing up.

"I know. I'll try."

"Good."

"Just, please. Tell me you'll try to improve things."

"You're doing it again."

She cringed. "Sorry. Sorry."

Alex took a napkin to dab his own tears. "Alright. Look. I'm not accepting your apology. I appreciate it, I know you mean it, but I'm not sure I can forgive you. And I don't think you're ready right now. I think, as it is, you're going to keep doing this. And if you keep doing this, we're not going to get along."

Sarah nodded, disappointed but understanding. "I can try."

Alex nodded in return. "Then try. And when you work it out, when you can go through the day without trying to control everyone, then you can come find me."

A silence. "So," Sarah muttered, "we're done? That's it?"

"To be fair, it's been four years. I'm tired of being bossed around by someone I love."

Wait. I thought he was over me?

"Alright." She couldn't fight anymore. There was nothing to be said that wouldn't agitate Alex further.

He got up to leave. He paused as if he had something else to say, but instead walked out the door silently.

Sarah sat with her head on her crossed arms, trying to conceal her crying. The restaurant was mostly empty, and the sidewalk offered little foot traffic, yet she felt utterly exposed.

"You musta been a real bitch to her, huh?" Tommy called out from behind the counter.

Sarah's ear perked up. She turned her head to look at him. "Yeah. Guess so."

"Well, these things happen. Just don't go kill yourself over it."

"I... wasn't going to, but thanks."

"No problem. And maybe don't be so much of a bitch to your next girlfriend."

"Boyfriend. Alex is a guy."

Tommy chuckled. "All due respect, that otter looks like more of a girl than you do."

"You don't have to point it out."

Sarah stared at the table beneath her crossed arms, taking focused breaths.

CHAPTER FIFTY-THREE

The movers looked like linebackers. Sarah figured the two wolves must spend every day at the gym, considering how buff they looked. But then, moving people out of their apartments had to be physically demanding. There was probably plenty of work for them, too. No need for a gym.

Lee was small to begin with, but the movers dwarfed him. He kept dodging out of their way as they grabbed Sarah's furniture. She was surprised he was even there to begin with. He offered to help the week before, but in a non-committal way, the sort of "maybe" that's best treated as a "no".

He and Sarah ducked into the kitchen, allowing the movers space to move the couch. Her focus bounced around the room. Anything to keep her from thinking about Alex.

"Starting to think you didn't need me," Lee said.

"Couldn't hurt," she said, grabbing a box of cookware. "Besides, I'm paying these guys by the hour. I'm hoping you can speed it up."

"No promises." He grabbed a second box, and they followed the movers out of the apartment. "How'd it go with Alex?"

Sarah sighed. "About what I should've expected, honestly."

"Bad?"

"Well, he doesn't want to talk to me anymore. So."

"Bad."

"Yeah. It sucks. I don't like getting kicked out of his life like that, but I guess he's right. I do like to have things in control."

"Who doesn't? Chaos sucks."

"Yeah, but I've been getting too controlling."

"You're not controlling." Sarah held a door open, allowing him to see her confused expression. "You're not! Sean's controlling."

"Sean's in charge. That's different."

"Because you want him in charge?"

"Well. It's not like we voted."

Lee dropped his box at the foot of the moving truck. One of the wolves, now finished positioning the couch, grabbed it and put it in its place. Sarah hopped into the truck, avoiding any assistance, and put her box next to it.

"I would've voted for him, though," Lee said. "He's good at it."

Sarah paused. "I don't actually know if I would. Maybe I would've voted for myself."

"Well, it's not like it's high-stakes or anything. It's just a little group."

"I know. I guess Alex was right, I do like to be in charge. Like, I would organize things all the time for work."

"Tell people what to do?"

"A bit, yeah. It's a management job. I get teams together for campaigns, keep everyone on task. If someone gets off course, I have to go corral them." She stopped in her tracks. "Fuck. I do like controlling people."

Lee stopped and turned around. "Well, it's not a big deal, I guess. Nothing to beat yourself up over."

"I ruined things with Alex because of it. I can beat myself up over that."

"You can. Doesn't mean you should."

"If I can't now, when could I?"

"Never? I mean, these things happen."

"Eh. I'd rather they didn't."

They stepped into her half-empty apartment. Only a few boxes remained along with furniture the movers were yet to get to. Lee leaned against an interior wall for a rest.

"Look at it this way. Did you really want to stay friends with him forever?"

She leaned against the opposite wall. "I guess it'd be kinda nice, but if he's not gonna-" She sighed. "That's what I mean. If he's not gonna do

266

what I think he should then I wouldn't want to stick with him. It'd get too frustrating. That's my problem."

Lee nodded, looking satisfied. "You and Sean are never gonna make a good couple."

"Come on, man." She slouched.

"Well, you know him. If you're going to keep getting frustrated when someone doesn't do what you tell them, then..."

"Yeah, okay. I get that. But with Sean, at least he does things. It's whatever he wants, but he'll do stuff."

"True. And you can get him to do stuff. I got him to go with us to that magic show that one time."

"But you convinced him it was his idea."

"Exactly." Lee smiled.

The movers arrived to interrupt them. "Bed's all clear to grab next?"

"Yeah, go ahead," Sarah said, pushing herself off the wall. "Anything I should grab next?"

"No, you're good," the mover said. "We can take care of this, don't worry."

The movers went to the bedroom and quickly carried a bed frame out the door. All the while, Lee looked at Sarah with a wry smile.

"You're doing it again," he said.

"Shush, you."

"You're admitting you do it, though. That's good."

"I guess." She fidgeted, trying to keep herself from helping the movers. "But, anyway. I think the whole thing with Alex was, he just doesn't want to do anything. He never called that designer guy I told him about. Which is fine if he was ever like 'I'm gonna go do this thing so I can get better and it's my job' but he wouldn't even do that."

"He's not doing anything?"

"Nothing I've ever heard about."

"Doesn't mean he's doing nothing."

"Well, he's painting, obviously. And he's not that bad with it, I think he's getting better. It's just the business side of it. He told me, straight out, he won't do it. Doesn't want to."

"So you're both stubborn."

She nodded. "We always have been."

She started pacing around the living room, eventually stopping in front of the window. There were no boxes there stacked up, so she could resist the temptation. The view was never anything spectacular, but she would still miss it.

"So how did it ever work between you two?"

"I... I don't know. It just kinda did."

"Until it didn't." Lee stepped closer. "If you're gonna be stubborn, you're just gonna keep getting frustrated with people. That's why you got angry."

"Of course it is. I'm at least that self-aware."

"I know. So, you just gotta learn to let that go."

Sarah sighed. "Easier said than done."

"You'll figure it out." He put a paw on her shoulder. "Just takes time."

Sarah looked at him, skeptical. "Since when did you get all talkative and Zen?"

"Since Kate left."

"Kate left?"

Lee's face had a flash of confusion. "Oh, right, right. You left early. Yeah, she asked Sean out last week, after the movie. She was like, 'if you're not dating Sarah, how about dating me?' and he turned her down. Got her really angry. Kinda cursed you out a little bit."

She sighed. "Yeah, I think I know why. Can't really blame her."

"It's alright. I mean, she's totally gone now. Facebook group and everything."

"Damn. She really was just there to sleep with Sean."

"Yep. Not a huge surprise."

Sarah laughed to herself. "So now Sean's your type?"

"No. The taller mover guy, he's my type."

"I get that a lot," the mover said from the hallway.

Sarah started laughing harder. "Don't worry, the ferret's got a boyfriend."

"So does he," the other mover said, entering the apartment. "Anyway, just three more trips, it looks like. Fifteen minutes or so."

"Thanks."

Lee slumped against the wall, blushing and smiling. Sarah smiled back, enjoying the company.

"I get to tease you for this now," she said.

Lee gave a relieved laugh. "Not in front of the whole gang, though, alright?"

"Fair. Do we know who's coming tonight? Other than Sean and us."

"Well, Eric said he might show up."

"So he won't."

"Right. Ian said he's in, you've got Daniel."

"Just me and a bunch of guys, then." She chuckled. "On the plus side, two of you are dating, so it's not that awkward."

"And you could ask Sean out. Make it two couples. Then it's just Daniel being awkward."

"I'm not asking him at the theater."

Lee laughed. "Oh, God no. Then it'd be awkward for everybody."

Sarah smiled. "Well. That's if he says no."

CHAPTER FIFTY-FOUR

A rabbit sat in a coffee shop. It was a simple and narrow venue; one row of laminated wood tables filled a wall, a pair sat next to the window, and that was all there was to sit at. The checkered floor and chrome behind the counter reminded her of a diner; one remembered by someone whose grandmother took them for the occasional weekend lunch. Not an exact replica, but close enough.

She lived a few blocks away in an old building, about as old as the one housing the cafe. They both let in a little bit of the cold November air in their roundabout ways. They both hummed when the heat came on. She had only come twice before, but already it was starting to feel a bit like home.

It helped that they made a good latte.

A raccoon sat across from her, sipping tea. He lived across the river and worked not too far from another of the coffee shop's locations. Despite that, he never went in before; he wasn't a coffee drinker, so he always assumed a coffee shop wouldn't be his sort of thing. The warm smile on his face proved him wrong.

"You seem pretty pleased with yourself," Sarah said, smiling. "Trying new things and all that."

"It's nice!" Sean said. "I didn't think this place would be so... laid back. Like, I expected a cafe to be all snooty and stuff."

"Oh, there are definitely snooty ones." She sipped her latte. "But it feels nice here. Better than all the stuff downtown, for sure."

"I know. Went to a Starbucks one time, the guy was so growly about tea. Like, dude, it's tea."

"Why would he get grumpy about tea? Like, they do that. It's on the menu."

"Yeah. It's the whole, like, stuck-up chai soy latte sort of thing. Bet that's where it comes from."

"Guy was probably just an asshole."

"Probably." He sipped at his tea.

Sarah looked around. "Glad I found this place. It works. It's no Deadline, though."

"Still miss that place, huh?"

"Still miss the whole neighborhood, honestly. Liked it there. I'm still figuring out my routines here."

Sean smiled. "Sure do like your routines."

She smiled back, playfully indignant. Her mood was lifting as of late. The chaos of moving was over with. The time away from work helped, allowing her to settle in and explore at her own pace. She felt like she might get back to normal.

"Been an experience," she eventually said. "Changed a lot of stuff. Job, house."

"That's two things."

"They're big things! It'll take some time to get used to it."

"Probably, but you kinda have to."

"I know." She looked forward to being used to things again.

Sean looked over her shoulder, watching the light traffic outside. For being along a major road, there were few people out driving. "Find a roommate yet?"

"Daniel's on board. Moving in at the end of the year."

He smiled with a light laugh. "You two sure are moving fast, huh. Already living together."

"Trust me. I am not his type."

"What's his type?"

"Kate."

He grimaced. "Fair point."

"Yeah. So, like, I'm not worried about that."

"You gonna be okay? I mean, having a coyote for a roommate?"

She chuckled. "Just having a roommate is probably a terrible idea. But I mean, if I have to, rather someone I'm friends with than some stranger off Craigslist."

"Exactly. Could've ended up with someone like Dave."

"Coworker?"

"Yep. Replaced Jeremy."

"I'm assuming you don't like him."

Sean shook his head as he sipped.

"Sheesh. Do you guys exclusively hire assholes?"

"Eh. He's not an asshole. He's annoying and a total idiot, but he's not an asshole."

"Honestly, have you ever had a coworker you liked?"

Sean looked up in thought. "Not here. Maybe one or two back in California, but even then it was just... eh. Most of them are just okay, some are really pretty arrogant."

"You could look for a new job. From what I've seen, you've got options."

"Job hunting sucks, though."

Sarah grumbled. "Don't get me started."

"You brought it up."

"I know, I know. It's not even that bad. Might actually have an offer soon. Perfect timing, too. Started to worry the severance would run out before I got anything."

"Congrats. Who with?"

"Sevent. A startup downtown."

Sean winced. "Dude."

"Hey," Sarah apologized, "it's my best lead. They need a brand manager, it sounds like something I can do. I mean, I have no idea, but what they're asking for is pretty close. And I nailed the interview. It's even a pay raise, which surprised me."

Sean glared.

"Look, I sure as hell would not go to Criticalas, okay? I respect you too much."

"Good. They'd be worse to you."

"I can totally believe that. Didn't sound like they'd be good with women."

"Yeah. Watch your tail with those sorts of people."

"I know. I'll stand up for myself if I have to."

"You sure?" Sean asked, skeptical.

She sighed, knowing it was an unlikely promise. "I'll try to."

"Good." He paused for a sip. "Thought you hated the whole startup scene, anyway."

Sarah shrugged. "Kinda? I mean, I'm a little concerned, but I think most of my problem was that I lost a lot of coworkers to startups. And they were people I actually liked. So, like, if it weren't for them those guys would still be around."

"And now you don't have that job anyway."

"Yeah! Now I'm like, why did I give a shit? Feel so dumb getting wound up about it."

"Well, try not to do that with the new job."

Sarah nodded and sipped her latte.

They sat and drank quietly, watching each other with small smiles. She found it romantic, almost, the two of them quietly enjoying each other's company in a cozy cafe. It was a simple, calm moment. She could see how artists would pull inspiration from such a sense of peace.

"By the way," Sean said, "I ran into Alex."

"You went to that bar? That place is really not your style."

"Nope. She's working at a Starbucks now."

Sarah blinked. "Okay, three things to unpack there. One, we're going with 'she' now?"

"Sounded like."

"Okay." She wasn't too surprised. Alex had been acting more female than usual lately. "Two, I thought you didn't go to coffee shops."

"I'm here, aren't I?"

Sarah gave him a flat look.

"I know, I know. I went to lunch with Kevin, he wanted to duck in on the way back. Happened to be the one she works at."

"A convenient excuse," she said dryly.

"You think I'm just making this up?"

"Well, kinda. Because, three, she hates Starbucks. So if she's working there, things must be really shitty. And, like... I don't know. Maybe you'd think it'd make me feel better?"

"How would that make you feel better?"

She stammered and came up empty.

"Think you just don't want to believe it."

She shook her head. "Not really."

"Who knows, maybe she changed lately."

They sat silently, letting a heavy air fall over the conversation. Sarah struggled to believe Sean. She knew that Alex would change from time to time, but never very widely. Not widely enough to start liking things she always detested.

"Just wish I knew how she got to that point," Sarah said.

"Working there?"

"Yeah. Wonder what changed."

"Well, gender, apparently."

She shrugged. "Knowing Alex, that's not even a huge change."

"Man, how were you ever a couple?"

"No idea." She shook her head. "Now we're not even talking."

"Still?" Sean asked in a voice that already knew the answer.

She sighed. "Haven't tried to, honestly. Don't think I'll be trying for a while."

"Why not?"

"Because, if I did, I'm just gonna try to help again. And that's not a good idea. Besides, she doesn't want to talk to me. And if that's what she wants, then..."

"Maybe, maybe not. She could've just said that out of frustration."

"No. I said a lot of things out of frustration, but that... she definitely meant it."

He frowned. "Sorry."

"It's fine."

"Is it? Really?"

She hesitated. "I mean, yeah. I'm not happy about it. It's probably gonna be a while before I'm okay with it, if ever."

"I was gonna say, there's no way you're over it so quickly."

She laughed nervously. "I can be a bitch, but I'm not that cold."

"You're not a bitch." Sarah cringed slightly. "Seriously! You're not. Like, the whole thing with Alex sucked-"

"And it was my fault."

"Even so. Dwelling isn't going to help."

She stared out the window. "I guess."

Sean reached across the table to give her arm a sympathetic pat. It brought her back to the moment. They took alternating sips, glancing out the window beside them, occasionally catching each other's eyes. Each time, Sarah grew slightly nervous. She did a good job of hiding it.

A smile grew on Sean's face. "So when are you coming back to movie night?"

Sarah gained a smile to match. "Ah, okay. That's your little game, huh?"

"We miss you! The group just doesn't work right without you."

"I wasn't aware I had that much power."

"Well, you don't."

Sarah laughed. "You just want me around so you can tease me."

"Isn't that why you invited me here?"

Alright. This is the best opening you're gonna get. You can do it, Sarah. You're ready.

"I have my own motives," she said with a smile.

"But of course. You're not exactly subtle."

"Well, you're not exactly observant."

"True."

She gave it a moment. "So, you do know why I asked you to stop by, then."

He shook his head. "Not really."

She blinked. "Seriously?"

"Seriously. If it's anything other than you just missing me 'cause we haven't talked a while, then... no, I don't know."

"Sean." She leaned forward and made eye contact. "I mean it, you get really oblivious sometimes. Like, Kate had been hitting on you for a long time. Danielle hit on you hard when we went to see the apartment."

"I know, you told me."

"And... I've been way too subtle with it, 'cause I've been nervous, but-"

"Wait." Sean's eyes widened. "You're not..." He fell back into his chair. "I swear, everyone wants to date me."

"Well, you're awesome."

He sighed, blushing. "If I say no, are you gonna stop coming to movies with us too?"

"Of course not! I'm not Kate. I mean, how often do we just bullshit about movies? You're fun to be around." She sighed. "I just think we could make a good couple. And I guess I want to try." Silence. "Just figured I'd ask."

Sean nodded, looking at his tea. "It's weird."

"I know."

"How long have you been waiting to ask?"

"A while. Months, I guess. I just didn't want to mess things up, we have a good relationship going. And then the whole Kate thing happened, and I didn't want to make that worse but I was like 'if I don't say anything he'll go with her' and it was just..." She trailed off, aware that she was rambling.

Sean nodded. "So, you finally felt ready?"

"I guess so."

He sipped his tea. "Lee told me a couple months ago that you had a crush on me."

Sarah stared blankly. Sean gave a sly smile, satisfaction for a long con executed without a hitch. She couldn't believe he did it, but she could easily believe he could pull it off.

So she kicked his leg under the table.

"Ow!"

"You little bastard!" She started laughing. "You just wanted to fuck with me!"

Sean, laughing along, leaned down to rub his leg. "It's fun!"

"You gonna be this much of a pain in the ass if we date?"

"Probably! I'm not exactly gonna change."

"Bullshit. If I can change, you can change."

"Fine, fine! I'm still gonna be annoying, though."

"Well, yeah. I would hope."

They calmed down and leaned back in their respective chairs. Sarah was already plotting how she would get him back.

"I assume this is a 'yes' from you, then," Sarah said.

"Of course."

She nodded. "You're willing to trust me like that?"

Sean shrugged. "I think I'm ready. Long as you're willing to trust me."

"Well, clearly I can't."

Sean laughed. "I'll give you that. I didn't know how to handle it."

"It's okay. Neither did I. I probably should've said something a while ago instead of just sitting around and waiting."

"That's fine. I haven't had a girlfriend in forever, not sure I know how to do it."

"Just be yourself. You're who I fell for."

Sean smiled. "Thanks."

"Other than that, I've always just seen it as friends who have sex."

He chuckled. "That's one way to put it." His eyes widened as he finished his tea. "Wait. That marathon night we did?"

"Yeah?" Sarah asked, concerned.

"We didn't...?"

Sarah blinked. "If we did, I don't remember it."

"Okay. That would've been... I mean, I'd rather have sex sober. Just gonna put that on the table."

She nodded. "Good thing to know. I think we're in agreement there."

"Hey, gotta discuss these things, right?"

"I guess so. I mean, Alex and I just winged it, but I don't think I want to do that again. With how that turned out."

"Can't blame you."

278

Sarah looked out the window. Their relationship would be difficult. They both had things they still needed to work on, things that could ruin a relationship. Sean would have to trust Sarah. She would have to stop trying to control everything. But they both knew the problems were there. Maybe that would be enough.

"So, Sean." Sarah leaned forward with a slight smile. "I cede control to you. What would you like to do on our first date?"

"Aren't we already on it?"

She paused. "Yeah. Guess so." She sipped her latte and smiled at her boyfriend.

ACKNOWLEDGMENTS

More than anyone, I need to thank Amit Gupta. He gave a talk at the XOXO Festival in 2015 that drastically changed how I look at life. (I strongly recommend looking up the talk on YouTube; trust me, it had much more emotional weight in person.) I had lingering, even suppressed, dreams of being an author for much of my life, but it was his talk that pulled them out of me and shoved them in my face. Because of him, I finally acknowledged what I wanted to do with my life, and got both the courage and the urgency to finally do it. This book would not exist without him.

By extension, I must thank the two Andys, Baio and McMillan, who organized the festival. I came within hours of losing the invite they sent, and every day I'm glad I didn't.

This book started its life as a National Novel Writing Month project. Naturally, I have to thank the organizers and volunteers who keep NaNoWriMo running every year. I also want to thank everyone who helped me during that month, whether as writing group buddies or just by offering emotional support. Special thanks to Ian for guiding me towards the right story.

I have many months of chat logs with Ariana, a good friend and fellow writer, as she supported me through the revision and editing process far beyond what I could ever ask for. Her patience and advice kept me from making dozens of bad decisions, up to and including canning the whole project.

Many thanks and apologies to Mike, Britney, Adam, and the rest of our trivia crew. I hope the many games I missed in pursuit of this manuscript can be forgiven. Rest assured that none of the characters are directly based on any of you. When you approach me later to argue the point, note that I said "directly."

As a software developer by trade, I feel obligated to thank the people behind the tools I used to prepare this book. So, thank you to the developers and maintainers of Scrivener, Pronoun, and Grammarly, as well as the admins and moderators of Scribophile. All of these tools and sites come well recommended.

You might have predicted that this book took shape in several coffee shops. In particular, many words were written and revised in Coffee Time and Ford Food & Drink, both in Portland, Oregon. Portions were also written in various Starbucks, an Ikea, and on a particularly long bus ride. (One writes where she can.)

As cliche as it may be, I always feel the need to thank the reader. It's in the sharing of art that it takes form, and it's when the art affects a person, whether positively or negatively, that it meets its duty. I hope you enjoyed it, and I apologize if you didn't.